How to Lose a Demon in 10 Days

How to Lose a Demon in 10 Days

Saranna DeWylde

BRAVA

KENSINGTON PUBLISHING CORP.

www.kensingtonbooks.com

BRAVA BOOKS are published by

Kensington Publishing Corp.
119 West 40th Street
New York, NY 10018

All Kensington titles, imprints, and distributed lines are available at special quantity discounts for bulk purchases for sales promotions, premiums, fund-raising, educational, or institutional use.

Special book excerpts or customized printings can also be created to fit specific needs. For details, write or phone the office of the Kensington special sales manager: Kensington Publishing Corp., 119 West 40th Street, New York, NY 10018, attn: Special Sales Department; phone: 1-800-221-2647.

ISBN-13: 978-0-7582-6915-7
ISBN-10: 0-7582-6915-3

First Kensington Trade Paperback Printing: September 2012

10 9 8 7 6 5 4 3 2 1

Printed in the United States of America

CHAPTER ONE
Technicalities

Caspian was technically a Crown Prince of Hell. Technically. And technically, he was royally fucked. Or was about to be, if he could manage it.

How did he get himself into these things? He felt the pull, and there was no use in fighting it. The Big Boss had seen to that. Fighting would just make this harder.

Caspian gave a dramatic sigh and followed the call up into the mortal world. Which he hated. Not the mortal world per se, but the bitch work. He materialized in the middle of what was obviously a woman's bedroom. There was enough purple to choke a unicorn. He quickly realized he was trapped within a chalklike circle drawn with finely ground bone.

Correction, not ground up. It was old. It smelled like rot. It had turned to dust on its own. What *was* this happy-crappy, another weekend warrior? How come he always got the freaks? No one sensible ever tried to summon a demon. Perhaps that should have been a consideration when he'd been frolicking down the primrose path that led to his current career.

She wasn't bad to look at, aside from the sneer, which was a bit scary. He was willing to overlook it because the rest of her real estate thrilled him. On the other hoof, as some of his co-workers would say, she didn't look at all impressed at his entrance, and Caspian was a showman.

"WHY HAST THOU SUMMONED ME?" he began in a large, thunderous voice that rattled the windows and made books and knickknacks fall off the shelves in a most pleasing way. Pleasing to him, anyway.

"I hope you know you're cleaning that up." The voluptuous woman put her fist on her hip and tossed long dark hair over her shoulder.

"WHAT?" Caspian would have clapped a hand over his mouth had she not been staring at him so intently with those large chocolate eyes. Who was she to tell him that he was going to do anything of the sort?

Chocolate eyes? Where the hell had that come from? Did he care what her eyes looked like? No. Not in any meaningful sense, anyway. He wouldn't remember them in a hundred years and describe them like foodstuffs he could get lost in or whatever.

"I know you don't have to bellow like that. It's not cute. I am not impressed."

What did she mean, she wasn't impressed? Of course, she was impressed. He was Caspian, Crown Prince of Hell and demon extraordinaire. He was Infernal Royalty. While Caspian couldn't imagine the Big Boss being rendered somehow impotent and unable to perform his cosmic duties, on the off chance he was, it would be Caspian's turn to pull the strings. No matter what the other twelve Crown Princes had to say about it.

"Look, lady. You summoned me. You take what you get."

She damn well better take what she got and like it. He used his demon sight to look at himself. No broccoli in the teeth; they were all straight, white, and perfect. There was the hard jaw, broad shoulders, wicked tongue—check, check, and check.

"Why, pray tell, did I have to get stuck with the metrosexual demon concerned with making an entrance? You should be on Broadway. Do you sing?"

Apparently, the question was serious. She was looking at him expectantly. Not only that, but she'd insulted his manhood. Demonhood. Whatever. She'd challenged his prowess.

Caspian looked at himself again. Metrosexual? He didn't think Regency GQ was metrosexual. He rather liked cravats, velvet coats, and breeches. Especially the breeches because they showed off his considerable package and his ass. All the girlies liked it, thought he was going to spout poetry and fling a sword about and . . . *oh.*

"Well, do you? I need to know."

"Why?" he grunted.

Wow. That was intelligent. Way to make her understand that she was in the presence of Caspian, a Crown Prince of Hell, his power second only to that of the Devil himself. Way to make her quake. If it wouldn't totally shoot his credibility to shit, he would have palmed his forehead.

"I can't have you bippity-bopping along behind me, now can I?" She sneered again, her cute little mouth curling in a very un-cute way.

Bippity-bopping?

His gaze lingered on her lips. They were making them better these days, human women. For a while, when summoning demons had last been all the rage, the women had been very skinny and worn ugly clothes. The '70s hadn't been a pleasant time for Caspian. Lots of offers for sex, though. He had actually inspired many of those gothics where the heroine gets it on with the Big Boss. Of course, he wasn't the Big Boss, so that had gone over like an airborne pisser. See, the Big Boss was a showman, too. He didn't really care to be upstaged.

This summoner really would be prettier if she smiled. He opened his mouth to tell her so.

"Oh, for the love of Hell. Not you, too."

"Not me, what?" Again, he had yet to put her in her place, to make her quail before the might of—

"'You'd be prettier if you smiled,'" she mimicked in a nasal little voice. "I can see the look on your face."

"Well, you would be. I'm not gonna lie."

"Why not? You're a demon."

He sighed. "Because lying is bad for business and it's boring. Can we just get on with this? What do you want? Riches? Power? The ability to eat anything you like and not gain a pound . . . ?"

She looked down at herself for a moment and snorted. "I like my figure fine, thanks. What I want—"

Caspian cut her off. "Really? Because you know most women are unhappy with themselves, regardless of size. It's nice to see a woman with real hips and"—he paused to look her up and down again—"very nice breasts who—"

"Excuse me?" she practically growled. "Can I send you back and get another? Because this is not working."

"No. And I'm offended." He pulled at his sleeve for a moment. "I really don't want to have to drag out the fire and the tail and the—"

"Fine! Let's get on with it. Vengeance. I want vengeance."

Caspian snorted. Hell, she was a woman scorned, which meant she didn't need him. "Lady, I don't know if someone forgot to tell you, but you're a woman. You don't need a demon to help you with vengeance. Most chicks do just fine on their own."

"You don't understand who he is. I definitely need help."

"Let me give you some advice," Caspian began. He could feel himself about to get into trouble again. He really shouldn't be spouting off at the suck hole, offering free suggestions. He should get something from her.

She sighed loudly, as if anything he might say would be superfluous. It annoyed him far more than made sense.

"Sleep with all of his friends," Caspian suggested. "They hate that."

"Uh, he'd *kill* them . . . ?" She let it hang like a question, almost with a Valley Girl inflection, as if he were the stupidest of all creatures.

"Oh." Well. Yeah, killing could definitely put a damper on that sort of plan, especially if one had a conscience. Which this chick seemed to have. Caspian supposed she hadn't actually killed anybody for the bone dust, which was why it smelled old. He wasn't sure if she was just enterprising enough to acquire what she needed in the simplest way or if she was against staining her soul with murder. He hadn't pinned that down yet, but he was definitely interested in finding out. Which was bad. He shouldn't care one way or the other.

"Well?" she demanded.

"Well, what, gorgeous?" He found his gaze zeroed in on those magnificent breasts. And they were magnificent. Creamy scoops of mouth-watering—

"Are you going to help me or not?"

"Yeah, yeah." Caspian waved her off. He could stare at that rack for hours, imagining it in a push-up bra, in a corset, or just running wild and free, as he could tell those breasts so obviously yearned to do. Really, that was what he wanted for them. It was wrong to capture something so beautiful, unless it was using his mouth, which—

"But?"

"But what?" Caspian said, still pondering the pleasures of that milky flesh. If she would just shut up.

"Demon! Hello? Up here." She crossed her arms over her chest. "They can't talk."

"I know. That's part of the appeal."

"Can we just get to the part where we make the deal?"

"Just a second," he grumbled. He wanted to ogle the chest some more before he dealt with the head. Why did something so delicious have to be sour in the mouth?

"I'm not making one of those open-ended deals," she growled. "I want to know the price up front. And I want it in writing."

"By the Sulfuric Rod, you are a difficult little baggage, aren't you?" He hated when they wanted things in writing. He sighed. "Yes, fine."

"Signed in blood. I won't settle for anything less."

"No. You wouldn't." He rolled his eyes.

"You still haven't told me the price. Don't we need to haggle?"

"There will be no haggling, witch."

"I'm n— a witch." It was a pointless denial. She couldn't even get the *not* out of her mouth.

"Aren't you?"

"Mother of Christ!"

She was screaming at him now. Not that anyone would blame her. He was being difficult. But what could you expect from a demon? Really.

Caspian cringed. "Heed your tongue, witch!"

"Don't call me . . ." She trailed off, then sighed. "I really don't like you."

"That hurts. I like you." He eyed her lasciviously. "I like you very much."

"I'm sure. Your price, demon. Now."

"Well, usually it's virgin's blood. But I'm thinking you don't have any of that." He looked her up and down lasciviously again. "Do you?"

"A gentleman wouldn't ask."

"But I am no gentleman. I'm a demon." Why did he feel the constant need to remind himself—and her—of the fact?

"This is so much more trouble than it's worth."

"Is it really? If you were angry enough to summon a demon, a Crown Prince of Hell, no less, it should be worth plenty of trouble. Because that's what you are going to get."

She smirked. "Oh? So you're a Crown Prince? How did you get stuck with this gig, then, answering summonses in the middle of the night? Isn't that like busting a detective down to traffic?"

He narrowed his eyes at her. "No. More like vice president down to jizz mopper."

"Thank you for the visual."

"You're welcome."

"So polite," she volleyed.

"I try."

"So, barring the virgin blood? What's your price?"

Tenacious, wasn't she? Caspian sighed, a very loud and bothered noise. Snide or not, he really wanted to get between this mortal's thighs. How badly did she want vengeance? And also . . . how badly did her state of non-virginity concern him? It was something he had to consider.

See, there were rules to the game. Demons went around deflowering virgins not because they liked their purity. Oh, no. It was more because virgins wouldn't ripen with fruit grown from the seed of demons. However, a more experienced Daughter of Eve? Well, her experience decided how fast and how easily she would ripen. One couldn't go around banging the corrupted willy-nilly or else hordes of imps would destroy the world. And, contrary to popular belief, the Big Boss was happy with the status quo.

It was an ugly mess, denying demons their nature. See, angels on both sides of the Eternal War still found the daughters of Men to be beautiful. Hell, the Book even talked about it. So, how badly did he want this chit? It had been a long time.

A very, very, very long time.

His decision had been made for him the moment he was summoned, really. She was hot. Hotter than the Diablo peppers the Big Boss kept in a jar on his dining room table. Caspian had to corrupt her for all mortal men. It would be a good day's work.

He'd forgotten that it was dangerous to conspire against women, who are at their core capable of much stranger plots than any simple demon. Even a Crown Prince of Hell.

CHAPTER TWO

Sign on the Dotted Line

Damn, if he wasn't the sexiest thing she'd ever laid eyes on. Grace almost had to fan herself. Of course, she couldn't go around thinking things like that. He might hear her. Though, she was sure the personal fanfare in his head was louder than anything she might be thinking. Demons were like that. If he did hear her, she'd just blame it on hot flashes. Not that she was old enough to have them, but what would he know about such things? He was too busy trying to play with his toy rather than learn how it worked.

That lacy jabot thing had to go. It wasn't the eighteenth century, after all. His hair was obnoxiously pristine. She wanted to run her fingers through it, muss it all up. And his eyes? Oh, saints and devils, his eyes! The irises raged with hellfire—though she kind of figured she wasn't supposed to find that attractive.

Those eyes were still on her breasts. She was drawn to ogle him in return, just a little bit more. That jawline? She almost shivered. He had a jaw so smooth, so defined, that it should be a sin. She was sure that somewhere it was. Maybe that's why he was doing time in Hell: because he was so devilishly handsome.

Of course, Grace couldn't have him running around thinking she was impressed. She'd never get anything out of him, then. Demons were like that, vain and incorrigible creatures. She'd also read they could be fun—at least until they pulled out the brimstone and damnation and whatnot.

She stole a peek at his fingers. You could always tell a powerful demon by his hands—or hoofs, if you'd gotten one of those. But she'd been specific. Her granny Seraphim didn't raise no dummy. Despite her previous protestations of ignorance, Grace had tried to conjure Caspian specifically, and he had nice hands indeed. The fingers were long and tapered. Elegant. He could work great magicks.

Also, the thing about Caspian was that he hadn't always been all demon. He wasn't even particularly evil. It was more like he'd run with a bad crowd. Been born into a bad place. Guilt by association.

Or so she'd read.

"Okay, then. For my boon, I want some poon."

"Excuse me, *what?*" Grace snorted. If she'd been a different woman, she would have blushed.

"Poon. Pussy. Love cave. Velvet sheath. Horizontal mambo. Any of this ringing a bell?"

"I don't think I heard you correctly."

"You heard me all right, girly."

"Number one, I am not a 'girly.' Number two, I'm not a virgin. I thought all of that cavorting had to be with innocent flesh?"

He raised a black brow. "How un–virgin are you?"

"*Un-virgin?* Is that even a word?"

"Does it matter?"

Grace sighed. "Yes. If you are going to drop bad Netherworld pickup lines and invoke outdated Mephisthophelean contracts, you should at least have your grammar down. I mean, Faust never used any tripe like that."

"Faust never got laid."

She opened her mouth to say something and then realized she really couldn't. How was she to know what Faust did with his male parts? Caspian could have been there for all she knew. "I suppose there is that."

"So, is it a deal?"

"I don't know. It's not going to end up like that scene from *Devil's Advocate,* is it? I don't fancy all the scratches and psychosis, thank you very much."

Caspian grinned, flashing very white and unnaturally perfect teeth at her. "If every deal turned out bad, why would women keep doing this?"

"Duh. Because the virgins don't know any better. The rest of us want whatever we want more than we *don't* want a few minutes of discomfort."

"There you go. You must make your choice based on those criteria." Caspian paused his pacing in the small circle of decayed bone. He looked pleased with himself. "But I can assure you, it will be more than just a few minutes."

"Of discomfort?"

"Whatever." Now he looked annoyed. "Stop impugning my manhood or I will not be nice to you when you let me out of this circle."

"Who says I'm letting you out? How stupid do you think I am?"

He sighed. "You have to let me out to fulfill both ends of the bargain. I can't shag you senseless if I'm in here, now, can I? Nor can I wreak misery and despair upon your chosen victim."

Grace hadn't thought about that, really. The specifics hadn't been mentioned in any of the books she'd read.

"You can't just, you know . . ." She waved her hand in the air.

"No, I can't 'just,'" he sneered, "'you know,'" and waved his arms in a similarly wild but mocking gesture. "I'm a hands-on kind of guy. I've gotta make sure it goes as intended."

"Why don't I trust you?" Grace asked sarcastically.

"I don't know. You're the first. I have a very honest face." Caspian winked.

She snorted. "My ass."

"Yes, it's nice. What would you like me to do with it?"

"Nothing!" He'd actually sounded sincere. "Not a damn thing. I want you to—"

"Let me remind you, we still need to sign the contract. That was one of *your* stipulations. I wouldn't feel right beginning without it," he interrupted.

"Fine. Get the damn thing already."

She experienced a moment of contrition. What had she just agreed to—besides possibly life-threatening or, alternately, mind-blowing sex? Either way, the possibilities were . . .

He produced something from his sleeve with a grand flourish reminiscent of the great turn-of-the-century showman magicians. His hands were probably slicker, quicker . . . Whatever.

The parchment unrolled of its own volition; again, this appeared to be orchestrated for the show. With his other diabolically elegant hand, Caspian produced a black quill that appeared to be made from a raven's wing. The nib was wickedly sharp and bright. Like a razor. Well, how else was she going to sign a contract in blood?

Grace eyed the parchment carefully, her gaze going from it to the quill, to the ridiculously pleased look on the demon's face. She wasn't sure that sat well with her. He was looking way too self-impressed. She needed to read that contract carefully. Carefully, indeed.

Again, Grace contemplated what she was getting herself into. At the time she did the research, the cost hadn't mattered—only that she pay Michael back in spades for what he'd done to her, because she was the kind of girl who would cut off her nose to spite her face. A contract with a

Crown Prince of Hell seemed just her bad-girl speed. Now she had a feeling she would live to regret it.

Or die to regret it, for that matter. Of course, where Michael was involved, she'd exhausted all of her other options.

She read the scrolling and calligraphic script of the contract, thankful that it was surprisingly to the point. But that gave her another worry: If Caspian wasn't trying to trick her with legal language, there had to be another angle.

Before she could think any more about it, Grace pushed the nub into her thumb. "Goddamn it!" she shrieked. "That hurts."

"Um, hello, little girl? You're the one that demanded the contract be signed in blood, not I."

"Whatever, demon," she hissed. "Fork the thing over."

He rolled up the parchment and thrust it toward her. Grace couldn't help but realize how very phallic the action was, presenting the scroll as if he were going to impale her with its long, tumescent shape. The demon himself was puffed up with a certain pride and watched her with a weighted expectation she'd seen on the faces of previous lovers when they'd first exposed their bodies to her view.

She scribbled her name on the line, then handed back the quill. He signed as well, and did some fancy finger-dancing before making the scroll disappear back into thin air.

"That it?" Grace asked.

Caspian looked offended. "Obviously not."

"With the contract."

"Not exactly. You need to break the circle to let me out."

"I'm still not feeling good about that."

Caspian sighed. "Is this going to be an encounter session where we talk about feelings and your childhood, or a summoning?"

"Fine," Grace snapped, and she wiped her foot across the part of the circle closest to her, smearing the dust.

"Nuh-uh." He shook his head. "It all needs to go."

Grace was annoyed. "Why does the book call for the bone dust to start with, if I'm just going to break the circle?"

"Uh, to keep me trapped until you get what you want?"

"I know that, smart guy. But, I mean, why does it have to be something I'd likely have to kill for if it's not vital to keeping your presence on this plane?"

Caspian grinned. "Demon-summoning is a gateway sin. It leads to other sins, like murder for bone dust. It's a slippery slope, sugar."

"Don't call me 'sugar.' "

"Then get to business. It's not like I have eternity to sit here and verbally spar with you."

She glowered at him.

"Not to say you aren't lovely just standing there, but that only makes our other activities more pressing."

Grace swallowed hard as he cocked his hips at a rakish angle. "You mean you want that part *now*?"

"When did you think I was going to want it?"

She sighed heavily. "Now, I suppose."

He motioned for her to continue wiping the dust away, and she obliged him. When she finished, he just stood there, like he couldn't believe she'd actually broken the circle. That couldn't be good. Not at all. She backed up a few steps.

"I'm not going to chase you," he said.

"Well, I'm not going to come to you."

"Your choice. It was in the contract. You don't fulfill your end, I don't fulfill mine. Easy, really."

"Just sex? It can't be that easy."

His eyes twinkled—or blazed. "I assure you it is."

"Why?"

"Why not?"

"Because you're a demon."

He shrugged. "We get bored. And you're hot. That's it, really. I have my share of souls, locks of granny's hair, and still-beating hearts. This is a better deal. It's something I want more. You'd be surprised how horny a demon can get."

"Uh-huh." Grace still didn't believe him that it would be this easy, but what choice did she have? If she wanted this thing done, she'd have to sleep with him. After all of her blabbing to Michael about how she was going to make him pay, well . . . there was just no option anymore. It had been four years. She'd waited four long years and gotten nothing, so this was her only recourse.

She tentatively stepped toward Caspian. He really was good looking, considering he was a demon. Of course, who knew what he was like under the skin? He could be all scaly and snaggletoothed. But, hell. What did she care? This had to be done. She just wouldn't think about it.

Grace took a deep breath and began peeling her nightgown off her shoulders.

"No, no. And no." Caspian shook his head. "That's not going to work."

Grace blew out a puff of breath, which caused her fringe of hair to flutter against her forehead, almost as if even it was exasperated with the ordeal. "What, then? I don't see how you can shag me properly—or get shagged for that matter—if I'm not naked."

He rolled his eyes and she found herself staring at those sinfully long lashes. "Well, yes. But no to the oh-so dramatic and put-upon removal of said garments. This is supposed to be fun."

"For you, maybe. I didn't conjure a demon because I can't get laid."

Caspian took another step forward, and she took another step back.

"This isn't going to work, Daughter of Eve, if you keep backing away from me. Come here. Or do not. I have pressing business." He glanced grumpily away.

For all that he was a demon, a Crown Prince of Hell, in fact, Grace was no longer afraid. Though, perhaps she should have been. If she'd had the common sense God gave a housefly, she would have been quaking in her fuzzy little slippers. She took a step toward him.

"That's better."

Grace took another step, but as his grin got wider she paused.

"I'm really not used to working so hard."

"What, like, I should fall over on my back like a turtle? Lie flailing and waiting for my doom?" She snorted again, but was now very close.

"Yes. Usually that's how it works. Though it's hardly 'doom.' Is there something in my teeth?" He bared them at her, a scintillating smile. "No? Then what's the problem? The sulfur smell will wash out of your hair, I promise."

"I'm really not relishing the thought of going to Hell for this."

He stretched out one of those long, elegant fingers and let one of her dark curls wrap itself around the digit. Fingering the texture, he murmured, "Like silk." And when he pressed his lips to her cheek, it was anything but platonic.

He shook his head. "You won't go to Hell, silly witch. Not unless this becomes a habit, you know—the summoning." He pressed a kiss to the corner of her mouth, his tongue darting out across the edge of her lip. "You have righteousness in your heart, do you not?"

"The road to Hell is paved with good intentions," she mumbled.

He filled his hand with her breast through the thin material of her nightgown. His tongue pushed past her lips, invading her very senses as if she already belonged to him. "Ah, like honey," he said.

She supposed it would have been fitting if he tasted like sulfur. It would be just what she deserved, but he didn't. He tasted like innocence, like childhood summers hiding in tall grasses after the rains, and there was something else that Grace just couldn't put her finger on—an intangible that made the feeling of innocence seem all the more real. Which, of course, it couldn't be. He was a demon, after all.

Grace pushed him away.

"Look here." He made a frustrated sound. "I don't usually put forth this much effort, but I like you." Her vision of Caspian shimmered before her eyes and his features softened. His generous mouth, the hard planes of his angular jaw, everything became smoother. Those beautiful hands became even more slender, feminine. In fact, his deliciously broad chest was now—

It was *wrong*. That was the only description she could manage. Grace was watching it happen right before her eyes, yet somehow it was still amazingly unreal. Unnatural. Caspian was becoming a woman.

"No, no. Stop that! What are you doing?" Grace sounded to herself much like one of those yipping, little ankle-biter dogs. If Caspian didn't knock off this stunt directly, she was probably going to start bouncing around like one as well.

"I figured," he/she began in a sultry voice, "that my shape must be the problem. I've never had a non-virgin be as reluctant as your most desirable self. . . ."

His features realigned and he was again devastatingly handsome and male, the bastard. As a woman he'd been beautiful. It was unfair. Was it too much to hope for that the creature had known a day of ugly, ever?

Well, of course, there was the fact that he lived in Hell. That had to suck.

With that thought in mind, she sucked in a deep gulp of air and walked with stiff shoulders into Caspian's arms, which were really quite nice, if she were honest. And unfortunately, she was. She was always honest. That was how her dear sweet granny Seraphim had raised her. There were some people who believed that her granny wasn't really dead, that she was the Baba Yaga herself—an immortal witch more powerful than any who'd ever walked the earth. But that was crap. Grace had sobbed at her funeral and watched as the last bit of dirt had covered her coffin and taken Seraphim away from her forever.

She mentally sighed. *Oh, Gran.* Grace missed her so much.

"Okay, chickadee. I need you to not be thinking about your grandmother while I'm plowing your field, if you know what I mean."

"Get out of my head!" Grace demanded. "We didn't agree on any Vulcan Mind Meld, buddy."

"I can't help it. You think loud. Not to mention you weren't forthcoming with pertinent information—like your name. That's what you get when you leave a demon to his own devices, *Grace*." He tested her name on his tongue, a first bite of the myriad confections he'd stolen from her mind.

"Oh, so it couldn't be that you're just nosy? Rude?" She shrugged her shoulders beneath the heat of his palms. When she got no response, she continued. "Uncouth? Pretentious? Invas—"

If he hadn't kissed her then, she would have continued to spew insults, so perhaps it was self-preservation on his part. Though, he'd already said that he wanted her. But . . . how many lips had his touched? How many places had he put the tongue that was now stroking her bottom lip, for that matter? The thought made her stomach a little queasy. Maybe more than just a little.

Those elegantly strong hands splayed across her waist and pulled her hard against him. His defined body was taut, his skin hot and seeming to beg for her touch . . . To Grace's chagrin, all of the thoughts in her head seemed to leak out of her ear and onto the floor. Ah, well, she had always been a fool for broad shoulders, and who could blame her? She sighed into his mouth and realized she might as well just enjoy herself. It's not like *this* was a sin. Nowhere in the Book did it say, "Thou Shalt Not Shag Angels, Be They Fallen or Otherwise."

She tangled his hair in her fist and, while it was like silk, what gave her the most pleasure wasn't the texture but knowing his coiffure wasn't perfect anymore. She grinned as her hands slid down to his shoulders, and she found her fingers sliding beneath his greatcoat and pushing it off.

"That's much better," he said.

"Shut up, or this isn't going to work." She was still fighting the brocade and velvet of his coat.

"Oh, it will work. I promise you that."

Grace snorted again. "Yes, yes, great demon prince. I'm sure *it* works fine. I meant 'it' as in the sex. Not your cock."

Caspian gasped. "Such perversion from that seemingly sweet mouth. Do it again."

"What? Belittle your cock?"

"Don't be deliberately obtuse." He sighed. "You know what I mean."

"The deal was for skin, not for 1-900-Gracie Talks Nasty."

Caspian was kissing the corner of her mouth. "So, *does* Gracie talk nasty? Hmm?" He accented this last with a swipe of his tongue across her lip.

"Only to curse you back to—"

That was enough of that, or so Caspian must have decided. The teasing swipe of his tongue became another full-on military campaign, another invasion. Grace wasn't complaining, though, even if she could do so with him ravaging her mouth in such a way. She melted against him, knowing that it had to be an illusion—the way that she fit perfectly against him, the way the curve of his shoulder was just right for her cheek, the way that her hands already seemed to know him. He was a demon, after all.

She kissed him back, using her tongue like a weapon, capturing and invading him just as he'd done to her. Of course, he liked it. It was obvious. What demon wouldn't? Hell, what *male* wouldn't?

Grace ran her tongue and mouth along the hard angle of his jaw, the corded column of his throat, the deliciously sculpted outline of his pectorals, down farther still to that valley of sin itself, that road to Hell—or to Heaven, as the case was turning out—those hard, hard abdominals. She found herself on her knees, prostrate before his maleness. Caspian didn't take it as his due, however. He watched her with glittering eyes, no expectation there, only desire. Only unbridled lust. He didn't thread his fingers through her hair only to get at the back of her neck and push her lips toward his cock. He waited to see what she would do next.

Because he didn't ask, didn't demand, didn't expect, Grace found that she wanted to taste him, wanted to bring him pleasure. She'd given over to this illusion. It wasn't the mortal and the demon having sex here, or even Grace and the harbinger of Michael's destruction. This was just a man and woman coming together for a moment of ecstasy.

She freed his cock from his breeches and drew her thumb across its velvet head, pearly fluid welling at her touch. Grace's lips were whisper close to the tip, her tongue darting out to follow her thumb. He tasted of salt and sweet, and she swirled her tongue across the swollen flesh, down to the base, then back up again before she took him fully in her mouth, her talented tongue working his need.

A sound began low in his throat, almost like a growl. "Grace."

She dug her fingers into his hips, pulling him forward, and opened her eyes to glance up and meet his gaze. Hellfire burned in those depths, and when she flicked her tongue, it blazed brighter. Closing her fingers around his member, she drew back to talk, stroking up and down to keep her momentum.

"Yes?" She raised an eyebrow.

"Enough." Magick crackled in the air.

Suddenly Grace found herself on her back, naked and splayed for his pleasure. Caspian covered her with his body, his weight pressing her down into the mattress, his mouth hot on her throat, his hands on her breasts, her hips, sliding between her thighs. She allowed him to anchor her hands above her head with one hand, but locked her legs around his waist. This wasn't right. Not yet.

"No," she said sweetly.

"What?" Caspian sounded disbelieving of what he'd heard. "What do you mean, 'no'?"

"I mean: on your back, demon."

Looking intrigued, he shifted his weight and rolled so that she was sitting astride him.

"I'm going to finish what I started," Grace explained. But she wouldn't deny him what he wanted. She swung her long legs across him and worked her hips up his torso to press herself against his lips as she took his cock in her mouth.

CHAPTER THREE
Goings and Comings

Caspian was afraid that he was going to embarrass himself. He hadn't had a woman in years, and he couldn't remember the last time any was so aggressive. He wanted to come, but he also wanted this to last forever, the delicious sensation of her mouth bobbing up and down on his rod. He had visions of spraying her face with his seed and watching that hot little tongue lap it up, or maybe to finish on those glorious tits . . .

His cock surged, but he held on to his control. Barely.

While tempted to just lie back and enjoy her ministrations, he refused to be outdone. He kept saying it over and over: He was a showman. So he grinned and pressed his face into her slit, his tongue sliding the length of it. Those sweet lips parted. His tongue forked and split, curling both around her clit and thrusting deep into her slick passage.

She cried out, pausing in her task to mash herself down hard on his face. Caspian reacted with pleasure, thrusting harder and then replacing his tongue with his fingers. Then he licked her from slit to arse.

Grace paused in her writhing, as if startled, but she didn't tell him to stop; nor did she stop what she was doing to him. In fact, she took him fully into her mouth, deep-throating his cock. It broke his control, and he was suddenly surging inside her mouth. But he wanted her to come as well, wanted her screaming his name—

He slipped his tongue back inside her, half of his oral member working her clit and the other driving past the rosebud ring of muscles several inches above. She was sweet and hot, her cries spurring him onward, and she was sitting upright now, her thighs braced on either side of his face, grinding against his mouth, begging him for more, for release.

Caspian slipped another finger inside her, and then she was screaming as her orgasm hit and pleading for him to stop, but her hips were still thrusting her forward against him. She dug her fingers into his hair to tug his head away from her clit, but he was latched on like a familiar seeking a teat. He would not let go. Caspian could sense there was another peak building inside her and he wanted to shove her off it with extreme prejudice.

Her screams hit an impossibly high pitch and he kept them there, playing her like a finely tuned instrument, and only when it sounded as if she were dying did he allow her bliss to ebb. There was evidence of her pleasure all over his face, and he licked his lips as he allowed her to crawl off him. She collapsed boneless and sated, curled against him, spasms still shaking her body. After a few moments, he spoke, though the sound was muffled. "You know, it's a good thing I don't need to breathe. Death by pussy is not one of my goals, even if it is a pussy as glorious as yours."

Grace crawled around to lay her head in the crook of his arm. "I thought most men wanted to die fucking."

"I can't die," he pointed out. No, he couldn't die, but he could wish he was dead. He shuddered, thinking back to that ill-fated affair with Lilith.

"Well, in that case." She moved like she was going to straddle him again. Caspian laughed and moved his hands to her hips to help out, licking his lips with a forked and primed tongue. He felt her slit spasm and clench against his thigh just from watching him, and she bit her bottom lip.

"Okay, you win. For now." She settled back down, clearly ready for a nap.

"You haven't fulfilled your end of the contract yet. This wasn't the big show, you know. Just foreplay."

"Oh, yeah?" Grace sounded intrigued, interested even, but it was clear she was spent.

"Yeah. But, it's a good down payment."

She burrowed closer, her eyes closing. "I should think so."

"So, we can begin plotting your revenge," he pointed out.

She yawned. "Later, I think. Sleep now. This has waited four years; I suppose it can wait one more night."

Caspian smirked. He'd enjoy taking advantage of this whole revenge plot. Just like he'd told her earlier, men hated to see their women, exes or not, with someone else. And if Grace wasn't completely over her relationship with her evil ex, she would be by the time he was done with her. Everyone knew the fastest way to get over one man was to get under another—or a Crown Prince of Hell like himself.

By morning he was having second thoughts. Grace had been sleeping for some time, but he, Caspian, great Crown Prince of Hell, next in line for the great Throne of the Damned, was having chest pain. A heart attack. That's the only thing it could be. He'd stayed all night and fucked the woman every which way from Sunday and she'd still been ready for more. If he could die, he might be worried.

Okay, so he *was* worried. This pain in his chest, he didn't like it. There was a nagging in the back of his head that told him this wasn't a physical malady; it was because he actually liked this woman. Wasn't that just a rancid bitch?

Sure, Caspian had always been a lover of women. He

loved how they looked, how they smelled, how they tasted; he loved the little sounds they made when he was riding them like horses at the track. He even liked to listen to them talk, liked the sound of their voices. And it was all women, really. Thick ones, thin ones, large breasts, small breasts, she of the childbearing hips and backyard, and those less gifted. Short hair, long hair, blue eyes, brown eyes . . . Earth was a smorgasbord to him. So much so, that he had never really paid attention enough to his lovers to know if he liked them as people. But, he liked *Grace*.

Caspian cringed as the pain in his chest doubled. It was sharp like a pinch from a clamp on his nipple, twisting because he liked her.

Damn! Again, he had to stop thinking about her. Especially as a person. Too bad he'd let her talk him into a contract, because he would leave her high and dry if he could get away with it. For his own protection, of course. He'd never broken a deal before. For a demon, he was reliable. While some of his cronies thought it was terrible, having a reputation as being dependable, he'd found it good for business. It meant more summonings, which meant more corruption ultimately spread around. Sure, most of it was bitch work, but it kept him in the Big Boss's good graces—which was important to everyone who didn't fancy roasting on a spit.

Grace rolled over and laid her head on his chest. From her light snore, he could tell that she was still asleep.

Sleep. That was something Caspian loved about being topside. Only when he was corporeal did he get to sleep and eat corn dogs. And chocolate. Oh, by the Adversary, did he ever love chocolate. And Warcraft. The game was a personal triumph for the Big Boss, originally designed for demon R and R. He played every chance he got. If he'd been a mortal man, Caspian knew he would have started out handsome but ended up a sloppy fatso living in his mom's basement and subsisting on corn dogs and Milky Way bars, jacking off to cybersex on one screen while gaming on another. With that thought, he looked at Grace. Once again, he was very interested in her naked breasts, in the curve of her bottom lip and—

An eye cracked open. "You'll just have to wait. My snatch is not a Bag of Holding. Nothing else will fit today. I am not a demon; therefore, I have no regenerative powers. I've had a baby, so I don't think it's going to just snap back into place. Sorry."

She didn't sound the least bit sorry, but Caspian found he couldn't be miffed with her when she curled into him like that. But, again with the nipple-twisting pain. Was she a virus only a demon could catch? That had to be it.

Wait, what did she mean by "baby"? There was no baby smell to the house, no maternal scent to her.

"Is *that* why you want to get Michael Grigorovich?" he asked.

"Yeah. Why do you care?"

"I don't," he said. But he felt a cold chill up his spine and wasn't sure of the reason. Whatever it was, he didn't like it. "I just need to know what I'm dealing with. To be effective."

Grace opened her eyes and propped herself up on her elbow. "He stole my child from me. I know that the parental bond probably doesn't mean much to a demon, but I want my son. He doesn't even know what I look like. Michael took him from me as soon as he was born. It's been four years. I just lost my last court appeal—and all without ever getting a physical hearing."

Caspian felt another tightening in his chest. "How did he get away with that?"

"Money. Power. Connections. All things that he's gotten from trafficking with demons."

"Who am I up against? You should have told me this at

the summoning. This information was not figured into the contract." Caspian felt a faint glimmer of hope that he'd be able to get out of the deal by exploiting a loophole. Then, no more torture.

"I knew you would try to find a way out of this."

The look on her face would have broken his heart if he'd had one. Not to mention that damnable pain in his chest doubled down again with the cold chill on his back. He thought for a moment the sensation might be guilt, but how could that happen? Guilt wasn't possible for a demon. "Damn it, who is it? Which demon did he make his deal with?"

"Ethelred."

"Oh." Caspian laughed. "For a minute there I thought this was going to be a challenge. If it had been Lilith or maybe, say, someone closer in line for the throne, that might have been a problem."

"That's why I summoned you specifically. I want my son back."

"I can do that," Caspian said.

"I want to be safe from Michael."

"I can do that, too."

He would have provided her safety regardless. The thought of someone hurting Grace did not sit well with him. Not that he cared to examine the thought at any length. Neither did he care to examine the hellfire that raged within him when he thought of Grace afraid. Or what this Michael person had done to her. Caspian was a demon. He shouldn't be having feelings, of hellfire or otherwise.

A damnable voice in the back of his head reminded him that he'd once been human. Yeah, a long time ago and even, yes, in a land far away, he'd been mortal. Once. But he was too far gone for that now. This was his fate, his destiny. His mother had not been of virgin flesh when she'd made her deal, so Caspian was always meant for this. Unlike those who were fully human, he'd been denied free will. Caspian had always known demonhood lay at the end of any path he chose in life. He'd been born of demon flesh, so what other option was there?

He realized suddenly the enormity of what he'd done with Grace. They could possibly have a child. Before he'd touched her, this sort of thing hadn't mattered: Demon spawn didn't much concern him, other than the Big Boss's reaction. Not until now had he cared about the rest. Not until this woman. She made him feel all sorts of things he didn't want to face.

It was all by virtue of her body, he supposed. Which was a laugh. It was like he was a virgin who'd fallen in love with the first girl that would fuck him. Now he was wrapped around her little finger, the Poindexter slavering after the cheerleader for a peek up her skirt. This was no longer a simple business transaction. Because he *liked* her. He might have spawn with her, and worse, he was worried about that fact. Sure, he'd tagged other pieces more than once, but he never planned it, never thought of tomorrow, and never worried about consequences. This was unacceptable!

He suddenly doubled over in pain, though a low growl was the only sign he gave of his distress. "Consider your part paid in full," he ground out. "I will fulfill my end." He had to get away from her. The very breath in her body made him ache somehow, and he'd had enough.

He dematerialized.

CHAPTER FOUR

Revenge Is Best Served Cold

She found it odd in the extreme that Caspian had stayed the night and then abruptly vanished after asking about her son. She'd expected him to leave immediately after they concluded her part of the contract: the payment in flesh. And, oh, dear saints in Heaven, how she'd paid. She ached everywhere. But it was that good kind of pain that let her know she'd definitely been in the company of a sex god. She hadn't enjoyed a time like that in . . . well, ever.

A nice, hot bath was just what she needed. With bubbles and a glass of wine. Yes, Grace felt languorous and leisurely, considering that a demon had just vacated her house—and her body, for that matter. Plans of vengeance could wait.

She paused, wondering if part of her brain would kick in and scream like a banshee on the rag, asking her what in the name of Hell she'd just done, even though the little voice in her head would know what she'd done because it was there. Or not. Where had that little voice gotten off to? Was it on vacation? Did it have an answering machine? Could Grace leave it a message?

On second thought, Grace really didn't want to leave a message. It was kind of nice not listening to her conscience shrieking into her ear all the time. Maybe it would stay gone forever.

Part of her knew that these were extremely dangerous

thoughts. These were the type of reflections that littered that amazingly glittery path to damnation, like so many primrose petals. But, seeing as her conscience was away from its desk, the concern wasn't as great as it might have been. She'd worry about it later.

Grace sank deeply into some hot water and wished that for once she could have a bath that would do more than cover her rump or her breasts. She wanted a tub that fit both. If she sank down far enough to cover her chest, her legs were in the air. If she sat up, the rest of her was cold. It sort of ruined the effect of soaking in a hot bath. This was more like dipping. When she got her money and her son back from Michael, after she admitted to him that she was behind the demon tormenting him and only she could stop it, she was going to buy a house in the nicest suburb of Kansas City. Somewhere with a homeowners' association, gated entry, and no damn demons, witches, supernatural creatures, or mobsters. It was going to have a bathroom the size of a living room. It was going to have a tub big enough for eight people, and two hot-water heaters. And the showerhead would be to die for. Then she wouldn't need a man. Or a demon. She and her son would have a nice, normal, safe life.

She wondered what Caspian was going to do to Michael, then snorted. Michael. Michael Grigorovich. He'd sworn on a stack of Bibles that he was descended from the great Rasputin. Grace would believe that when Madame Tussaud sculpted his likeness out of her earwax. She knew now he was just another thug from Brighton, a thug who had her son, Nikoli.

He'd stolen the child as soon as Nikoli was born, kicking her out of their penthouse and refusing to see her. Grace didn't know why he wanted the boy, but it wasn't to raise him or to be a father. He'd actually acted angry when he found out she was pregnant. He'd only begun seeing her, she'd learned, because he was into the occult and had heard that she was a witch raised in the old tradition.

For her part, Grace had been blind to him and his slimy ways. Stupid. She'd liked his power back then, liked his money. Best of all, she'd liked his promise to take care of her as long as she took care of him. Ha! As if. She'd finally found out what he was *really* like. How had she not known earlier? Maybe because she didn't want to. She didn't want to believe it even now.

She'd never dunked her fists into anything as wrong as demon-summoning before; Michael had done that all on his own. But she would fight fire with fire, and her fire was bigger. It was a bonfire. Caspian was very powerful, like the will of a mother trying to regain her child. Michael could summon the Devil himself and Grace would get Nikoli back. She would do whatever it took, as last night clearly showed.

She wondered briefly if she was going to see Caspian again. He'd said that he would keep up his end of the bargain, which wouldn't necessarily require a second visit, but wasn't it just like a demon to come back and demand a second payment? If she was honest with herself, the idea caused her a little thrill of pleasure. Grace *wanted* to see him again, to be close to him. She'd never been touched the way Caspian touched her. Not even when she'd been fooled into believing that she was in love with Michael.

Wait. This was a dangerous path she trod. No matter how great the sex, Caspian was still a demon—a Crown Prince of Hell, no less. If she planned to be one of those foolish girls who confused sex and love, this was the wrong time. There was nothing but misery down this path. Nothing at all.

A loud banging on the door jarred her unceremoniously from her languid dip, but Grace would be double damned if she was going to get out of the delicious hot water to answer. She didn't have that many friends, and none who would stop by without calling. Michael had seen to that, actually. He'd secluded her from her friends, her hobbies, her life. She was well rid of him. All that mattered now was her son, and when she got Nikoli back from his asshat father, she was going to make sure that neither of them ever had to deal with Michael again.

She debated slipping under the water to escape listening to the incessant pounding. That was when she had another epiphany: Only cops and thugs banged on doors like that.

"Open the door, Grace." It was Sasha, Michael's right-hand man. She hadn't seen him since the last rescheduled court date regarding Nikoli. "Grace, I'll be letting Petru break this door down if you don't open it."

Petru. Where Sasha went, that Cro-Mag followed. Petru could have worked in the circus as a dancing bear, he was so large and hairy. All he did was growl. She didn't know how Sasha understood him.

She hurried to the door. The robe draped around her slick, wet body was provocatively clingy, but she didn't care. They'd seen much more of her already. They'd been in the room when Nikoli was born. In fact, Sasha had delivered him.

Grace stopped short of the door. "What do you want?" she called through it.

"Open up."

"No." She had no doubt that Petru *would* break it down, but she defied Sasha anyway. Even knowing none of her neighbors would call the police, and even if they did, Michael owned all the police. People who fucked with the Russian mob had a nasty habit of turning up dead.

"Grace, Michael knows what you did."

"I don't care. He can rot in Hell."

"Some third-level demon isn't enough to thwart him, so

I hope you got the best. He's only going to get angry. I don't want to see you hurt."

"Then why are you pounding on my door and threatening to break it down?"

"Let me in, Grace. I just want to talk."

Grace could hear Petru puffing like a pregnant hippopotamus trying to run straight up Mount Everest. With his large bulk likely rearing back to locomotive through her poor, defenseless door, she had no choice but to open up.

Actually, she could have hexed him so that mosquito larvae hatched in his sinuses and flew out his nose, but this was much more fun; she'd get immediate gratification. She opened up and stepped out of the way just as the bull moose charged. The look on his face was priceless: a startled yak with lost footing. He bashed his round melon-head straight into the opposite wall, straight into the hanging silhouette portrait of Grace's grandmother, Seraphim Stregaria, and fell to the ground.

A long, low sound started in the back of his throat. "Baba Yaga," the large mobster whimpered, falling in seeming slow motion to land on his rump. He was staring at the silhouette portrait, clearly horrified at the thought of violating a likeness of Seraphim Stregaria.

Grace was amused. Her granny's name had been whispered in what Seraphim had called the old country, in Russia—a tale told to frighten little children—or so she'd claimed, though Grace always thought that her dear old gran was a bit of a ham. She had liked living in that rundown Victorian in that bad neighborhood, daring kids to play "ding-dong ditch" or to come get their ball from her porch. Once, Grace had seen a child's face go white as the bloated belly of a dead fish in her gran's presence. While his eyes darted here and there for any manner of escape, Gran had laughed so hard that she'd choked on her false teeth.

Not that she'd done anything to the child; in fact, she'd tried to give him a cookie. But the hysterical cackle had indeed sounded like a stereotypical Halloween hag and sent the boy running. Which had tickled her more, of course. Gran never minded the "witch" moniker; she was always happy to play it up.

Petru was still sniveling as Grace finished her little jaunt down memory lane. She put a fist on her hip and demanded an answer. "If you fear Seraphim so much, why did you almost break down her granddaughter's door?"

"I didn't know," he howled like a child who'd stepped in a great pile of dog shit and had just been told it wouldn't wash off. "How did I not know?"

Sasha bowed his head to the remains of the portrait, also clearly surprised. Grace raised her eyebrow at him. "Just wait until I hang up an actual *photograph* of Gran. That should be interesting." In some small villages in the Eastern Bloc, there were people who still believed that a photograph could hold a person's essence, even their soul.

She closed the door and put the latch on it. Not that anyone other than Michael's thugs would bother her, but it was a habit.

Sasha eyed Petru as if the man were his life's great cross to bear. He rubbed his blondish beard, which by all rights should have been threaded with gray for all of his hard fifty years. "Look what you did, you great *govniuk*."

Petru slapped his meaty fists on the ground, a child throwing a tantrum. "I said I didn't know."

Grace didn't have the patience. "So, what is it that you want?"

"I swear, Grace. We did only come to talk." Sasha held out his palms, as if that alone would convince her of his innocence.

"You're a bad man, Sasha Dubenko. You do bad things. Why should I believe you?"

"For one thing, because you're Seraphim Stregaria's granddaughter."

"You fear her wrath even from the grave? Then, how could you take my child from me when he was born?"

"That's what I'm here to talk about. Your grandmother is alive." Sasha bowed his golden head to look at Petru again. "And, dear Heaven, will you please tell this *govniuk* that Baba Yaga will not come and carry him off for her dinner?"

"I don't know, Petru. You did destroy her likeness. She might think you did it on purpose. . . ." Grace trailed off and shrugged, figuring they both deserved it for saying her grandmother was alive. That was just cruel.

The mobster grabbed the hem of her robe and pulled so hard that the garment was practically torn from her shoulders, revealing flushed skin beneath. Sasha almost choked, turning a bright shade of red before spinning around to face the wall. He managed to work in a kick at Petru, who looked up at Grace and saw what he had done.

Grace sighed. It was her own fault, egging the dancing bear on when he was so obviously frightened. Gran had been such a powerful witch that it was believed she'd shrugged off the dark embrace of Death and returned as Baba Yaga, the goddess witch incarnate said to devour human flesh to keep her magick strong. Grace could just see it: her dear old gran standing over some gargantuan black kettle, stirring the thing madly with a gleam in her eye and reciting in a singsong voice, something from *Macbeth* about "Filet of a fenny snake, double-double toil and trouble, boil cauldron burn and bake . . ." She'd have gotten a kick out of it.

"Petru, it's okay. Really. Just don't try to break my door down again."

"*Slavny*, Grace! Thank you." He was on his knees, still trying to kiss the hem of her robe.

"Petru, I need my robe back."

He looked up again, only then seeming to realize that she was half-naked. It was as if he'd been bitten by a rattlesnake. He threw himself against the floor, prostrate.

Grace could tell his comrade wanted to kick him again. "It's okay, Sasha." She pulled up her robe and made herself decent. "You, too, Petru. Come, sit, tell me what you came to tell me."

"*Slavny, slavny,* Grace!" Petru gushed.

From hours at her gran's knee, she was sure that he was saying something kind. He kept calling her "nice" or "good"—which was totally off the mark, because she'd just summoned a Crown Prince of Hell to deal with their employer. She hadn't thought too much about the other people who might get in the way.

Then again, what did she care if these two idiots got hurt? They were the ones who chose to work for Michael Jizzhat Grigorovich. That wasn't her fault. They'd helped Michael steal Nikoli from her. They deserved everything they had coming.

Unfortunately, this was when the little voice in the back of her head, the thing called a conscience, decided to return from its extended "vay-cay" wherever the hell it was sipping little drinks with umbrellas while she'd been naked and sweating with a demon. She *did* care what happened to these two. Especially when she looked at simple Petru. Double damn.

"So, what did you want to tell me, Sasha? I'd really like to get back to my bath. Although, my water is most likely the temperature of a current off the coast of Iceland by now."

Petru was mumbling to himself. He had apparently decided to make himself at home, sure now that Grace had forgiven him. He was rummaging through her refrigerator and, like any good carnivore, was shoving everything into his mouth that could be remotely described as meat.

Sasha was watching him with something that seemed akin to loving disgust, if such a thing were possible. The sort of look a mother would give a monstrous child that had torn down fruit displays in the grocery store after biting a clerk and sat among the ruins happily stuffing food in his mouth. "I apologize for him. He . . ." The blond mobster shrugged.

"Dear God in Heaven, get on with it! Petru can have whatever he wants in that fridge, as long as he doesn't strip me naked again." The thought occurred to Grace that keeping these men on track was like trying to corral a few hundred preschoolers hyped up on gummi bears and chocolate milk. She motioned irritably for him to continue.

"Nikoli isn't your son."

Sasha waited, and Grace blinked owlishly, not sure if she'd heard correctly.

"I know this is hard to hear, but Nikoli is just a memory implant. He isn't real. He's part of Michael's bargains with the demon Ethelred to send you on a sleigh ride down the slippery slope to damnation. He needs you to make the ultimate sacrifice for Nikoli's return—your life—so he can achieve demonhood. Four years he's wasted, or you've outmaneuvered him. He's only got thirteen more days to do it or his soul is forfeit."

Grace's bodily reaction to the news seemed to cover the gamut of the animal kingdom. Her eyelids fluttered like the wings of an inebriated hummingbird, her eyes were mosquitoes buzzing around in her head—or was that the ringing in her ears? Her mouth fell open like a largemouth bass with a hook in its lip, and she was gasping so much that she sounded like a hiccupping mouse, which included the strange little sound coming out of her nose.

As the squeaking mouse act was not allowing enough air into her lungs, or into her brain for that matter, she promptly fell over. On the way down, she cracked her head on the ornately carved and expensive corner of her coffee table, the one her granny had brought from the old country. The last things she saw were the beautifully lacquered scenes of the Baba Yaga fairy tale that had been etched into the top of the table. The colors swirled in her narrowing vision in the most pleasing way.

CHAPTER FIVE
The Colder the Better

Michael Ivan Grigorovich was a bastard in every sense of the word. It was a badge he wore proudly. He was calculating and cruel, and he took every opportunity to showcase these traits. Also, his mother never married his father.

His father had been a bastard first—and a dickhead. Ivan Vasilyev was a firm believer that sparing the rod spoiled the child. He'd believed the same about lovers, like Michael's mother, Nadja, from whom Michael got his magickal powers. Not a day went by in all of their time together that Ivan didn't lay his hands on her. Even when she surpassed all of his expectations and demands, he still gave her a healthy slap just to remind her of her place. Michael had never done that to Grace, so he didn't see what exactly she had to complain about. Nikoli? Bah. Even if the kid were real, she was better off without him. At least, that's what his mother would say.

Nadja claimed it was somehow Michael's own fault that he'd been born; her son was so determined to come into the world that even a mandrake-infused hot chocolate had refused to root him from her womb. If not for Michael, Nadja would have left Ivan a hundred times over. There had never been any love there. No, what kept Nadja from leaving Ivan had nothing to do with affection for her son. It was simply a desire for power.

While she'd never wanted him, Nadja was willing to use Michael. She'd wanted to make sure that when his blood—Rasputin's blood—drove him to seek magick and power, it would be her influence that guided him. It would be her darkness that would take root in his heart. Nadja would wield him as a weapon against his father and the world. So, when her son came to her, his blood urging him to seek the old magicks and arcane knowledge, she'd taught him what she knew and had no problem whatsoever explaining the ritual for taking Ivan's head to offer the demon Ethelred. Yes, Nadja had held her son's hand down the primrose path to Hell. It had been her pleasure, and her son knew it.

That didn't stop him from wishing for her counsel. There were thirteen days to make this mess of a plan come together. If she were here, it would already be done; he wouldn't have been deterred from the original design at all. But she was gone and Michael couldn't think that way. Nadja was trapped somewhere, imprisoned by the Baba Yaga for her arrogance. She'd be no help to him; she couldn't even help herself.

Grace had been a convenient choice for the original plan and she'd been especially suited for his mother's purposes, being the granddaughter of her enemy. Michael was to seduce a girl and make her fall in love with him, and then sacrifice her. He'd first planned to slit Grace's throat on their wedding night, but when she started to disobey him he knew they'd never make it that long. Especially after she refused to summon Ethelred. That's when he and his mother hatched the idea of Nikoli.

He'd had to be patient for this to germinate, layer after layer of touch and memory implanted in Grace's mind. She had to believe it had all happened, her separation from her baby. Four long years of memories, of the birthing, of court battles and lawyers, all the while that ache growing for her son, the magick making her dwell on the hollow sensation of arms empty of a child. It was a carefully measured poison administered in precise doses. Yes, four years was a long time to wait, but Michael had cultivated Grace's pain like an exotic flower, feeding and tending it from afar. Grace would soon do *any*thing for the child he'd conjured, even give up her own life. It was worth the wait, for this sacrifice was no longer simply a step to demonhood, but a deal that would fulfill all his other bargains.

Michael rubbed his hands together absently, pondering his machinations until an unwelcome voice shrilled him out of his thoughts.

"Are you going to fuck it or stare at it all night? I got things to do, Michael."

He didn't pay these bitches to talk or think; he just wanted them flat on their backs. Who did this hooker have to do that was more important than he? Didn't she know who he was? He was the son of Ivan Vasilyev. He'd been inked with stars on his kneecaps and shoulders; the tattoos signified his heritage, that he bowed to no one and was a man of status and tradition. He was a leader of men. He was motherfucking *royalty*.

He slapped the hooker with just enough force so that she got to keep her teeth. The next blow wouldn't be so forgiving. She didn't flinch, didn't cry. He assumed that she knew better. She damn well should.

His voice was deceptively calm. "If I want to stare at your pussy all night long, I'll do it. If I want to watch you ex-fucking-sanguinate into my bathtub and splash my goddamn ceiling in a modern art mural with your blood, I'll do it."

"I'm sorry." The whore pursed her now-swollen lips.

Yeah, she was sorry. And she had no idea how much sorrier she was going to be before this night was over. Michael positioned his fingers at the soft indentation of her throat and then spanned the pale column of her neck. He could feel her pulse pounding there, the drumbeat of a scared little rabbit in the mouth of the wolf.

Her mouth fell open and she screamed. It was a huge sound for such a little mouth, especially with the pressure of his hand on her throat. But the whore's wide eyes weren't looking at him. They were focused on something else.

That was when he felt the first sting—no, maybe "sting" wasn't the correct word. It was a pain like no other he'd known, followed by an itching that felt like a sheath of poison ivy had wrapped his dick, which was where the prostitute was staring. He didn't want to look. Yes, for maybe the first time in years, Michael Ivan Grigorovich was afraid.

He felt the sensation again and looked down involuntarily, closing his eyes at the very last second. He didn't want to open them; he fought to keep them closed, afraid of what he might see. The whore was still screaming, a high-pitched wail that made a place in his spine tic with homicidal rage. He clenched his hand.

Forcing himself to breathe, Michael opened his eyes. There, doing an Irish jig on the end of his cock, was the most horrible thing he'd ever seen. It was small and red, fat and round like a bloated tick. It was the size of a clementine "cutie" orange, its skin smooth but for the hair that hung off the end of a phallic tail, and it smiled at Michael and revealed a mouth full of tiny razors.

The thing then flipped its tail up, revealing a second smiling mouth. Using its crustacean-like appendages, it dug into his skin and flipped, biting down alternately with the rump mouth and the front mouth. And it was excreting some sort of fluid that made Michael itch so badly that he debated completely cutting off the affected area. But it was his cock.

He grabbed the obscenity and smashed it in his fist, various parts of the creature dripping out of his still-fisted hand. It had popped like a tick. He shook the material from his grip but, as he did, two more monstrosities appeared on the length of his still-hard dick. They scuttled down into the nest of his pubic hair, which did little to hide their bloated bodies. In fact, even though he was gifted in the size department, there was little space for any more of the creatures.

Michael heard more screaming, but this time it couldn't be the whore—he'd cut her air off and killed her already. No, it was his.

The dead whore forgotten, he scrambled off the bed and into the bathroom, where he grabbed a razor and immediately shaved his pubic hair, hoping that would root out the disgusting little bastards. But it didn't. It just forced them to dig their claws into his flesh as opposed to swinging like Tarzan through the foliage. And what messed with him most was that they seemed intelligent. The bugs smiled at him with those predator's teeth before flipping themselves over like maniac gymnasts to bite with both mouths. It was *disgusting*.

Michael found a pair of pliers and a lighter. If they popped like ticks, maybe he could get rid of them like ticks. He was no longer concerned about what they were, but rather whom they were from. He was doubly glad now that Grace was going to die. These little horrors could only have come from her, from that demon she had summoned. This was definitely a trick inspired in the seventh ring of Hell.

A sulfuric odor burned his nostrils, and a low menacing laugh sounded from the shadows. "I wouldn't do that if I were you."

"Well, you're not me, so fuck off. And you weren't invited here."

A figure stepped forward, shedding the shadows like a cloak. It was clearly a demon. "Grace invited me."

Michael met his visitor's eyes as he grabbed one of the creatures with the pliers, its little appendages flailing in protest. "I'm not impressed."

The demon shrugged. "Suit yourself."

Michael squeezed, taking a special delight in killing the creature he'd wrenched off his privates—only to find that two more had appeared in its place. Now there were three.

"I told you so. Demon crabs are a bitch, huh? No fun, my man. No fun at all." His demon guest whacked him on the shoulder in a good-natured gesture of male bonding, unmindful of Michael's nakedness.

"How do I . . . ?" Michael began, but the demon was gone.

Crap. He was definitely going to have to summon Ethelred again, barter more of his soul to get rid of these things. Goddamn it, he was fucked. He was fucked like the two dead hookers in the trunk of his Lexus. He was fucked facedown. And it didn't look like anyone was looking to flip him over.

CHAPTER SIX
Ain't Life a Bitch?

Grace came around slowly but wished she was still in oblivion. There was something under her nose that smelled like death.

Another hot puff of the putrid stench was blown up her nose. Before she thought better, she opened her mouth to protest. She was immediately and heartily sorry, as a blast shot right into her mouth, like something out of an Internet shock vid. That was when she realized it was just Petru's breath.

She opened her eyes and gagged as he moved closer into her breathing space, peering at her intently. "I'm going to pass out again if you don't get out of my face, Petru," she warned.

"He had borscht and lamb for breakfast," Sasha said by way of apology.

Grace struggled to turn her head. "I'm going to spew *my* breakfast."

"You hit your head," Petru said. "You fell."

He was suddenly yanked out of her immediate vicinity, and for that she was grateful.

"Yes, Petru. Thank you." Grace realized that she was starting to feel sorry for him again; he was really just a big, dumb animal that needed a guiding hand. It had been a while since she'd seen him, and she'd forgotten what he was like. "Sasha, why don't you try to tell me once more? Please use small words, because I find it hard to believe that my son—my Nikoli—isn't real."

"I know he's real to you, Grace. Which is why Michael believes that you'll make the ultimate sacrifice for him."

"But I remember you taking him from my arms. I remember being pregnant. I remember Michael getting me anchovies and ice cream." Grace's voice cracked with emotion.

"Grace," Sasha admonished. "How many women do you know who've ever actually craved anchovy ice cream? It's a stereotype. Look at your belly, Grace. With your genes, there's no way you would have made it through a pregnancy without stretch marks. I saw you when your robe slid open. Your stomach is as smooth and flat as it was when you were a teenager."

"How do you know what my belly looked like when I was a teenager?"

The mobster sighed. "It's an expression."

"Why are you telling me this?"

"Look, Michael has plans for you."

"Why me?" Grace wrapped her arms around her body, suddenly frightened. Why couldn't he just leave her alone? The whole world she'd created for herself seemed to be crumbling like the bone dust still littering her bedroom.

"Nadja, his mother. She chose you."

"Michael said she was dead."

"Nadja can only pray for death now." Sasha looked sad.

Grace took his hand in hers. "And I ask you again, why are you telling me this, Sasha? Michael will kill you." She knew this could very well be a ploy, because for as long as she'd known Michael, Sasha had been loyal to him.

"Because I love Nadja. I always have. Since Ivan introduced me to her on their first date. I have to find a way to set her free."

Nadja? Really? Things were getting more complicated by the moment.

"How is helping me going to help her?"

"Gaining the Baba Yaga powers through deceit will surely damn her. I just pieced together the details of her plans from Michael's own."

Grace sighed tiredly. "There is no Baba Yaga, Sasha."

"There is, Grace Stregaria. And her blood runs through your veins."

"No one knows whose blood I carry. I never even knew my father's name."

"Your father's blood doesn't matter. It's Seraphim's blood and magick that runs through you, that's made you as powerful as you are, and has marked you for Nadja's vengeance."

"If I were to believe any of this, why does Nadja hate my grandmother so much?" Grace was sure it was all a fetid crock of crap, but if Sasha believed it, maybe Michael did, too. It could be something that she and Caspian could use against him.

"There was a prophecy about the Baba Yaga power. I don't know the specifics, only that it had been narrowed down to two witches. Nadja and Seraphim. And rather than fight the Nazis with her power, she aligned with them and had Seraphim arrested. She believed that if Seraphim died in a camp, it would take the stain of her death off Nadja's hands and she would ascend. But it didn't work out that way."

"She never spoke about that time with me. But it makes no sense. Nadja isn't old enough to—"

"You're from a family of magick users. There are ways to prolong youth and life."

"I'm sorry, Sasha. This sounds so surreal."

"And summoning a demon sounds more reasonable than an immortal witch? Look, you have to believe me. You're in serious danger from more than just Michael Grigorovich. Nadja's shadow is everywhere."

"Nadja is dead, just like my grandmother."

"No." The big man shook his head. "She's waiting for me and I'm going to save her. Even if it's from herself. I've done some terrible things, but it's been to survive. Even without a father, you've never had that burden. It changes you at your core."

"And Michael? What has he had to do to survive? No, this is pure selfish greed on his part inspired by his mother. We make our own choices, no matter what we go through."

"You're so rigid, Grace. How can you see the world in black and white when nothing is ever so simple?"

"You *need* the shades of gray, because you loved a woman who was evil to the tips of her pedicured toes. If everything you said was true, then Nadja tried to kill my grandmother and wants her son to kill me. She conspired with her bastard son to give me pain and suffering like no parent should ever endure and you're talking to me about saving her? Why should I care what happens to the witch?"

"I don't suppose you should, *malenkaya*." He patted her hand and withdrew from her grasp.

Grace shrugged her shoulders. "This all too much. It's unreal. Unbelievable."

"Ask your demon for the answer. He'll give it to you," Petru interjected.

"Oh, yeah. I'll just ask a demon for the truth and he'll give it to me?" Grace stared at him. "Wait, how does anyone know I summoned a demon?"

"Bone dust. I can see it on the floor in your bedroom. That only proves what Michael suspects. Now, I've helped you, Grace. Are you going to help me?" Sasha asked.

"This is too much, Sasha. More to the point, I wouldn't even know where to begin to help you."

"Just ask your demon what he knows. Decide whether to trust us. We'll be back."

Sasha grabbed Petru and shoved him out the door.

Was he trying to drive her crazy? He must be really pissed that she'd summoned a demon to thwart him. It made sense, especially considering that she'd refused to summon a demon for him. There was no way that her son, the child of her body, was not real. It had been four years since she'd seen him, but the memories were as fresh as ever. She'd sung to him as he grew beneath her heart, as they'd shared dreams, made promises.

Yet, the look in Sasha's dark eyes had been so sincere.

Grace really just wanted to take another bath and go to bed. That would be ideal. It probably wasn't the best idea, though, considering that she'd just knocked brain juice out of her ears when she'd hit her head on that damn coffee table. Was it possible that her grandmother was still alive? Was the Baba Yaga myth a reality?

All of these questions were making her head hurt even worse. She couldn't be expected to process everything at once; she needed some downtime where she didn't have to think about anything. Not her grandmother, not Michael, not what Sasha had told her, certainly. Not even Caspian. Definitely not Caspian.

She would go shopping, she decided. Credit therapy, she liked to call it. She was going to buy some new underwear for dating nice mortal men and a few nice lacy little things to sleep in, maybe a new outfit or two. And shoes, definitely shoes. There was also a new chocolatier that had opened in the River Market district, and she wanted some gourmet chocolate-covered graham crackers. Best of all, this wasn't even going to be on her credit. Grace had applied for a card in Michael's name and, surprisingly enough, had gotten it. It was one of those lovely no-limit numbers. She'd only have a short time before they canceled it for lack of payment. If she'd had more time, she'd have flown to Paris and Italy during Fashion Week and given that card a real workout.

She supposed in some circles this would be called identity theft. Grace called it monies owed for services rendered. She would be careful not to pay any bills related to her apartment with the thing. In the eyes of the law, it could be considered his domicile if she did. That was the last thing she needed, especially as she'd spent the last four years ridding her life of anything reminding her of him.

Damn it! She wasn't supposed to be thinking about Michael. The whole point of shopping with his credit card was to enjoy sticking it to him. But could she shop, spend his money, and not think about him? She'd give it a try.

It worked. The next day, she found herself naked in a dressing room at Avenue, one of the only shops that carried lingerie that looked good on her lush figure, debating the balconette or the push-up bra and feeling much better. Even though she'd always loved the push-up, she wondered if it was time for something new. Grace couldn't deny that she liked her lines better in the push-up. She didn't need it so much for making her look like she had more—this little witch was generously endowed—but she liked the support.

She caught a glance of herself in the mirror and smiled, pleased that there wasn't one stretch mark in sight, not even on the rounded curve of her hip or the slightly rounded part of her abdomen where her baby would have first started growing. That thought brought a sigh. Tracing her fingers down the same path, she couldn't help but think of Nikoli. She'd been determined not to, but he was her son. What would she do if none of it had ever happened, if she'd never given birth to her amazing child? It would be like a death. No, not *like* a death. It would be murder—the death of an ideal, a dream. It would indeed be the death of her son, because he would still be real to her.

"Waiting for me, Gracie?"

Grace screamed and jumped back against the wall, jamming the hook into her back that had been thoughtfully installed on the dressing room wall for hanging clothes, which in turn propelled her forward into Caspian's waiting arms. Actually, it was more like it propelled her *rack* into his waiting hands. He was holding her up by her breasts, and it was none too pleasant a sensation.

"If you required my attention, all you had to do was ask." Caspian squeezed once, twice, and then he rubbed his thumbs over the nipples before looking back up at her scowling face. The sensation got a hell of a lot better.

"Don't call me Gracie," she hissed.

"Why not? I like it. It's sweet and tastes good on my tongue, just like you." He still had hold of her breasts.

He made the mistake of winking at her. That small action seemed to stop time, or at least slow it down. Grace had had enough. Her hand reared back behind her head, her fingers curling into a fist before it shot forward. For both of them, it was like they were moving through water. Caspian's eyes seemed to grow ever wider. Her fist plowed through time and space to finally connect with his face.

The crash of her flesh against his was electric, and the force of her blow was enough to turn his head. He still didn't loosen his grip on her breasts.

"Are you going to let go or what?"

Caspian looked tempted to rub his jaw. Instead, he said, "It was worth it."

She started whacking at his hands. "Let. Go. Of. Me." An ineffectual little slap punctuated each of her words.

"Hot pokers couldn't make me let go."

He smirked again, and double damn if Grace didn't find that to be sexy as hell. Damn him! She pulled her fist back, but this time Caspian was ready. He let go of one breast to catch her arm midair. So, Grace did what was logical. She used the other. Granted, she wouldn't be able to hit as hard, but it would get her point across.

Caspian wasn't about to be clobbered again, so he let go of the other breast to catch her other arm. Now Grace found herself in a much more precarious situation. She was pressed against the flimsy wall of the Avenue dressing room, naked but for her brand-new, cheeky-lace panties and a push-up bra, with a demon that looked like he could win the Ultimate Fighting Championship tournament rubbing up against her in all the right places. Her body tightened with anticipation at the same time that it cried out for her stop. If her pussy had a voice, it would have said, "Hell no! What the fuck is wrong with you? He might be hot, girl, but that dick is just *too* big. We are closed for business."

Grace was in trouble. She wasn't listening to her pussy. Caspian's voice was like silk, smooth and seductive, and she burned for more of his touch.

"I thought you said you weren't going to let go," she growled, trying to fight her attraction. "Some B.S. about hot pokers. You can't tell me that my fist is anything like a hot poker."

He brushed his lips against her cheek and throat; his breath was warm on her ear. He seemed to like to do that, and she liked it, too—it made her shiver every time. Which of course he knew. He'd been seducing women for thousands of years, and Grace doubted that her erogenous zones were that unique.

"It is to my heart, Gracie. You wound me through and through." His mouth settled on the pulse in her throat.

"You don't have a heart," she whispered.

He maneuvered her weak and aching body to suit his

pleasure. He was holding her hands above his head with one hand, but the other was now free to roam. It found her breast again. His skin was rough, something that still surprised her. He was a Crown Prince, so were there no moisturizers in Hell? Were his fingers rough from honest labor before he'd been damned? Who *was* Caspian, aside from the man—no, demon—that was making her so very wet?

"Caspian, please," she begged.

"Please, what?" he asked as a thumb and forefinger taunted her nipple. "Please make you scream? Please fuck you hard? Please what, Grace?"

"I can't," she cried out, though her hips angled forward and she arched into his touch.

"Oh, I think you can," the demon said.

"I'm still sore," she pleaded, but she was caught up in a spell. She was ensnared in a web of desire, and Caspian was the spider.

A spider. It wasn't a romantic image. In fact, it terrified her. But not only was this a matter of not being able to resist, she didn't want to try. The danger only made her hotter. That's how she'd gotten tangled up with Michael at first, and a demon was certainly more dangerous than a Russian mobster. He'd also proven better in bed, which was hard to do. Although Michael was a shit in all other aspects of his life, he was a generous and talented lover when he chose.

Caspian claimed her mouth, his lips brutal against hers. "A little pain can be fun," he said, his voice a physical force. It was a caress, as if it were a corporeal being sliding over her. *Inside* her.

"Caspian, I mean it." But Grace didn't sound like she meant it to even her own ears.

"How about a gift?" he asked as his hand drifted lower, past the filmy lace of her new "dating" knickers. He pushed one finger against her clit, inciting a divine pleasure-pain that was almost too much to bear. Grace didn't know what she would do when he moved that finger; she might not be able to stop herself from screaming, which would bring who knew how many people into the dressing room.

Caspian whispered something that sounded like Latin. "*Everto Iucunditas.* I give you the gift of demonic pleasure, regeneration, healing."

Grace panicked, wondering what he would demand in return. "I don't want to pay for it!" She was already worried about her soul.

"Oh, you'll pay, my Gracie. But not in the way you fear."

Grace felt something solid beneath her, but it wasn't Caspian. Something ethereal raised her up; her new knickers vanished to dust and manacles closed about her wrists and ankles, spreading her wide to his ministrations. Suddenly, she was afraid again. She was bound in the Avenue dressing room, awaiting the pleasure of a demon who'd just gifted her with the power of regeneration. What was he going to do with her? Hell, what was he going to do *to* her? What had she gotten herself into?

To make things stranger, there were quiet sounds of pleasure coming from the other dressing rooms: women masturbating to fantasies that they couldn't explain. They'd been overwhelmed by a sudden need that emanated from Caspian's presence, from the sex-magick he'd given her. But instead of turning her on, as it might have in other circumstances, this only made Grace feel more alone.

"Are you afraid, Gracie?"

"Yes," she whispered.

"Are you aroused?"

She didn't have to answer; with her womanhood displayed before him he could see the evidence of her desire and could smell it on her. But she didn't know if this was some kind of test, if he was going to hurt her. Had she made a mistake by summoning him? He was far too powerful. A lower-level demon she might have put in his place, might have banished back to Hell, but Caspian was too strong, and he had command of her flesh.

"Tell me to stop," Caspian said as he dipped his head to taste her. His tongue laved her clit.

It felt good enough to set her on fire . . . No, she was already burning. Grace ached to be filled by Caspian, to be possessed by him. Maybe not possessed in the traditional demon-human relationship, though. She hoped he hadn't heard that.

"Stop," she whispered, even though it felt so good.

He raised his head and drew back. "I thought this was what you wanted. I'm sorry, Gracie. Your body, it speaks to me. Your fear, it makes you wet." Caspian shrugged.

"You're stopping?" she asked, a little unsure of his intentions because she was still manacled.

"I don't want an unwilling partner." He paused when he saw the look in her eyes. "Before you go and make me out to be something all goody-goody that I'm not, unwilling is boring. I'm not some redeemable antihero," he sneered. "Don't make that mistake."

"Are you going to take these chains off?" Grace asked.

"Do you really want me to?"

Grace realized she didn't. This was suddenly fun again, now that she knew she had ultimate control, now that she knew her surrender was just a game. And her body was no longer sore. That demonic regeneration must really be working, whatever it was. "No, not really."

"Can I continue my meal then?" He didn't wait for her answer but bent to slip his tongue back inside her.

Grace wanted the last word. "Don't talk with your mouth full."

Caspian was nothing if not polite. He kept his mouth full and didn't say another word—at least, not while he was licking what he'd called her "passion flower." He could talk so hokey, but *oh,* could he ever use that tongue for better things.

She strained against the cuffs that held her tight to the wall at her wrists and ankles, wishing she could move, wishing to torture him the way he was torturing her. No, scratch that. This was bliss. She wanted him to keep doing what he was doing. His tongue was amazing. It felt as if it were sliding inside her at the same time as it ghosted over her clitoris. For all she knew, it was. Demon sex was going to ruin her.

He made a sound of pleasure as if he'd heard her thoughts. Grace would have said something suitably sharp-witted had he not suddenly started using his fingers. That deliciously masculine, calloused hand began working her along with his tongue. She couldn't get close enough, and she couldn't push herself away. Caspian continued to manipulate her swollen flesh, continued to lap at her with that wicked tongue.

She wanted to fight it, wanted to draw the pleasure out, but soon all she could do was submit to another mind-shattering orgasm. Grace came, stifling a scream that would have been drowned out anyway by cries of pleasure coming from the women in the rooms next to hers. It went on for some time.

Her body still trembling, she suddenly found herself on some sort of divan in what she imagined the Halls of Olympus would look like. Her restraints had disappeared as if they'd never been. She found herself splayed before Caspian like some sort of virginal sacrifice that gods knew she hadn't been in years. The velvet sheath of her slit was still shuddering with aftershock waves of pleasure.

"Scream here if you like, no one will hear you," he promised.

He claimed her mouth, and she could taste herself on him. That made her hot, to taste what he tasted, the sweet honey his mouth had coaxed from her. A shiver ran through Grace as he brought their bodies together. He entered her and she was instantly full—full of sensation, full of him—until he moved. Then it was like something inside her shattered, and she dug her nails into his shoulders, and raked his back. That inspired him to thrust harder, to lift his forearm and angle her hips up to meet his thrusts so that he hit the core of her again and again.

Grace was suddenly screaming, but the words were unintelligible. In the back of her mind she wondered if this was what happened to cause a body to speak in tongues— or maybe this was just speaking with Caspian's tongue. Wave after wave of ecstasy took her, and soon she couldn't feel her flesh anymore; she couldn't feel anything but the surreal, endlessly spiraling sensation. Her orgasm was like a portal to other joys where every touch rippled new pleasures like a stone dropped into a pool.

It finally ended. Her surroundings shimmered, and she saw the walls of the dressing room again. Grace knew then that she'd been changed irrevocably, without a doubt. In the heat of Caspian's arms, she couldn't find the strength to fear—or worry about facing the other occupants of the dressing room.

CHAPTER SEVEN
New Management

The Baba Yaga paced around her quaint little nowhere cottage and huffed and puffed. Some days she wondered if she should have taken that wicked-witch gig and got the gingerbread house with the really big kitchen.

It was all very frustrating to only be able to watch the goings-on of the real world from another plane of existence. She was stuck in a place out of space and time—a safe place to be sure, a place to grow her power and practice her skills, but entering the mortal realm had proved to be a real problem. Helping people was easy, but meddling in the lives of her immediate family required invocations and summonings on their part. Seraphim Stregaria hated that Grace thought she was dead, and she missed that child like nothing else, but her departure had been part of the sacrifice for the greater good—the world's as well as Grace's.

Seraphim wasn't sure if she dared another peek into the swirling black depths of her iron cauldron. The last time she'd checked, she'd had to drop her shawl over the top. Really, she didn't need *that* image of her granddaughter. Or the one before that. And definitely not the one before that!

All the silly girl was supposed to do was ask the demon for the truth, not shag him until his brain spewed out his . . . Well, she wasn't supposed to shag him, anyway.

Though, the Baba Yaga supposed, with all of the nonsense Grace had put up with from that hell-spawn Michael, the darling child deserved a treat. And Caspian was definitely a treat. Not that Seraphim knew from actual experience, but she knew someone who did. That witch had been ruined for mortal men for all time, forever and ever, amen!

Of course, all the demon shagging in the world had to be secondary to thwarting Nadja's machinations. Seraphim knew the woman had lived a hard life, but that was no excuse to be such an evil bitch. None at all. Seraphim had been enrolled in the school of hard knocks, too. In fact, they'd come from the same impoverished little village. But though Nadja was younger than Seraphim, she had more hate in her heart.

It was strange, in some ways. Seraphim had survived Auschwitz. She *still* didn't understand what a soul could do to earn torment like what she'd seen there, what she'd lived through. She didn't think there was anyone in the world who was evil enough to deserve *that*—unless those responsible were forced to live their deeds again and again, each time suffering another life that they themselves had destroyed.

When she'd first learned she could become the Baba Yaga, she'd been determined to use all her new power to make sure that the last of those responsible for the Holocaust would pay the ultimate price. She'd learned, however, that it wasn't her place to make such choices, not even when vengeance was in her grasp and her heart told her it was the right thing to do. Every person had a destiny, a wheel of rewards and trials that were his or hers to live. This had ended up being a comfort in the darkest parts of the night, when memories were newly sharpened daggers. She hadn't quite found it in herself to forgive, but Seraphim surrendered to a higher power. She took comfort in the fact that whether she called it God, the Goddess or both, the Universe knew better than she and everything would balance out.

Seraphim couldn't stand it anymore; she gave in and peeked into her cauldron. Thank the Goddess her granddaughter and Caspian weren't naked anymore. But what she saw was just as bad. In fact, now that she looked, Seraphim would have rather seen them naked and midfrolic. This was horrible. It was the worst thing that could happen, and Seraphim couldn't see how she was going to straighten out this tangle of thread that Fate had wrought. The grandchild for whom she'd had such high hopes, the one for whom she'd do anything, was staring up at a Crown Prince of Hell with stardust in her eyes. *Stardust,* damn it!

As if it couldn't get any worse, not only did the demon appear to like it, but he was holding her tenderly, looking down at her with the same foolishness. Seraphim was feeling nauseated, was sure she was going to spray her lunch in Technicolor disapproval all over her cauldron.

She was so mad she could cuss. So she did. "Fuck on a knock-kneed mare. Can you say rebound?" she muttered. What else could this be, after all? You take a demon used to shagging inexperienced virgins and an experienced woman used to shagging selfish mortals . . . ? It was a recipe for disaster.

"Oh, sweet bleeding damnation." The enormity of what was occurring had just hit her like a brick. No, *two* bricks. Grace wasn't a virgin. The impact of these coital relations could be catastrophic. Seraphim was sure she had taught Grace better.

"Ask and he shall appear," said a deep, sexy baritone.

Seraphim raised her hands, her power gathering in great, crackling halos. "How in the hell did *you* get in here?" she asked the newcomer.

"Hell is right, Sera darling."

"Sera?" she practically shrieked. What gall! She let fly a bolt of pure white energy at the intruder. It was a shame to have to fry him like a pan of bacon; he was as handsome a thing as she'd ever seen. He was tall, with jet-black hair and smooth pale skin. He had an immaculate, devilish-looking goatee, and he looked kind of like a vampire, with shoulders to die for. He also looked kind of familiar.

She was surprised to see him still standing there as the energy faded, but Seraphim prepared herself to strike again. She'd try something more like lightning. Still, it was a shame. Just because she was old didn't mean that she was dead. She could still appreciate a fine piece of meat.

He laughed, a rich sound that touched her in places that hadn't been touched for years. She was tempted to change form, to become the voluptuous seductress and have some fun of her own, but she rather liked wearing the shape of the crone. She could get away with more. No one suspected the grandmotherly type—no one but those from her part of the world, anyway. They could see her coming a mile away.

"Ah, Sera. I see you don't remember me."

"Should I? And don't call me Sera. No one calls me that but . . ." She trailed off and almost zapped herself in the mouth as she clamped her power-infused hand over it to stifle a scream. She let the energy dissipate.

"Is it coming back to you, love?"

Hades, the onetime god of the underworld, had gotten another job with a spiffy new title in this current pantheon. He was now upper management. In fact, he was the Big Boss. He was what the mortals commonly referred to as the Devil. In her youth, Seraphim Stregaria had shown great power for a mortal. She'd summoned a demon, made her deal, and it was with this very demon. He'd not been so high up back then, had still been a Crown Prince. Even though she'd been a virgin, the laws of nature had been somehow twisted. She'd gotten pregnant with Aurora, Grace's mother. Then the war was over and Seraphim came to the United States to give her child a better life. She'd never seen the demon again.

"Nothing from you for seventy years and you think I'm happy to see you?" Power gathered again at her palms.

"Ah, Sera, girl. Work's been a bitch. Kept me busy. What can I say?"

"That you're a thoughtless bastard?" she offered.

"That I am." He flashed her a wicked grin, baring straight, white, and inhumanly lovely teeth. She wanted to knock them out.

"What do you want?"

"You."

What? He could have knocked her over with a feather. Had his marbles rolled away from him and gotten lost in a fire pit?

"No," she said.

"What?"

"You heard me. You think you can just disappear and leave me with a child and never ever help me and then—"

"I *did* help you. You survived a concentration camp. You came to me a virgin, and you survived with your baby. How do you think you found the way to this Baba Yaga power, hmm? Did you really think it was all by yourself? And why do you think Grace got Caspian?"

"Because that's who I told her to summon."

"And you think you came up with that all on your lonesome?"

"As a matter of fact—" Seraphim began.

"She's my granddaughter. Of course, I—" he said at the same time.

Seraphim closed the distance between them, her form growing younger with every step so that she might stand upright and look him in the eye. "Then, why did you let Aurora die?" she whispered with a deadly calm. "You don't care about your half-spawn. Not mine, and none of them from any of the other women you bred with."

"You're wrong, Sera. Life and death are not in my purview."

"You're the Devil!" she shrieked. "How can it not be?"

"That belongs to Fate." He cast his eyes skyward. "Even *He* doesn't twist those threads. There are some things that can be changed and some that cannot. Man is the maker of all the evil in the world, I just hold an office. My duties are to test Man, to show him the faces of adversity and horror. Not to kill, not to murder, and certainly not to resurrect. Her soul was gone, Sera. She wanted to go. I can't put something back in a body that's not there."

Though he looked almost sad, Seraphim lifted her chin. "I don't believe anything you say." Demons were tricky.

Hades shrugged, as if he suddenly couldn't care one way or the other. That only pissed her off more.

"You never answered my question. What the hell do you want?"

"You," he repeated. Then he grabbed her around the waist and crushed her against him for a searing kiss.

"You wouldn't have done that if I hadn't changed into the maiden," she accused when she could breathe again.

"You think?" he asked, with a diabolically arched brow.

"Maybe not. You're just perverse enough to do it. Now, get out of here. I've got things to handle."

"Like, ensuring that our granddaughter doesn't get pregnant from frolicking with a Crown Prince of Hell?"

"There is that, yes. And I need to stop her from falling in love."

"That love thing you can't interfere with, but number one I've already fixed. There will be no imps from this union. I have to tell you, I was kind of pissed when he demanded sex as payment for the deal. I saw it was time to come talk to you."

She narrowed her eyes. "You're just making a booty call."

"Oh, Sera. Listen to yourself, using terms like 'booty call.' You were always better at keeping up with the times than I. We'll see how long that lasts before you're tired of trying."

"You aren't denying it, though."

"No, I'm not." He grinned.

"It's been so long for me, there's nothing down there but cobwebs and dust. In fact, I'm sure the hinges would creak if you tried to open *that* door."

Hades still hadn't let go of her. "You don't think I remember how to grease the hinges?"

"Now that's just disgusting."

"But you like it."

"Not really. I—"

She was rudely interrupted by the Devil's mouth again crushing her own. When he pulled away, he eyed her for a long moment. "I see it's inherited."

"What is?" Seraphim asked, breathless.

"Kissing shuts *you* up, too."

CHAPTER EIGHT
Big-Girl Pants

A few days later, Grace was pleased with her purchases and still incredulous no one had given her the hairy eyeball on the way out of the Avenue dressing room. She'd had a moment when she'd thought for sure that when she opened the door cops would be there to arrest her for public indecency. Then there'd come the fear she'd never get Nikoli back and she damned her own impulsive behavior.

But Caspian had been a gentleman, soundproofing the dressing room—or so she'd assumed. Perhaps the others were too embarrassed by their own impromptu self-pleasuring to bother with her. Or he'd wiped their memories? She didn't know if he could do that. It was definitely something to ask him, along with the question about Nikoli. Grace couldn't get over how incredibly stupid she'd sound, asking if the son, the one she remembered pushing from her body, was real. It wasn't like he was Pinocchio and made out of wood.

Grace knew she needed to ask Caspian the question, but what was nagging at her now, practically chewing on her in fact, was a need to talk to Michael. She wasn't sure where such a meeting was going to get her, but she had to see him. The visit from Sasha dictated it.

Though Grace was a powerful witch, a snake of fear coiled upward from the bottom of her stomach and wrapped around her heart. She was afraid of her ex. And yet, this fear for Nikoli was worse than anything Michael could do to her physically. She was going to see him. She had to pull up her big-girl panties.

Not that her knickers themselves were large; she was currently having a passionate affair with a lacy, cheeky variety. But metaphorically she would pull them high enough up to walk into his club. They felt pretty far up her ass already, so she figured they were high enough for her to walk through the door. But she'd been wrong before.

Soon she was standing alone at the back entrance to an after-hours club that was home to bookmaking, smuggling, and anything else that Michael could dip his paws into. Goddess, but the guy was scum. What had she been thinking when she got herself tangled up with him? Certainly not about a child, a future, or dealing with demons, that was for sure.

A tall, lanky man dressed in a pin-striped suit leaned against the brick wall of the alley. "You comin' in or what, kid?"

"Maybe 'or what.' Don't know yet."

"Sure ya do. Sure, doll. You want to talk to Michael. He's really hot about those crabs." He grinned.

Grace was confused. "What crabs?"

"The ones you sicced on him. Nasty little buggers." The guy tipped his hat at her as if saluting.

"I don't understand."

"No need to play coy with me, sweet face. I know a witch's work when I see it. Unless it was Caspian?"

The faint scent of sulfur tangled around her. *Ethelred,* she realized.

"Yeah, that was great, huh?" she agreed, even though she had no clue as to the details.

"Certainly."

Grace kicked at a rock with her shoe, suddenly engrossed, hoping against hope that Ethelred would just go away and leave her alone. She didn't think it was likely.

"You're a pretty little thing. I've always thought so," Ethelred said as he tilted her chin up with his finger. Grace was forced to look up into those hellfire eyes. They were nothing like Caspian's. Whereas Caspian's eyes sent shivers of desire down her back, Ethelred's Hell-gaze inspired a gut-twisting fear.

"Always thought so?"

"Little Gracie, I've kept an eye on you for some time. Orders from your gramps, don't ya know."

"No, I don't know." She narrowed her eyes at him. "So, is Michael's newest depravity your doing?"

"All will be revealed, Graciekins. In time." Ethelred held the door open, and it appeared Grace had no choice but to walk through. The demon didn't follow.

Gramps? Who the hell was he talking about, anyway? This was probably another plot to drive her absolutely, irrevocably insane. Also, she would ask next time why all demonkind was determined to call her Gracie. She hated it.

She walked the long, shadowed corridor. The room at the end wasn't much homier. It hadn't changed much in four years, either. There was still ugly, circa-1973 faux wood-paneling stained even darker with nicotine and despair. A cliché it might be, but this bar was dim and smoky. In fact, Grace was sure she could feel cancer about to stage a takeover in her lungs as she stood there scanning the room for her quarry.

A jukebox leaned to one side in the corner, one of the front lights hanging from it like a knocked-out tooth still attached by the root. All it played was Elvis covers, unless someone had changed things, and at any time during business hours you could hear the sad strains of English and Russian blending into horrible, riotous mockeries of the King.

The specialty of this "dinner club" was hot vodka. Michael called it his Russian Tea. The blackberry variety was particularly tasty, and Grace decided she might just need one. Especially since it looked like Michael wasn't there yet. She knew he would be soon, though. This was where he conducted business.

She flopped down at the bar, resting her fingers on the worn, scratched, and stained wood. Some of the darker spots she knew to be blood, marks from where a life had been ended. She couldn't think about that right now, though. Her plate was too full. She had to worry about herself.

"Blackberry Russian Tea, please."

The bartender was new, which surprised her. In four years, a person could expect the staff at most establishments to change, but Michael was very careful about those he kept at the bar. The new guy didn't know her, for which she was thankful. She could feel eyes boring into her back like dung beetles building condos. The sensation was hot and cold at the same time, and she didn't like it one bit.

The drink was delivered, and she took a sip of the hot, blackberry-flavored vodka. It burned all the way down, but damn was it good. Grace motioned for another. And then another. She wasn't sure, but she may have even had a couple more after that. They sure went down easy after the tongue and throat tingled into numbness. Soon she was lit up like a Christmas tree and her nose could have easily been mistaken for Rudolph's. Her cheeks were also a ruddy hue, and her pupils were small. And her heels were so very, very high.

She teetered backwards and almost fell off the bar stool, colliding with the wide, hard expanse of a chest that smelled of cherry cigar. It was hot and familiar, and it wasn't Caspian. A grip on her upper arms steadied her. Those hands were deceptively gentle.

" 'Are you lonesome tonight? Do you miss me tonight?' " a heavy Russian accent cooed in her ear, in unison with the King on the jukebox.

Grace struggled to pull free, but Michael's grip tightened, holding her there. She reached for more Russian Tea instead, planning to throw it in his face. Michael knew her too well, though, and pushed the glass out of reach.

"Let me go," Grace said in a voice that even she didn't believe held any power.

"If you wanted me to let go, you wouldn't be here." His fingers trailed down the pale skin of her arms.

"I want to know about Nikoli."

"So rude, Grace. Do I need to remind you of your manners? I'm being so patient with you, and this is how you repay me?"

She said, "You're being patient by waiting for me to kill myself instead of doing it for me, you mean?" She didn't mention the details Sasha had revealed and neither of them mentioned that this was the first time they'd spoken without lawyers in years.

He was digging half-moon marks into her skin with the pressure of his fingertips. "I haven't taken revenge for this latest little stunt of yours, have I? I even let you leave me. Nadja said I should have killed you for abandoning me and our son like you did."

Abandoning them? He was the one who'd kicked her out and taken her child from her arms. "Our son. There is no son." Was what Sasha said true? She needed Michael to confirm it.

His mouth was close to her ear now, and his voice dropped to a whisper. "Don't you remember our beautiful boy suckling at your breast? Don't you remember the pain of giving birth?"

Grace doubled over. She felt like she'd been slammed into an iron maiden, bombarded with sudden, stark memories of Nikoli and how she'd struggled to push him from her body. How the doctor told Michael in quiet tones that they would both die unless Grace made a choice. She could see the doctor's face before her now; he was asking her to choose . . . Only, he wasn't part of a memory. He was in her mind's eye, asking to trade her life for her son's. His fresh white coat was so bright it blinded her. He told her the pain would stop. All she had to do was say the words, and the memories, the pain, the suffering, it would all stop. She was ready. She would tumble into darkness with the name of her son on her lips and her heart full of a mother's love.

There came a strange buzzing in her ears, and also Michael's voice. There was chanting, and Ethelred shimmered into her field of vision. The room began to spin and she could hear her own voice chanting words she didn't recognize. Clarity hit her like a brick: Michael was using magick to make her feel this way, magick he'd gotten from Ethelred. If she agreed to die for him, for her *son,* Michael's deal would be fulfilled and he would become a demon. Just like he wanted.

She didn't know where that knowledge came from, but the influence of the blackberry vodka was suddenly gone and so was Michael's manipulative magick. Grace wanted to scan the room to see who was helping her, for someone had to be; her sudden realization had come from somewhere. But she didn't dare draw Michael's attention—and in turn, Ethelred's—to whomever it was.

The ache in her body continued despite her insight, a horrible ripping pain through her abdomen. Nor did the revelation fill the emptiness in her heart. This was an acute pain, so real, and she knew its source. Her need for Nikoli was like an infection, and it was gnawing away at her.

"He's not real, our son?" Michael continued, mocking her accusation. His lips were on the column of her throat.

"What a cold, unnatural mother you are. A fitting mate for the next ruler of Hell."

Grace didn't process his words. Instead, she felt terror sluice down her spine like ice water. A toddler with Michael's eyes peered out from the bar's office door. His blond hair was mussed and curly; there was a familiar baby-soft roundness to his cheeks that was also present in the small fingers that clutched the door. He smiled at her and held out his arms as if he wanted to be picked up.

"Four years is a long time to be away from your son. The courts can't help you, as you've seen, and neither can your demon. Get rid of him and we'll be a happy family again. You have ten days. Get. Rid. Of. Him. Or else."

He bit her hard on the neck, his teeth tearing at the soft-ness of her skin. Grace tried to scream, but he cut off her air. Not that anyone in the bar would have done anything to help. If she'd had the breath, she would have cursed him. She was reliving now all the horrible things he'd done, all the things she'd learned just before they'd split. She'd seen the bodies of the whores who had tried to leave Michael's employ. Why had she even come here? Why hadn't she just begged Caspian to act before Michael could counter him? Was it too late now?

Magick crackled around her fingers, but she couldn't stop clawing at Michael long enough to direct it. Rationally, she knew that if she just relaxed she could use her arms, her hands, her magick, but she couldn't force her body to obey. She could feel her life slipping away. Strangulation was an art to him, and not only that, it made him hard. She could feel his erection digging into her hip, and the less breath she had, the bigger it felt. She wanted to vomit. How could she ever have been attracted to this man? How could she not have realized what he was?

He released her just as she started to really fight. Kissing her cheek, he gave her a bloody-minded smile. "Oh, my love," he crooned. "Such times we shall have when you come back to me."

She cursed him with her first returned breath. *"Ego vomica vos ut persolvo pro vestri spiritus per spiritus."* The next time he choked or bit a woman, he himself would feel himself the victim of whatever he inflicted. If he killed her . . . well, Karma could be a bitch.

Michael grinned. "I can hardly wait."

He obviously had no idea what she'd said or done to him, but he would. She had the urge to run out of the bar screaming—it was taking all her willpower not to do just that—but she couldn't show him that she was afraid.

"Ten days, Grace. Or I'll kill Nikoli. The spell is already in place that will end his life if you fail to meet your obligations to me. If you or your demon tries to take him from me, Nikoli's dead and so are you. Ten days. Get rid of the demon."

"I understand," she said. She reached over the bar and grabbed the bottle of vodka from which the bartender had been pouring her drinks. She took a long final swig. Then, with blood still streaming down her neck from Michael's bite, she walked with her head held high through the front door. The quiet notes of "Kentucky Rain" echoed behind her.

Ten days to get rid of Caspian. And, she had to do it. Michael was on to the demon, and she didn't doubt for a minute her onetime lover would kill Nikoli just as he threatened. She'd been naïve to think otherwise, been so damned caught up in getting revenge that she hadn't considered the outcome. She knew now that she'd been foolish to think even a Crown Prince of Hell could stand between Michael and something he wanted.

So, Sasha had lied? Grace didn't know why and wasn't sure it mattered. Nikoli was real. She'd seen him. More memories came flooding back: late nights with Nikoli in her arms, his sweet baby scent, those quiet times with his mouth on her breast taking nourishment from her body. Such peace she'd felt in those moments. And now Michael was using the boy as a weapon.

She suddenly couldn't breathe. Her chest was tight and she felt her face spasm with sorrow. She hated that people were so ugly when they cried. No one ever did the couple-of-lone-wolf-teardrops-meandering-elegantly-down-the-alabaster-cheek thing that you saw in the movies; that was such bullshit. If sorrow was real, it meant full-on twisted features, mascara racooning around the peepers to stream in ugly, toxic-looking stains down red cheeks. That was why men hated to see women cry, she figured—because, damn, it made them ugly.

Grace made a couple of swipes at her face with the back of her hand, took a shaky breath, and turned down an alley. Sasha and Petru were there, trying to shove a plastic-wrapped something into a Dumpster.

Upon closer inspection, it wasn't plastic wrap but a clear garbage bag. A woman's face was staring out from it, peeking up behind Petru's shoulder. The eyes were wide and empty, dead. The mouth was open. And if Petru and Sasha were disposing of the corpse, it was Michael who'd murdered her.

A cold feeling slid over Grace like a shroud. This was how she was going to end up: a nameless face wrapped in a garbage bag, dropped in a Dumpster like trash. Like she'd never had breath, never had a voice, never had people to love her. Grace knew what lay at the end of Michael's scheming. Sasha was right about that, at least.

No. Things weren't going to happen that way. She'd get Nikoli away. Somehow.

"Grace," Petru huffed in acknowledgment, still holding the body.

"Why did you lie to me, Sasha? I saw Nikoli," Grace growled, getting straight to the point.

Sasha's mouth was set in a grim line. "I've never lied to you, Grace. Never. Not when you were first sitting in that bar making calf-eyes at Grigorovich, and not now."

"Then how did I see my son? How did he hold his arms out to me, his mother, if he's not real?"

Sasha let go of his burden. He'd been holding the dead woman's legs so Petru could do some maneuvering, but they weren't making much headway. "Grace, do you remember his birth? You said I was there. You said I took Nikoli from your arms."

"It's vague but it's there. The doctor sedated me."

Sasha shook his head. "Did he sedate me, too? Why don't *I* remember it? And, why would I lie to you, Grace? Don't you remember your first date with Michael? When I took you home, do you remember what I said?"

"You told me I was getting in deep water. Over my head."

"Was that a lie?"

Grace grabbed the lapels of his Dior trench, curling her fists around the fabric. "No. So, why are you lying to me about Nikoli?"

"I'm not!" Sasha's large hands engulfed her wrists, and he extracted himself from her grasp. "Why don't you just summon your grandmother and have done? She could end this nonsense right now. Why do you engage Grigorovich in these games? Do you still love him? Is that possible? Are you—?"

"No!" She fought off nausea. "But my grandmother is dead. Your quaint little bits of folklore are nothing. Nothing! I can call my granny all night long, but she's not going to miraculously get her ass here because, as I mentioned before, she's *fucking dead*."

"Grace, no. Shh." Petru held fingers to his lips, looking terrified. "Granddaughter or no, she's the Baba Yaga."

"Petru!" She spun on her heel, ready to give the moronic mobster a full dose of verbal venom. Unfortunately, the dumb innocence in his eyes was enough to curb her tongue. Just barely. She took a deep breath. "The adults are talking."

He turned back to his task, the dead prostitute hoisted over his massive shoulder, his hand firmly on her rump like he was carrying a keg of beer rather than a woman. His face showed no comprehension of that at all. His sausage fingers were having trouble pulling open the cover meant to keep Dumpster divers and animals out of Michael's personal waste. Many a body had been transported to Garbage Island this way, never to be found again.

"He believes. I do, too," Sasha said quietly.

Grace sneered. "Why do *you* buy into all this superstitious nonsense?"

"How is the Baba Yaga superstitious nonsense but a demon conjured from Hell is not?"

Grace opened her mouth, but there was nothing there waiting to come out. She had no answer other than the fact that it just wasn't possible. Her granny was dead and gone, and no amount of wishing would bring her back.

"If Seraphim Stregaria ever had a maxim in her whole life, it was this: want in one hand and shit in the other and see which one fills up first. No, there's no point in hoping. If my granny were still around, she'd have let me know."

"Sasha?" Petru called.

They both turned to see the dead prostitute's legs sticking out of the Dumpster. Petru was unable to push them down any farther.

"Can you see it from the street?" Sasha asked.

"Probably," Grace announced cheerfully. Then she

pushed past them to continue home. She would make a stop at a pay phone. The Dumpster would probably be gone by the time the police got there, and if it wasn't, Michael had a lot of the guys on his payroll for just such occasions, but she would make the effort anyway.

Caspian could have made the situation unbearable for Michael. She wished she didn't have to send the demon packing, but with Nikoli's life at risk, she had no other choice. Goddess above. He was delicious. He'd been nothing but good to her, and she chuckled as she imagined the demonic crabs Michael was suffering from. She also wondered what the gift of demonic healing encompassed. Would it stay once Caspian was gone? If it did, maybe she'd have a chance against Michael, after all.

CHAPTER NINE

Opinions Are Like Arseholes

Caspian didn't like Michael Grigorovich. The feeling was something he'd pondered at length.

Generally, his likes and dislikes were irrelevant. He'd always been rather passive in his assessment of humans. Some were pretty, some were ugly. Some made him laugh, some didn't. Some were good and some were bad. Then there were those that were *really* bad.

This last variety bothered him a bit. They didn't really get the point. The whole reason for evil was to test Man, not to inspire him to further acts of depravity. But that's what seemed to be going on here, what seemed to be happening with Michael and all his deal brokering. Why in the name of Mephistopheles would a mortal choose to be a demon? There was a hierarchy to follow down below, just like there was above with the Really Big Boss. Sure, everybody got to be "a unique and special snowflake," but there were orders everyone had to follow, rules that went with the magick. Most of the time, those aspiring to demonhood just didn't understand. They thought it was all about the power and the pain; they didn't understand being a demon meant providing a public service. Caspian knew for damn sure that Michael Grigorovich didn't get it.

Of course, all this reflection was relatively new. Caspian had once been content as he was, and he didn't really care for this new introspection that seemed to coincide with his recent chest pain. It was damned uncomfortable all around. But, this disliking business, he really couldn't give it up. He *did not like* Michael Grigorovich.

Caspian wondered how Ethelred could stand the mortal's stench. The Russian mobster smelled funny, like goat cheese, old socks, and vodka—not a good mix. Even his borscht-snorkeling crony Petru didn't smell as bad. Caspian knew that scents played a strong role in human sexuality, so he had yet to see how the Russian ever got any tail that he didn't take violently or pay for. What had Grace ever seen in him? He'd *touched* her. Every time Caspian thought of Grigorovich laying hands on her, it made something prickle on the back of his neck.

He didn't like that, either.

Yes, there was quite a bit about Grace that Caspian didn't like, but he knew that it all stemmed from what he did.

Caspian, Crown Prince of Hell, was jealous.

Admitting that was like kicking himself in the balls with soccer cleats. He was a demon. He had nothing to be jealous of. Grace didn't even like Ass-o-vich.

Caspian's prowess was legendary, he reminded himself. He'd pleasured thousands of women, been pleasured by many more. He was no stranger to the carnal arts, and he'd never left an unsatisfied customer. Hell, he'd always left his lovers enraptured. But his Gracie seemed unmoved. Maybe she didn't like him, either. Sure, she'd enjoyed their time together, but he hadn't heard from her since their encounter in the Avenue dressing room. He'd expected a summoning, a mention, a muttered curse under her breath . . . Nothing. This made her different—a *challenge*. Add to that the fact that she'd been fixated on a douche bag like Michael Grigorovich, and Caspian's disgruntlement only grew.

He chose to ignore the hollow feeling at the base of his spine. When taken as a part of the big picture, it didn't really matter. Caspian was a Crown Prince of Hell, and Grace was just a witch venting her fury at a man who'd done her and many other women wrong. Very, very wrong. Caspian was only here to do a job. Grace was that job.

Caspian's mouth curved in a smile as he followed his own logic. He was here to do a job, and if Grace was that job . . . well, then, he was here to do her. It was time to get back to work.

If guilt had been an emotion he could feel, Caspian might have felt bad about his circular reasoning. He'd been contracted to make Michael's existence a living hell, but while that was all fun and good, he liked playing with Grace more. He could have done this job, been in, out, spells in place to torment Michael until Cerberus wore pink ballerina slippers and himself back drinking shots of Flaming Nipples in his fireside condo by the very first evening. But he was drawing this out. He was going to make it last, all while doing lots of customer service. Caspian liked the "hands-on" approach to customer service. Especially with Grace.

It was definitely time for some customer service.

Materializing at her place, he found Grace naked in her kitchen. Her deliciously round rump was calling to him as she leaned over a little island to drop a bit of this and a pinch of that into her cauldron. He knew that she was working some kind of spell, but it looked for all the world like she was cooking.

What man or demon could resist naked hausfrau-ery? Certainly not Caspian. His favorite decades were the 1930s, 1940s, and 1950s. The women were all so shapely then; they'd worn stockings, which were a bitch to get off but looked divine. Silk hose were his favorite. He'd loved the hairstyles of the period; even when hair was short, it was always coiffed. And the makeup! Caspian loved painted women in high heels. Just watching Greta Garbo movies and Donna Reed reruns made him hard. Not to mention the work of that goddess Marilyn Monroe.

Caspian licked his lips, envisioning scenarios as he watched Grace. Greta and Grace would have been lovely to see together. Not that he could have kept his hands to himself long enough to just watch. And, Greta had told him that when women chose to love one another it wasn't for his enjoyment. Caspian didn't see why not. *Everything* about women was for his enjoyment. Especially everything about Grace.

She raised her hands to the sky and called out an invocation, slowly lowering her hands and arms and charging her brew with power. It was beautiful to watch: her sheer elegance, the way her body moved. The way her arms were shaped, the way they curved into that secret place beneath her shoulder, the gentle yet generous profile of her breast. The curve of her hips, and those long, long legs—they most certainly went all the way up.

Caspian suddenly realized that the Donna Reed reruns playing in his head now all starred Grace. The Marilyn and Greta movies showcased Grace, too. Rather than spend any time worrying about that, however, he considered asking her to put on an apron and heels while she double, double, toil, and troubled. Or maybe a cone of power. She'd be hot as hell wearing just a little witch hat. She would—

His thoughts were interrupted. Lucifer, Beelzebub, and Ozymandias, what in the name of all that was unholy had the woman put in her cauldron? It was worse than sour lamb and olive turds filling a Greek outhouse in high summer after a garlic festival. Maybe he didn't want her to cook for him, after all. They could just order takeout, and she could dance around the kitchen naked with a wooden spoon in her hand that he could spank her with and . . .

He took another look at that inviting arse. Even though it sang songs of frolicking and debauchery, he was going to have to ask either what was wrong with her or whom she was trying to banish. She could banish just about anything with this olfactory assault.

"Son of a . . . Why do these things happen to me?" Leaning farther over her wicked-witch workstation, Grace suddenly glanced skyward, as if she really thought she was going to get an answer. Caspian saw that she'd mistakenly dunked one of her sweater cows into the mixture, which dripped down onto the plane of her belly as she turned to the side to grab a hand towel.

"Great! I hope my boob doesn't disappear," she grumbled.

"Whatcha doin' there, sweet cheeks?" Caspian inquired.

Grace screamed six kinds of murder and, if it were possible, would have literally jumped out of her skin. Her expression reminded Caspian of a cat stuck to the ceiling, claws embedded in the plaster like some startling new kind of chandelier. He thought this was funny until her flailing arms sent her bowl flying through the air like a mortar shell of Hell-stench. Of course, that wasn't the worst. It landed upside down on top of his head, a proper bowler hat but for the sludge dripping down through his supernaturally perfect hair.

Caspian froze as a particularly nasty yellowish glob raced down between his eyes and off the end of his nose like a ski jump. He thanked whoever happened to be listening that his mouth wasn't open. If it had been, he would have been reenacting Linda Blair and her pea-soup scene all over Grace's kitchen.

The corner of her mouth turned up, and she raised an eyebrow.

"Think that's funny, do you?" he asked, wiping his face on the back of his sleeve.

"It's no less than you deserve for popping in without an invitation."

Caspian narrowed his eyes. "Really?"

For some people, *really* just means . . . well, really. For others it's more of a challenge. It's rhetorical. It's a warning. Caspian was one such as this. His *really,* though in the form of a question, was a genial and polite way of snorting, like a bull that had been stuck in the hindquarters by sharp objects.

Grace obviously wasn't aware of any such nuances of interaction. She gave her own little snort and said, "Yeah, really." Then she turned around, dismissing him as if she couldn't possibly conceive of anything he could do about it.

This was the equivalent of waving a red flag at that same bull. Caspian charged.

CHAPTER TEN
Banishing Cream

Grace was delighted and terrified all at once to see two-hundred-some-odd pounds of raging, well-built demon charge her. She would have tittered like a schoolmarm in a too-tight corset if she could have laughed at all. But, nope, she couldn't laugh too hard when she was unceremoniously hauled over Caspian's shoulder like a sack of potatoes. She was reminded of Petru, with his hand on that dead—

Except, she felt very much alive, and Caspian was only making that feeling increase. His fingers seemed to have doubled in number before creeping into places they shouldn't. Was he trying to pick her up like a bowling ball or a six-pack of Budweiser?

She slapped at his shoulders and biceps, but this was ineffectual at best. She wasn't sure what would happen if she got any of the smelly goo she'd been making on herself, so she didn't struggle too much. If there was a way for a witch to banish herself, Grace figured she'd be the one who discovered it.

Sometimes she wondered if her name was a curse. She'd learned a lesson while naming her pets: Giving a cat a name like Diablo was always a bad idea—the animal invariably felt a need to live up to it. Her first familiar, which she'd unwisely saddled with that name, always bit her on the backside whenever it was time to get up. Correction: He'd bit her when *he* decided it was time to get up.

It was the opposite with humans. Name a girl-child Helen for Helen of Troy and she'd end up not just ugly and dumpy, but with an *assalanche*—an avalanche of buttocks that just sort of sagged down past her knees

Of course, it could simply be the klutz gene she'd inherited that had landed her in Caspian's arms. And she was lucky. If she were honest with herself, she wanted this. She liked the feel of his large hand splayed across her backside. He knew exactly what he was doing with those fingers, and she knew what was coming next.

Grace sighed, but her languorous sigh turned into a howl as that large hand smacked her soundly on the rump.

"What was that for?!"

"Because you're a bad girl." His hand cupped the rounded globe of her buttock before he slapped it again. He rubbed like he was sizing up the target for a more serious assault, and Grace wasn't really sure if she was into that. She'd liked being handcuffed and told what was what in the Avenue dressing room, but spanked?

Suddenly, the most curious throbbing began where he'd swatted her. Radiating inward, the sensation moved from her bottom to between her tightly clamped thighs, and tightly clamped or not, she couldn't have blocked his fingers if she'd wanted. One slipped inside her, and her body tightened as if to trap it and force it to continue delivering those delicious sensations.

He pulled out slowly and then pushed back inside with two fingers, then smacked her ass again. "Yes, you *are* a bad girl," Caspian said.

"No, I'm not," Grace replied, breathlessly shifting against his fingers. "I'm so very good." And to prove it, she turned her head to nip his earlobe and pressed her lips to the corner of his jaw.

"I guess I can't argue with that."

He leaned over, with her still on his shoulder. Grace thought for sure he was going to drop her, but neither his balance nor his grip wavered. She could feel his biceps working and wondered dreamily if he was using his perfect abs and hard thighs, or if he was lifting incorrectly with his back. She noticed that he was still wearing her goo hat. She had to bite her lip to keep from giggling.

Caspian promptly dislodged her from her perch and dumped her into the shower. "You made the mess; you're going to clean it up."

"You can't just . . . ? You know." She made little motions in the air.

"Why do you always seem to think I can 'just . . .'?" He mimicked her gestures.

"You're a demon. I thought you were supposed to be all-powerful." Grace shook her head and fought off a grumble. The potion she'd been concocting obviously didn't work, because she still had a Crown Prince of Hell staring at her naked self in her bathroom, wearing a whole batch of the stuff on his head like a *ushanka,* one of those furry Russian ear-hats. What was even funnier, he was now otherwise naked.

Wait, maybe that wasn't so funny. They were both naked but she was trying to get rid of the guy, not ride him like a mustang. Naked proximity didn't tend to make a man go away. Neither did squirming against his fingers when he was fondling places he shouldn't.

Wicked inspiration struck like lightning. It did make them go away if it was *bad.* How did one ride a pony badly? An improper seat? Grace supposed she was lucky that she didn't know. Whom could she ask?

Caspian stepped into the shower stall with her, interrupting her thoughts. "I don't know what's going through that devious brain of yours, but let's get to it."

Against her will, the slick walls of her sex tightened. Why did everything this demon said have to go down like a Fuck Smoothie infused with *yes*? Couldn't he just speak the way normal people did? Getting rid of him was going to be so very hard. Hard, thick and . . .

Damn it! Difficult. It was going to be *difficult*. It was going to be especially difficult, since he was hard. She glanced down once. Twice.

She was daring a third peek when Caspian lifted her chin with his fingers. "Up here, sweet face. It can't talk."

Grace seemed to remember telling him the same thing about her boobs. The shoe was on the other damn foot now, wasn't it? And it was certainly a big shoe—

"Grace. Goo. Hair. Not a happy demon," Caspian reminded her.

"Well, don't get your thong in a knot. Jesus Harold, you're worse than a woman. You better remember denying me later when you're trying to hide the bald-headed hermit. Because it's not going to happen."

Caspian smirked, but he didn't say anything. He didn't have to; she knew she'd be on her back like a turtle as soon as he snapped his fingers. She only hoped that Caspian wasn't a Mack truck that would turn her into turtle soup. Or a mean kid with a magnifying glass. The truck would be quicker.

Caspian touched her cheek. "Look, Grace, I apparently can't just will this crap off me. It's magick. And you are the magick weaver, so you need to unweave it, got it?"

Grace considered. "Does it hurt?"

"No, it just stinks like an outhouse. So that means *I* stink like an outhouse. Why you'd want to climb on before I have a shower is beyond me . . . Though, I suppose it does explain the attraction to Michael Grigorovich."

The demon closed his eyes and bent his head like a supplicant, waiting for her to clean him off. Grace narrowed her eyes. His arrogance was staggering. He just expected her to wash his hair like he was some kind of prince and her a serving wench? Oh, hell no.

Though, he was a prince—a Crown Prince of Hell no less. But that didn't matter to Grace one bit.

She flattened herself against the stall and angled the showerhead just so, then flipped on the cold water full blast. It shot Caspian in the face, a payback that some woman somewhere surely owed him. To counter his annoyance, however, the spray and her general intention took the magick goo off. Mostly. When she turned down the cold and made a big show of adjusting the hot, she chanced a glance at him, seeing his hair standing up like a crazy anime character's. A blob of the magick-banishing goo was plastered like a centuries-old gum ball to the back of the shower.

Caspian hadn't made a sound when the cold water hit him, but he was wearing a look of startled incredulity.

"Grace," he growled through gritted teeth.

"Yes, my lord Caspian?" Grace replied in the sweetest voice she could manage.

"If you were a man, I would strangle you. Slowly."

"If I was a man, I don't think you'd be naked in the shower with me." She paused and looked contemplative. "Would you?"

"The hair, Grace."

"I was trying, but then you got all growly."

"Grace." He took a deep breath and, if he were her gran, she would have sworn that he was praying to the saints for patience. She wondered to whom he did pray for patience. If he prayed at all.

"Stop fucking around." Caspian punctuated this with another slap of her ass. The blow stung a little bit, but that didn't stop the heat that went spiraling through her—which pissed Grace off even more. She didn't want to feel this way. She *couldn't*. Not considering Michael's threat.

She slathered almost half the bottle of her Burt's Bees pomegranate shampoo on Caspian's head. Too bad it wasn't something like Head & Shoulders that, when it ran into his eyes, would sting like being stood up on prom night. His nose twitched peculiarly as the fruity scent filled his nostrils. Good. Grace hoped he hated it.

She was doubly mad at him—for being so grumpy and also because she had to get rid of him while she still felt desire. She wasn't used to that. Grace was always the one to send lovers packing. She didn't want Caspian to go, and she'd never had to face that before. She'd been *quite* finished with Michael when he'd given her the boot.

This was all Caspian's fault. Why did he have to be so damn hot? Worse, why did his hair have to feel like silk when she ran her fingers through it, even fully loaded up with her banishing cream like a blue plate special? She allowed herself to enjoy the sensation just a tiny bit as she raked her fingers through his locks, massaging his scalp and giggling at making him smell like a girl.

Such yummy pomegranate shampoo. And the banishing cream smelled like mangos to her. She moved Caspian beneath the cascading water and rinsed it all away.

This was such an intimate act, washing someone's hair. Not to mention the delight of ogling him at her leisure— which was completely counterproductive to what she should be doing. But that cherubim-molded mouth was open in blatant pleasure as he enjoyed her ministrations.

The water sluiced down his tanned skin, and as his eyes fluttered closed, his black lashes swept the curve of his cheek. A rivulet of water ran down that hard, defined line of his jaw, down the corded muscles of his neck, farther down those Goddess-sculpted pectorals. They *were* Goddess sculpted, because no man would be able design a creature so perfect and pleasing to the female eye. Caspian had been designed by a woman, for a woman, and he was built for pleasure.

Everything about him screamed sex, like an alarm clock she couldn't shut off. Grace lost track of the rivulet of water in her contemplation of his physical deliciousness, but she soon found another. This one was gliding down his abs to—

She was lucky that she could multitask. She was still rinsing his hair, and Grace saw something that he would enjoy as much as a trip to a drunken proctologist. Slipping away with Burt and his fruit-flavored bees was the dark color of Caspian's hair. Some witch she was! She tried to banish a demon and she banished his hair color? Pathetic.

But, perhaps this would be the catalyst for getting rid of him. He was clearly fussy about his hair, so when he found out that he was blond he would have a stroke. It'd be the end. Kaput. They'd be through. He was worse than a woman in that respect—unless he'd just been annoyed because he realized she was planning on banishing him. She imagined if she was on the receiving end of said intended banishment, she would feel insulted, too. Either way, he'd soon consider his part of their contract fulfilled and would be done with her completely.

But . . . if that was the case, she might as well grab a one-off. It'd be their last, so she could wholeheartedly enjoy it. She was secretly thankful that she wouldn't have to try to figure out bad sex. That research would have been a jewel in the Hurts-Me-More-Than-You crown, of that she was certain. She was also certain she needed an unholy good time.

Since his hair was now clean, she looked down at her demon's pitchfork and contemplated her next move. She debated sinking to her knees and taking him into her mouth . . . or maybe she'd just reach out and grab herself a handful. He seemed to think that it was fine for him to do with her, so why not turn the tables? Sometimes she thought that penises were separate creatures from the men they belonged to, anyway. His seemed to beckon her, whether he mentally wanted her to grab him or not. It had been staring at her for the entirety of her contemplations.

Grace splayed her hand across his abdomen, her fingers teasing Caspian as they slid toward her target. "Is your hair clean enough now, Miss Priss?" she asked with a playful curve of her lips.

His eyes were dark with desire, and there was nothing light in the hard set of his jaw, the sculpted perfection of his face. His responding kiss was brutal, his mouth demanding, yet his grip on her was tender—something entirely at odds with their previous encounters. Each time with Caspian was new and exciting.

She melted into his embrace, wondering if he was going to spank her again and deciding that she would let him. Everywhere their skin touched was afire, her nipples tight peaks scraping the broad expanse of his chest, her belly joined to the thick length of his erection. The back of her thigh tingled where his fingertips skimmed, guiding her leg up around his waist. She laid claim to the hard planes of his water-slicked body with her hands, tracing the lines of his back and shoulders, his hips.

And that ass! It should be illegal for a man to have that ass.

Just as the water grew cold, Grace found herself up to her neck in a hot tub. When she could think, she would have to remember to ask Caspian why he always teleported them when they were having sex. And, why not to a hot spring? This hot tub was familiar, but it was hard to place, especially when his tongue was doing things to her that made it impossible for her to think.

His mouth closed over her nipple. Caspian had positioned her so that his cock was rubbing her clit, and she threw her head back in abandon and didn't give two damns about the hot tub any longer.

Just as she was about to demand more, he shifted again so

that she was straddling him in a reverse-cowgirl position, leaning forward to use the side of the tub for support. She could feel his breath on her shoulder. Not that she needed it, but his arms were around her, his hands on her breasts, and she was anchored to him. And just as he entered her, she discovered a strategically placed water jet that doubled her pleasure as she rocked her hips against him.

He moved inside her, slowly, deliberately. There was a different kind of intensity to this encounter, something urgent but unknown. His movement, his ministrations—everything was measured and controlled and designed for her pleasure. The feel of him against her back was new, the breath on her skin and the slow caress of his hands on her breasts. And it was good. It was all so damn good.

Grace met his thrusts, grinding herself against him as she tightened herself around his cock only to release and pull him in again. She was so close, but she didn't want to come yet. She wanted this sensation to last. She never wanted it to end.

"Not yet," she whispered.

"Come for me, Grace." Caspian pressed his mouth to her shoulder blade. "Come for me now. I want to hear my name on your lips as you do."

"Caspian," she cried softly.

"No. Louder. I want everyone to know who's making you come. Whose cock are you riding? Tell him!"

"Caspian!" She gasped as the water jet increased in pressure like his thrusts. "Oh, *God,* Caspian!"

Electric pleasure shot through her, and her entire body contracted against the onslaught to release in a galaxy of stars and sensation. She relaxed against Caspian and realized that she didn't even know if he'd gotten off. She took a deep breath and figured if he hadn't, he would do something about it. And if not . . . ? Well, that was his problem.

"That was so good," she sighed. "It's always so good with you."

The demon pushed her wet hair away from her forehead, kissed her softly and asked, "If it's always so good, why did you try to banish me?"

Chapter Eleven
A Night at the Opera

Michael Grigorovich was watching a show. His bill to the demon Ethelred was about to come due and he needed to relax. *Carmen* was in town and it was a particular favorite, especially the end. Of course, if he'd been Don José, he never would have been so stupid as to confess. Who gave a damn about a gypsy whore?

He smirked to himself as he looked at his new arm candy. Dina was blond, thin, and rich—everything that would have made Grace gnash her teeth together like junkyard machinery chewing through a rusted-out El Camino. She wasn't physically attractive to him; he fucked her because he liked the power. It was like the ultimate grudge fuck.

She looked a bit like a famine victim, always hungry. He liked that. Also, she was more than willing to let him do all sorts of cruel things to her. She even enjoyed them. Of course, she liked to starve herself, too. That made him wonder how far he could push her before she snapped, how much pain he could convince her she liked. She was a new toy. He'd play with it until it broke.

Dina's father leaned over and spoke. "You've got great taste. I'm impressed, Grigorovich."

Of course you are, you pretentious bastard. You *couldn't get these tickets.* The seats were practically impossible to obtain. But he waved his hand as if it were nothing.

"Let's talk business after the show, shall we?" Dina's father suggested.

Michael inclined his head and nodded. He'd just as soon shoot him in the face and take what he wanted, but Ethelred had told him to make nice and benefits would be forthcoming. This wasn't turning out anything like he'd imagined. He'd thought he'd be a demon by now. Instead, his ass was in a sling, and it would be until Grace came to her senses—or until he talked her out of them.

A voice in the back of his head wondered if he should have actually bred with her. He should have at least told her he wanted a baby. Women seemed to think that meant something. And then he wouldn't have added to his Hell-debt by implanting those memories, because they would have been real.

Of course, it was possible Grace would have been equally recalcitrant if a child existed. After all, there was no way Michael's mother would sacrifice her life to save *him*. He couldn't blame Nadja—he wasn't about to go hanging his ass out on the line for her, either. He hoped she remembered that as she stewed in her limbo prison, neither living or dead, waiting for someone devoted enough to use the old magicks to release her. He pitied the creature who loved his mother enough to free her.

Sasha harbored soft feelings for Nadja. Michael knew that, but he hadn't decided how to work it to his advantage. He was most thankful that no one knew where his mother rotted, waiting for her chance to vent her poison. Michael was torn between admiring his mother's strength and yearning for her approval and fearing her great power while hating it at the same time. And all the while, he coveted it as well.

Dina slipped her hand into his as the tenor sang. Michael allowed it, since her father was watching with an approving eye, but he couldn't help but wish that she were Grace.

Grace wouldn't have tried to hold his hand or make any other public display of affection she knew he hated. Maybe when he'd succeeded and was a demon, he would raise her from the dead and keep her with him. She'd always been a good lay, and he'd have complete power over her then.

He glanced at Dina's breasts. The low-cut dress did nothing for the flat, desolate plain of what was supposed to be her cleavage, and Michael was actually somewhat offended that she tried to pass herself off as a woman. If the bitch would eat, she might be hot. Then again, he did like her hungry look.

He smiled at his date, and she returned the expression. Sort of. That mouth too big for her sunken-in little face turned upward in a vulpine expression that was supposed to be a smile. He wanted to hold her down and force-feed her sausage gravy and chocolate cake. Together. Perhaps that's what he would do to her, make her fat. Not just the Marilyn Monroe sort of classic voluptuousness that he found attractive; he would see if he could push her beyond that. She'd hate herself even more than she did now.

He gave her hand a little squeeze, and Dina seemed content in her place in the great wheel of his machinations. Yes, Ethelred had been correct yet again. Making nice had its advantages.

Feeling very satisfied, he caught sight of an elegant blond man seated nearby. The stranger seemed familiar and inclined his head. Michael returned the gesture in acknowledgment but was unsettled by his smile. Frankly, it was a look that Michael recognized, having worn it on his own face quite often. It was a sort of horrific glee, and seeing it on someone else did not bode well.

The blond man smiled wider and then kissed the tips of his fingers, extending his hand as if blowing Michael a kiss. He mouthed something Michael couldn't quite catch but was clearly not a blessing on his mother. About five seconds later, the man was up and gone—the inconsiderate prick rose and left just as the gypsy hooker onstage was getting what was coming to her—and the most horrible sound gurgled out of Michael's stomach. It was not unlike a toilet chugging down a full bowl of the abuse it had suffered after a college frat house's taco night bender.

Dina's eyebrows scurried up into her hairline like fleeing mice. She turned to look at him. "Are you okay?"

Michael nodded and crossed his legs. A small squeal erupted under his chair like there were four piglets fighting for a single teat. Michael felt his face flame, and Dina slowly turned her head to face the stage, her cheeks tinged pink.

He didn't know why he was embarrassed. So he'd had some gas. So the fuck what? Everyone did. The average human male farted more times a day than he thought about sex. He was never going to see these people again, and if he did, they'd be puckering up for a good long blow on the rump horn just to get in his good graces. As far as he was concerned, he could perform the "William Tell Overture" out of his ass and these people should be thankful to hear it and expound upon his musical genius.

At least, that's what Michael told himself to get his face to return to a neutral color.

The gurgling started again, but this time it was accompanied by intense pain. The sound was deeper. He wasn't sure if he could get up, at least not without releasing a devil wind that was being restrained like the Kraken. With the pressure he was feeling, this was bound to be a tornadic assault. His entire body clenched, and he uncrossed his legs so he could better glue his cheeks together. He had a sudden terror of exploding there in the middle of the theater like some kind of new biological weapon.

Gritting his teeth against the stabbing in his gut, he glanced down at his belly as if he could will it into submission. If he'd been able to unclench his teeth, he would have gasped like a woman. His stomach was the size of a basket-ball and slowly inflating. He had to get up and get to the bathroom. If he didn't, there was no doubt that his stomach would burst. That blond man had obviously cursed him. Michael would remember the bastard's face, and when they next met there would be hell to pay—hell not unlike that he was in now.

Oh, no. He had to sneeze. The force of the sneeze would send atomic fire shooting out of his ass like a malfunction-ing death ray. If he held the sneeze . . . well, he just didn't think he could. Michael believed himself to be a man of few limitations, but this was one of them. He was in deep shit—or he soon would be. Literally.

He rose and fled, squeezing his thighs together, hoping that would help him at least make it to the mezzanine. Dina didn't spare him a glance. She kept her head solidly facing front, which was just as well. If she'd chanced a look at him, she would have been sorry, especially if she opened her mouth to speak. Because, when the scent reached his own nose, Michael was sure the paint was going to curl off the walls.

He gagged a little as he slammed through the door to the men's room. The attendant took one look and his left nos-tril flared, the rest of his face turning a garish purple. He coughed behind his hand, trying desperately to escape the stench.

A sound tore from Michael, an apocalyptic thunder that seemed to shake the very walls. The expelled air was some-thing of a self-propulsion engine, and he barreled right through a stall door. Unfortunately for everyone con-cerned, the stall was already occupied.

"Somebody in here," squeaked a high-pitched voice.

Michael looked down and saw a poor bastard sitting

there with his white boxers hanging around his ankles, studying his iPhone over horn-rimmed spectacles. The game app he was playing made happy little noises.

"D-D-Didn't you hear me?" the man stuttered.

Another thunderclap rattled Michael's glutes like windowpanes in a hurricane, and he grabbed the guy by the shirt and heaved him out of the stall. The hapless gent went sprawling across the floor, his boxers still around his ankles; his lily white cheeks flew up in the air, two marshmallows fighting for dominance.

"Didn't you hear *me*? Get out!"

Michael then slammed the door, and what followed was nothing short of Hiroshimic, mushroom cloud and all.

CHAPTER TWELVE

The Hot Tub

"I don't know exactly what you're talking about," Grace said as she took a redneck-like swig of the golden-hued champagne that Caspian handed her. Though, she did wonder why he hadn't just conjured it. He'd been gone an awfully long time after making that accusation about her banishing him. Had he really just popped out to get some bubbly?

"Oh, no?" Caspian's voice went up in pitch on the last word.

Grace shook her head. "Unh-uh," she mumbled through a mouthful of booze. It wasn't technically a lie.

"Grace. You don't lie for shit."

She set her glass down very carefully and ran her finger around its silver rim. "I don't lie."

"Then why is my hair blond?" He shouted the last word as if she were stone deaf.

"How am I supposed to know?"

"It's banishing cream, Grace. You were mixing it. I seriously doubt that you'd prepare a Hell-stench like that without knowing what you were going to use it for."

"Hell-stench?" She was indignant. He was impugning her potion-making skills, which was akin to insulting her cooking. "I thought it smelled like mangos. It was *supposed* to smell like mangos . . ." Her brow furrowed. Maybe demons smelled things differently. Especially banishing cream.

"Maybe mangos after they've been through someone-with-food-poisoning's intestines."

"Look, Caspian—"

He interrupted. "My hair, woman. Look what you've done to my hair!"

Grace had the good sense to act a bit sheepish. "Yeah, I'd noticed that. It's, uh, very striking."

"It's *balls* is what it is, witch. So it's quite obvious you were trying to banish me. Well, if not me, someone. But I'm thinking me. What other demons have you been carousing with?" He narrowed his eyes. "Have you been riding the demonic baloney pony with someone else now that I've given you powers of healing?"

"Jealous?" Grace taunted.

"Hell, yes. I broke you in for demon stick and now you're hopping on someone else's? Who wouldn't be jealous?"

"Jealousy is a *human* emotion," Grace shot back.

"So what?" Caspian said. "I was born to a human woman."

"Really? Because—"

"No. Enough. Stop trying to change the subject. Who were you trying to banish? And for future reference, a banishing cream will not work on a Crown Prince of Hell. Not with the deal we made. Once you open that circle, I can stay out until Daddy calls to tell me playtime is over."

"Maybe Ethelred," Grace suggested.

"Ethelred? What did he do to you? Did Michael sic him on you?" The dark depths of Caspian's eyes burned with intensity, and his demonic nature was never more evident. They were sitting in a hot tub that had been previously soothing, but now the heat bordered on unbearable.

She was sorely tempted to blurt out the truth, but if it wouldn't make him leave, why bother? He was a demon, and she couldn't exactly trust him. Demons had big egos and cocks, and often tiny brains. He'd just do something that would push Michael over the edge and Nikoli would be dead.

"Grace!" he demanded.

She didn't say anything. The flame had spread from Caspian's eyes into a black halo around him, and as his rage built, so did that fire. She knew that the water was going to boil her soon, but she couldn't speak. She couldn't even move, because her fear held her frozen. She'd always kept it in the back of her mind that Caspian was a demon, but she'd never seen his power spiraling out of control like this. It had just been great sex and word games. But now he was shedding his façade and displaying the power of Hell. Michael was dangerous, but he was mortal. Caspian was something else.

When he reached out to her to grab her arms, she screamed. That was when great black wings erupted from his shoulder blades, fire sluicing down all around them.

"Why are you so afraid?" he asked. "Ethelred? I will destroy him."

She realized that he wasn't aware of how his voice had taken on a thundering timbre, of how his flesh was shrouded in fire, or even of the beautiful downy wings of darkness that marked him as one of the fallen. They were splayed out behind him.

"I'm afraid of *you*," she whispered.

He looked surprised. "Me? I'm the same demon you've been shagging senseless. And, demon or no, I'm male. We all get jealous. It's normal. You're afraid of a little jealousy?" He paused. "Or is it because I offered to destroy Ethelred? Don't most women like that chivalric garbage—'destroying thine enemies' and all that crap?"

Her voice was shaky, and Grace hated how weak it sounded. "The water is really hot, Caspian."

Steam was rising in waves. Caspian looked down and reached out again to touch her, but Grace flinched away. That was when he saw he was wreathed in flames. If he stepped out of the water, she'd bet the whole place would go up.

"Get out of the tub," he said calmly, moving slightly away from her.

She scrambled, naked, out of the tub and wrapped herself in a towel just as the water began to boil. Her skin was red and tender all over, but she knew it was nothing compared to the damage that he might have unintentionally wrought.

Caspian repeated himself, as if he were talking to a child. "You need to answer me, Grace. What did he do to you? Ethelred."

"Nothing, Caspian. He didn't do anything but talk."

"Most women wouldn't banish someone for talking to them. Especially not a handsome man like Ethelred appears to be."

Grace desperately wanted to see Caspian as a man again. She *needed* to. What she saw now was horrifically beautiful, but it was both impossible to look at or away from. She wanted to see him as he'd been—dashing, funny, gorgeous, a means to an end who saw her as exactly the same, and who also happened to be delightfully talented at the carnal arts. Nothing less, nothing more.

"You think he's handsome?" She gave Caspian a weak smile that made the corners of his mouth curve and the flames began to recede. "I just know he's helping Michael. I wanted to take away the advantage. That's all."

He narrowed his eyes at her. "You're sure that cream wasn't for me? Because if you want me to leave, all you have to do is say so."

After this? She wasn't going to tell him shit from apple butter—and without having time to think better of it, she told him just that.

"I'd never hurt you," he promised.

Grace wanted to ask him why not. Why hadn't he hurt her before this, in fact? She wondered if he was like Michael. He'd said he would never hurt her either, not unless she forced his hand. She wondered just what it would take to force Caspian's.

"I was angry because I thought Ethelred hurt you," he continued. "I haven't been angry in a long time. I'd forgotten what it was like."

How did one forget what it was like to be angry? Probably the same way Grace forgot that Caspian was a demon. She couldn't imagine what it was like to have lived so long to forget feelings, to be so unaffected by the world. Sure, it would be wonderful to never be sad or lonely. To never feel pain. But Grace also knew that being without those things would mean existing without the other side of the coin. She wouldn't know the good things: the warmth of love and joy, awe at the beauty of the universe.

She wondered what it was like to be Caspian. How lonely it must be, and she doubted he even knew it. That part saddened her and she didn't know why.

Grace decided she needed another guzzle of champagne. Picking up her glass this time, she noticed the dramatic masks etched into it, and she recognized they were from the Kansas City Met opera house. She also recognized the hot tub. There was different greenery around it now, almost like from someone's backyard. But this wasn't a backyard. It was a magickally enhanced balcony on the hip side of Westport. Worse yet, it was Michael's.

She dropped her glass and it shattered. Droplets of golden champagne covered the ground. "What have you done?"

Caspian looked sheepish. "Which time, Gracie?"

She didn't correct the use of that name. "This time. Right now."

Caspian shrugged. "He's not here."

"Is my son?" Grace pulled the towel tighter around herself. *"Did my son hear his mother having sex with a demon?"*

"You don't have a son," Caspian said.

She spun to face him, irrationally angry. "And how would you know?" She went to the door and tried to enter the apartment, but found she could not. "Were you there?" she threw over her shoulder.

What if Nikoli was inside the apartment and alone? What if he was afraid? She felt an overwhelming urge to get through the door no matter the cost. How had Caspian walked right through it only moments earlier, holding their champagne? Grace was almost hysterical, banging on the door, trying to get through. Her power pooled around her fingertips, drawing energy from everything around her, including Caspian.

Her power turned to flame and she was just about to release the full force of her need upon the door when Caspian grabbed her hands. "The door is hexed, Grace. Whatever you cast on it will come back to strike you."

Her frantic fears were not allayed. "Then how did you get through?"

"I didn't. I went to the opera and stole Michael's champagne. He wasn't drinking it; he was launching Scud missiles in the men's room. Oops. My bad."

She couldn't resist the mirth that the image evoked, but it warred with her fear for her son. "I don't want to laugh right now, you ass!"

"Look, Grace." Caspian sighed. "This wasn't part of our deal, so I probably shouldn't be handing out freebies, but Nikoli is not real. You don't smell like a woman who has given birth."

Grace shook her head, unimpressed. "You don't understand. I *feel* him. I know he's real." Her hands were shaking. "I remember feeling him move inside of me. I remember his baby smell. I remember . . ."

Emotion choked her, and she couldn't say anything else. Her eyes fluttered closed and her dark lashes swept the curve of her cheek.

At last they opened wide. "Petru told me to ask you," she admitted. "He said you'd tell me the truth. So I ask you now: Is my son real?"

He drew her close, his ebony wings curling in to cradle her. He paused a moment and then said, "I swear to you, Grace. I swear if he *is* real, I'll get him back."

She felt shielded from the world in that dark embrace, and Grace was tempted to believe his promise. She also wanted to ask him why he'd asked her to scream his name while he fucked her here in Michael's hot tub. If it had been a mortal man, Grace would assume he was staking a claim. But, Caspian was a demon. He didn't have feelings. Not like mortals. This didn't make any sense.

She supposed it didn't matter. All that counted was his pledge. He'd made a promise, and a demon's word was not lightly given. Could she let him stay long enough to try to get Nikoli back? They had ten days. But if he failed, she'd have to get rid of him.

CHAPTER THIRTEEN

Vexing Verbiage

Last time he checked, Caspian was sure he hadn't had a bowl of stupid meal for breakfast with a side of idiot sausage. But you could have fooled him, what with that *I swear to you* nonsense. Really? Had that just happened: him promising to rescue her nonexistent child? It had to have happened *to* him? otherwise, he'd have to admit that he'd done it to himself, and a Crown Prince of Hell would do no such thing. Ever. Grace was a mark. She was nothing more than a contractee, and he the contractor. That was it. She'd paid him with her snatch to make Michael's life hell.

Oh. That's what it was. He just hadn't fulfilled his part. Michael wasn't in Hell yet. The demon crabs and operatic assplosion were just the beginnings. Caspian had to go see a man about a hooker. Specifically, the one Michael had strangled and tossed in a Dumpster. He'd had a few good ideas about her.

Unfortunately, while he was smirking about removing one plaguing question, another went bubonic: Why had he gotten so angry at the thought of Ethelred hurting Grace? And, damn, if the pain in his chest wasn't worse than being junk-punched.

He was also hearing a strange sound that he'd never heard before. Okay, he'd heard it before, but not when he was by himself, and not since he was a mortal child. Humans made that sound, not demons. Never demons. What could it be? It was a strange, foreign thudding in his chest. Caspian had to say that he didn't care for it in the least. It sounded like a heartbeat, which had to be a hallucination. There was no way there was anything alive in the black hole where his heart once was. Demons didn't have hearts.

As long as he was asking stupid questions, he might as well pose the big one Grace was dying to ask. It wasn't why he'd agreed to help her get her son, either; he could finagle that into being part of the contract if he so desired, could say that taking Michael's son away would indeed make his life worse. Such a loophole was perfect if the Big Boss asked, which was always important. But, no, the big question was why he'd transported them to Michael's hot tub. He could have teleported them anywhere in the world: Iceland, Poland, Missouri. Anywhere. But he'd chosen to set up their carnal carnival in her ex's hot tub, and he'd asked her to scream his name. Why?

Aside from the fact he just liked hearing women screaming his name through abject kitty-wrecking pleasure, he knew damn well why. He just didn't know if he should acknowledge it. He thought of her as his. She belonged to him, pure and simple. Grace Stregaria belonged to Caspian.

But, this was simply a territorial thing. It wasn't like—Lucifer and the Chorus of Hell forbid—he was having feelings or anything. All males were territorial, even demons. That was just nature.

If he was just being territorial, why had he offered—no, not offered, damn it. He'd *promised* to help her get her son back. She'd looked up at him with those chocolate eyes so full of hope that they'd painted him with a suit of shining armor, and like a dumbass he'd fallen into it.

And yet, she knew he was a demon. She had no illusions about what he was. She'd seen him in a raging, fiery fury. She was even afraid of him. He hadn't liked that fear in her eyes, and just about anything would be worth tackling to maintain that joy she'd shown when he gave her his vow.

What a fucking mess.

Why hadn't he just told her again that Nikoli wasn't real? The boy was a demon-magick-induced figment of her imagination that he couldn't counter. How in the name of Legion was he supposed to get Nikoli back? Oh, he could construct something from her planted memories, but it wouldn't be real.

For just a moment out of time he wished that he was something other than what he was. He wished that he could give her a baby, because demon spawn or no, she would be the child's true mother—something his own parent had been unable to do. And even though he couldn't be a proper father, he still liked the idea of Grace holding their son in her arms. Caspian couldn't help but wish for it, just a bit.

Grace was protected by powerful magick indeed if she hadn't ripened with his seed yet. Or she was barren. Considering how un-virgin she was, and the virility of demon seed, Grace should have been knocked up higher than a kite in the past few days.

He damn well wanted to know what Ethelred was doing talking to her. There was no reason for it, unless it was to taunt her or work more devilries upon her at Michael's behest. Well, here was something he could tackle. Caspian would put a stop to that in two shakes of a seven-headed dragon's tail. He and Ethelred were going to have a discussion immediately—and he might not even open the window before he threw the bastard out, depending on where Ethelred was.

The demon turned out to be visiting a café in Brussels when Caspian found him later that evening. Not, unfortunately, the best venue for demon chucking. If it had been the Scottish Highland Games, Caspian might have gotten away with it. Or even at the Punkin Chunkin Festival. But not a droll little café in Belgium, with its dainty, metal-scrollwork chairs, and quaint hand-carved tables. Not to mention the Old Country Roses china cup that was currently pressed to his slick-talking mouth, Ethelred, that cock-muncher.

Not that he knew for certain that Ethelred was a cock-muncher, and not that Caspian cared if he was. In fact, Caspian had been bored enough to experiment back in the 1700s, but that was neither here nor there. He was getting off track. It just felt good to call Ethelred a name, even if it was only in his head.

Seeing and acknowledging him, the other demon motioned for him to sit down. If he'd been wearing knickers, Caspian's would have been twisted into a tight knot at the thought of having to be cordial. Going commando did have its benefits. But he sank into the chair with the grace inherent to demonkind, and when a dainty cup with Irish Breakfast tea appeared before him in the same china Ethelred was using, Caspian added some milk and three cubes of sugar. Then he threw in another just because.

Ethelred raised a brow. "Some tea with your sugar, my prince?"

Caspian narrowed his eyes in contemplation and tossed in another cube. Really, he'd rather just put the sugar in his mouth and suck on it. Funny, how affectations from time as a human stayed with a mortal after accepting demonhood. His mother would have slapped his hands and clucked at him like an overwrought chicken for putting that much sugar in his tea.

It was also funny how he was thinking of his mother so often now. He'd gone years and not given the woman a moment's consideration. Now he could hear her voice clear as a church bell, as if he'd seen her yesterday.

Ethelred smirked. "To what do I owe your esteemed presence?"

"You know very well 'to what you owe my presence.' " Caspian sipped his tea.

"Michael Grigorovich, I assume. He's indebted to me for well nigh a thousand years should he fail to convince Grace to . . . ah . . ." He paused, looking for the right word. "*Save* him."

"You may also assume"—Caspian took another sip before continuing politely—"that if you torment the human Grace Stregaria with any more false visions of a son, I will bind you for all eternity as a dog rocket in Central Park."

Ethelred didn't answer. He picked up a pastry and popped the whole thing in his mouth before pushing the plate forward. "These are heavenly. You must try one."

Caspian fixed him with a glare that would induce death in a lesser being.

"That's quite a hefty threat considering this insignificant human woman. Especially since I'm next in line for Crown Prince status." Ethelred popped another pastry in his mouth, chewing while he talked. "Are you getting soft in your old age?"

Caspian turned up his nose. "Finish that bite before you speak."

Ethelred laughed. "You torment souls and see the blackest depths humanity has to offer and you're offended by *this*?" He opened his mouth to show Caspian his food.

"It's disgusting."

Ethelred swallowed and waited for Caspian to say something else. When he didn't, the lesser demon spoke. "So . . . you were threatening me with eternity as a canine rump biscuit in Central Park?"

"Yes, that. I was actually going to smite you, but the Big Boss would frown heavily upon such an obvious and public display of power. Instead I've decided to warn you. *Leave Grace alone.*"

Ethelred pursed his lips. "I'm afraid I can't do that. And before you go all avenging angel and send me back to perdition, let me tell you why."

Caspian was indeed about to "go all avenging angel" and smite the demon down. He could feel the flames this time, the heat gathering around his body. His tea was boiling in his cup and molten frosting slid off a nearby tart.

"My prince, control yourself before you burst into flames in front of all of these people! You know the Big Boss's greatest achievement was to convince the masses that he doesn't exist. You're going to fuck that up in five seconds, all over a piece of . . ." The demon stopped short, realizing his terminology would be the last sprinkle on the shit-fire sundae he was making himself. "Over a *woman,*" he corrected.

"I'm awaiting your explanation. And it had better be good because, Big Boss or no, I will own your demonic ass."

"Grace isn't human."

"That matters exactly how?"

"The Baba Yaga is indeed Grace's grandmother. Seraphim Stregaria wears the cone of power."

"Again, *so?*"

"Auschwitz? Her pregnancy and grand escape were all machinated by . . ." Ethelred let the words hang, hoping Caspian would figure everything out. Caspian didn't, so he had to continue. "The baby was Grace's mother, and a half-demon whelped on her by none other than a certain Crown Prince of Hell who is now . . ."

"The only one who outranks me," Caspian finished. "Sonofabitch."

"The real bitch of it is that she still has free will. Now,

Michael learned a powerful summoning spell from his mother. Someone had to come, and if it was anyone else everyone would be bitching that Hades has gone soft. A revolt in Hell is really not cool right now, *capiche*?"

"So, you can't remove that memory spell no matter what I do to you. Grace has to break it herself." Caspian's rage toward the other demon cooled slightly. "I suppose I can't just kill Michael, can I?"

"Nope. He's bought powerful wards. You can't kill him . . . but as you've already discovered, you can make him *wish* that he was dead." Ethelred picked up the teapot. "More tea?"

CHAPTER FOURTEEN

Witch Balls, Medium-Size

Seraphim Stregaria watched the happenings through her crystal orb and was not the slightest bit happy with what she was seeing. Again. In fact, she was downright pissed. But this time it was for different reasons.

She felt Grace's pain as acutely as her own and it was breaking her heart. Seraphim would have none of that, especially from that douche bag Michael. The mobster's mother was just as evil, and she, too, would have her day of reckoning. It would not be a blessed day in the Grigorovich household when Seraphim Stregaria came a-calling, which would happen soon. It was about to get pretty damned ugly, truth be told. Damn Michael. Damn the man straight to Hell, and not in the way that he wanted.

She'd called Hades earlier, but had gotten Ethelred and his platitudes about why a revolt in Hell right now could be a very bad thing. Not that Seraphim cared about the hierarchy of Hell when it was ranked against her granddaughter. Hades could fend quite well for himself. Even if he were deposed, he'd be fine. He could just hang out at her pad until he rallied his troops or whatever. Though, that would be a mess. Battle plans, armor, and war-demons hanging about everywhere . . . ? No, she really couldn't have that. Her enchanted forest was already smothering her, and she was by herself. No, she couldn't imagine her lovely little home packed to the gills with demons.

What was truly smothering her was frustration at not being able to do more for her granddaughter. Thunder boomed overhead, and Seraphim schooled her thoughts. This plane responded to her moods, and she took a deep breath and brought the sunshine back.

A new plan formed, and she knew just the necessary ingredients. First, there was a hooker. Not just any hooker, of course, but the one that Michael had strangled and left in a Dumpster. She knew that Grace wanted to raise her as a *Bean Sidhe,* but there were better options out there. To enact them, she needed a few rare ingredients only found in Haiti.

Well, to be honest, the ingredients were available in other places than just Haiti, but it was more likely that Stregaria would be able to find them all together there. She needed *Bresillet, Pomme Cajou, Calmador,* and *Pois Gratter.* Hell, she'd be able to find them already ground up into a fine powder in Haiti if she played her cards right. And she usually did play her cards right. It was a gift.

She needed the hooker first, though, and Seraphim did not fancy traipsing about through a landfill at this ungodly hour of the night. Not to mention that her shoes were new. *Witchy,* as she liked to say. Adorable little heels, purple-and-black spectator-style, she just loved them. She'd found them in the Pyramid Collection catalog, and she couldn't imagine what they would look like and of course smell like when she got back.

She briefly considered riding her broom, but that would be awfully obvious, and it wasn't a two-seater. She'd need a sidecar. If she reanimated the corpse before rubbing it down with the secondary potion, she could maybe get it back to her lair, but zombies hated flying and were no good at it. Puked-up entrails from motion sickness were not

Seraphim's idea of a good time, either, especially since they were usually crawling with things she'd rather not consider.

And, Seraphim didn't want a zombie. She wanted something else. The girl's soul had to be hanging around, crying for vengeance, and it could be given just that. Seraphim knew her own soul would be eager under the same circumstances.

"Hades," she called out, deciding to try again. He'd been gone for some time, but she fully expected an answer. In the old days, before his seventy-year vanishing trick, it wasn't like him to just go away after sex like a normal man. He'd seemed to like hanging around for the afterglow or something. Maybe she should write her own gothic about Devil-shagging and give the dark bastard a heart. Wouldn't that be funny? Better yet, she could make him fall in love with a mortal who didn't have one. It was no less than he deserved. Even after their recent encounter, she was still mad at him for leaving her high and dry—not to mention gravid.

Seraphim sighed heavily. Oh, how she missed Aurora. The loss of a child? Awful. It was the same pain that her beloved Grace was now feeling, though Seraphim had the comfort of knowing Aurora was safe, that she was in a better place, and preparing for another turn on the Great Wheel. Grace had no such comfort and she never would, no matter what happened. Even if she discovered Michael's ruse, it would be a kind of forever death for the child. Such was the magick he'd used. Rotten, misbegotten son of a whore! Oh, Seraphim would show Michael and Nadja, all right.

"Hades, I know you can hear me."

When still she received no reply, Seraphim stomped her foot in a fine fit. Sparks shot from the heel of her shoe and ignited, bursting forth into true flames and then a figure. Leave it to Hades to make an entrance.

"Too much?" He'd appeared with tail, cape, and pitch-fork. The little villain mustache was just overkill. Not to say it wasn't sexy as all hell. It was.

Seraphim pinched her fingers together with a small space in between. "Maybe a bit."

"You bellowed?"

"I certainly did not 'bellow.' I called because I need your help."

"*Again,* woman? Don't you know that's why you're the Baba Yaga? So that you can accomplish things on your own."

"I am the Baba Yaga, yes. But I don't fancy zombie juice all over my new broom or shoes."

Hades shook his head. "You're a difficult little baggage, just like your granddaughter."

"What's the common denominator there? Aside from the obvious."

He eyed her. "Oh, no *way* are you blaming this on me."

"I wasn't trying to blame anyone. Grace is a lovely and talented witch. You should be so lucky if any part of her is because of you."

Hades sighed. "Look, I'm kind of in the middle of some-thing. What is it that you want?"

"A dead hooker."

"You can't get that by yourself? Wait—what are you go-ing to do with a dead hooker?" Hades' brow furrowed.

"I want the one Michael killed."

"Honey, there's about forty-two of those at least. I stopped counting a few years back."

Seraphim clarified. "The most recent one, I think. She's a redheaded virago. Her soul burns as brightly as her hair."

"Oh, *that* dead hooker." Hades looked thoughtful again, an expression that always brought a lump of dread to her stomach like a gallon of thick oatmeal. "What do I get out of it?"

"What haven't you had already?"

Seraphim double-damned her tongue for running away with itself. This really wasn't the best way to bargain with the Devil. She should have made him think that she had something he didn't, something he'd have to have or suffer endless, eternal agonies. He'd always been a lot like a crow, lining his nest with shiny things, but as soon as he had them, they lost their glow and he was off in search of the next. Most people were like this, to her mind, but Hades in particular. Because he looked so damned good doing it, however, it was hard to deny him, with or without his deals, contracts, or fine print.

"Your heart."

Seraphim's mouth fell open like she was a largemouth bass with a hook in her cheek. It flopped around in a similar way. She couldn't quite seem to flap it shut. It was like the tendon was severed and her jaw was surfing gravity, just like most other parts of her had been doing recently—at least, until she'd run into Hades again. She hadn't been able to resist an urge to tighten certain things and lift others a little bit. Being a witch had to have some perks.

"I'm immortal and all that, but it would still hurt to have you take it out of my chest," she announced. "What would you do with it, anyway? Keep it in a jar on your fireplace to show company?"

"You are ever the thickheaded lass, aren't you? I just want you to say that you love me, Sera. *That*'s how I want your heart."

Seraphim tried to haggle. "Are you sure you wouldn't just rather pull it beating from my chest? I think I'd like that better."

"Nope. That's all you have left to give that I haven't had."

"I don't think I can do it," she said.

"You didn't even try." His cape deflated and his pitchfork

disappeared. The tail still wandered about. She'd bet it would be creeping up her leg in a minute.

"Oh, but I did. See what a lost cause this is?" Seraphim shrugged as if she were a helpless child.

Hades crossed his arms. "I guess you better try some more."

"Really, it just won't work," she said. "Besides, after I give that up, what would I have left to bargain with?"

What she'd really meant to say was: After she admitted she loved him, *then* what would she do? She'd be alone with her feelings. That love could be just as heavy a burden as hatred. Sometimes more so. If she didn't admit it to herself, she didn't have to acknowledge its existence.

"Think of Grace."

"*You* think of Grace, you sulfuric troglodyte. She's your granddaughter, too."

"Why am I always the one giving, hmm? Always you're asking for things. I saved your life, got you your dream job with kick-ass health benefits—as in, you're freaking immortal—and this is the thanks I get? You should be dressing me in shiny armor and envisioning me on romance novel covers. But do you? No. Always the same surly attitude. A lot of women would give their right ovary to be in your shoes." Hades looked like he was pouting but cast her a sly look from the corner of his eye. "Like Nadja."

Seraphim knew he meant to get a rise out of her. She happily obliged. "Like bloody hell she will!" She flung her arm back and was going to slap such nonsense out of his head when Hades caught her hand. At the same time, he pinned her other hand behind her back.

"Now what?" she demanded.

"Now I have all of the advantages. I won't let you go until you admit it."

"I thought you had pressing business."

"I thought you wanted that dead hooker." Hades arched a brow with a smug, superior look on that handsome face.

"I'll find another."

"Not as good as this one. Her name is Jill, I think. Yes, Jill. She's a spicy piece who will really give Michael a run for his money."

"I don't care." But they both knew that was a lie.

Seraphim stomped on Hades' foot, but he didn't let go. She tried to bite him, but he just laughed.

"Come on, Seraphim, angel of my heart, just admit you love me. You do, you know."

"No. I do not."

"Why not? Do I smell? Am I ugly?" Hades made a show of checking his most delectable and devilish person. He knew very well that he didn't smell, and he was hotter than sin. The damned man. No matter how immortal or devilish, he was still a man. A frustrating, irritating, sneaky man, but a sexy man. And she did love him.

If not for Hades, she wouldn't have survived the camp. Neither would hundreds of others. He'd openly defied the Pantheon of Gods to protect her and the others. It had only been one camp, only a few souls in the face of the sea who'd suffered, but even a Crown Prince of Hell couldn't stand in the face of the Nazi death machine.

At the time, she hadn't understood why he couldn't purge the evil from men's hearts and take it out of the world. She'd been so naïve to think evil originated with the Devil instead of in the souls of men.

But he'd defied the laws of the universe with his direct intervention and had been willing to trade his very existence for her. She'd tripped over her own feet and fallen in love with him and he'd become the Devil himself, but Seraphim's love for him was branded on her soul.

But there was no reason to tell him that. Nor was there

any reason to tell him that every time she lay down with another man, even the most "cunning linguist" she ever met, she always saw his face. Hades, with his easy charm and chiseled features, was always the dark head dipping between her thighs. Nope, he was hard enough to deal with as it was.

"You get your grand confession," she complained, "and I'll be left with exactly what you left me before. Nothing."

"I beg to differ. You'll have a hooker."

"I hate you," she said.

His smile grew wider. "No, you don't. You love me. Come on and say it."

"That's like inviting a vampire in. There's no way I'm just going to say that I l— No, won't work. Not going to happen. Now, let me go."

"Seraphim—" he began.

"What? You have to let go sometime. I mean, you have important business, like Infernal Insurrection or some such silliness."

"I love you."

"You're full of goat shit," Seraphim replied.

"I'm hurt."

He was still smiling but leaning in closer, as if he was going to kiss her. Seraphim tried to squirm away. "Then why are you still grinning like the town fool?"

"I'm bleeding on the inside."

Seraphim snorted and rolled her eyes.

"What do I have to do to convince you, angel?" Hades asked, the smile on his face suddenly softening. "What would you like? Shall I break one of the Seven Seals of the Apocalypse like a Communion wafer? What would make you happy, my love? Rivers of blood and plagues of—"

"Stop this nonsense for once. Get me the hooker and we can forget this insanity."

"I don't want to forget," Hades said.

"Fine. I love you. Get me the hooker." Seraphim struggled to keep her words monotone. Still, she couldn't deny that a tremendous weight was lifted off her shoulders. But, it wasn't like a Grand Confession or anything. He had to know she didn't mean it. Not really.

"More romantic words have never been spoken." Hades produced the required body, and it dropped unceremoniously on Seraphim's worktable. "A betrothal gift, perhaps?"

She stared at him. "Have you lost your mind?"

"We can keep a summerhouse in Texas. I've always liked Texas."

Seraphim eyed the heavens. "He's lost it. Really, he has." She glanced back at Hades. "I have some supplies I need to acquire, and I think you have a rebellion to quell."

"Not outright rebellion, no. But there is talk. I was thinking of retiring."

"Can you retire from being the Devil?" Seraphim was incredulous that he'd even suggested it.

"I don't know if anyone has tried. I guess we'll find out. But not until I've cleaned all this up, of course."

Seraphim was unconvinced. "Why now? You haven't even been in office a century."

He looked serious. "Honestly, because it wasn't what I thought it would be. I love you, Seraphim. I want to be with you."

If she'd been made of anything less than steel, she would have cried. She turned away to find her broom. "And you said you weren't going to rip my heart out of my chest."

"We're not done here. But we'll talk after you've raised Jill."

Damn him! Then Seraphim realized she'd have to get a more original curse. Something with more teeth. Hades was already damned, so this really wasn't much of an oath. She also realized that she'd said it about ten times since seeing him again. It didn't continually pack the same punch.

"And I hate Texas!" she snapped, but he was gone. She hated that he always had the last word.

He popped back. "You didn't hate that weekend on Padre Island." Then he disappeared again.

If he was serious, which she doubted, she'd take the house on Padre.

Sighing, Seraphim grabbed her broom and headed to Haiti. She liked Haiti. The children all knew her for what she was, though in Haiti they called her a *loa,* a type of guardian. So did the man she would see about the powder. They called him Papa, in reverence to *Papa Legba,* the spirit god that was said to possess him from time to time.

Then she would be off to Ireland for the best shea butter available. One had to keep the flesh pliant to get the soul back in, and long enough at least to bind mortal flesh to demonic.

CHAPTER FIFTEEN

A Rabid Rabbit Assassination

Grace was watching Caspian sleep after another wild romp between the sheets. They'd been rutting like rabbits on ambergris since he'd come topside a week ago to answer her summons. What was *with* her? She'd never been quite this into anyone. It was amazing.

Worse, this behavior was completely unacceptable—staring at him while he slept. For her, for him, for the masses that saw the Virgin Mary in a *gordita,* for the universe in general; she knew this was wrong for everyone. It was just that he looked so innocent when he slept; she was forced to recall the taste of him and the images that invoked. Such sweet innocence. The summer rain on her tongue, everything fresh and new. Was that one of his survival mechanisms? Was he like a chameleon; he could blend to match whatever she found most desirable? Or perhaps he mimicked that which she most lamented losing—her own innocence.

His scent wasn't pure at all. It was male, dominant and delicious. It made her tingle in all the right places. But his face made her soft. Black lashes against those tanned, sculpted cheeks. She wondered if he was tan from the glare of all that raging hellfire. Then she realized Hell was probably nothing like she thought.

She wanted to see his wings again, touch them. Grace remembered that they were downy and black like a raven's wings, not the hard, stretched skin like a bat's that she'd thought demons would have. Even those rolling waves of flame had been stunning. Yes, man or demon, Caspian was a beautiful specimen.

Grace ghosted her fingertips up to let his again-black hair curl around her finger. It still felt like silk, soft and shiny. It was hair that a woman would kill for, just like those decadent lashes. Yet, there was nothing feminine about him. He was all hard, caveman alpha dog.

She wondered again what it was like to be him, how he perceived the world. If he was lonely. If it was an unknown ache that had hurt so long that he didn't know anything else. She couldn't get past his admission that he'd forgotten what it was like to be angry. Grace had thought he was sub-human because he was a demon, that he didn't understand the workings of a human heart, but maybe he did. Maybe he comprehended more than any mortal.

He'd been born to a human mother, she knew. What was that like? Had he always known that he was to become a demon because of his heritage? She wanted to ask him so many questions, but she also needed him to leave. It was the strangest thing. This wasn't just about Michael and Nikoli anymore. She needed him to leave for her own peace of mind. She was starting to crave his touch. Sex with a mortal man was now going to always leave her wanting something more, which led to a different fear. This was supposed to be just a business transaction, these encounters. She wasn't supposed to look forward to them. But she did.

Grace knew where this would lead if it continued. She wasn't stupid. Of course, she'd fallen for Michael before she knew the full truth about him, and that had been pretty dumb. She just couldn't resist the bad boys, especially when they seemed slightly redeemable. That had to be where Caspian's power began. He'd said he wouldn't hurt her and suddenly she'd shoved him into armor that, albeit black, had its own special shine. Next thing she knew, she'd have him wielding a sword and asking her to let down her hair so he could climb up her tower and rescue her.

The reality of it was, however, if she fell in love with Caspian, painting him up like a French whore with her antihero cosmetics, she'd spend her life waiting for him to pop in and visit. She'd be alone with her spells and crochet, and the next time she looked in the mirror she'd be an old woman with no family, having never lived life. And, Caspian would almost certainly lose interest when she became too old to be exciting. He might like fucking her now, but demons didn't have hearts. He couldn't fall in love with her. It was all an exercise in futility. She didn't even know why she was thinking about love. It wasn't like she had such soft feelings anymore. She'd learned better.

Her fingers strayed to Caspian's shoulders, his biceps, down his forearm to his hands. Goddess, how she loved his hands. The things those hands had done to her, the way those fingers had moved inside her. His fingers were long and elegant but strong and talented.

She twined her fingers with his and exhaled deeply, rolled onto her back, and drifted off to sleep. But only seconds later she started awake again because his arm clamped down on her belly. It was like being caught in a Chinese finger trap; the more she struggled, the tighter he held her. She slapped at his hand to get him to let go, but of course, it did no good. He was still sleeping like a coma patient.

This was going to end in the "suck" column, because she really had to pee. And sweet bleeding hell of hells, it had begun raining outside. The gentle pitter-patter of the raindrops hitting the window would have been enough torture by themselves, but she could hear the water trickling through the downspout like a musical waterfall.

Grace tried to clamp her thighs together, but it didn't

seem to help. Dreaming of a trip to the porcelain god, she struggled against Caspian but accomplished nothing. Well, that wasn't completely true; she felt his erection pressing against her rump as she managed to roll over. So . . . she'd accomplished a hard-on. Or it could just be the Morning Wood fairy. She didn't know if demons were susceptible to that.

She squirmed some more, hoping that if she rubbed against him enough, it would wake him up and he'd let her go. No such luck was to be had. Grace only had enough room to roll over, back to Caspian. She did so and pinched his nose shut, hoping that would wake him up, waited patiently for his brain to tell the rest of the body that he was getting no oxygen and to rise before his life functions ceased. But after her arm ached from holding his nostrils together, she realized he didn't actually have any life functions.

She was about to let go when his eyes popped open. There was almost an audible snap. Grace shrieked and dropped her arm, and a moment later found herself flat on her back with a horny demon atop her.

"Not nice, Gracie," he said against the edge of her mouth. He didn't even have morning breath. She didn't know whether to be thankful or jealous.

"What's not nice is that I have to pee and you won't let go of me. Now, get off unless you want a . . ." She couldn't bring herself to say it, even as a silly threat. He might just be that perverse.

She suddenly found herself sitting atop the aforementioned porcelain god. Of course, Caspian had forgotten to miracle her knickers down.

"Will you stop that? You can't just transport—" she called out.

She was interrupted by the slamming of the bathroom door. Obviously, he wasn't as perverse as she'd thought.

This made her unreasonably happy. Grace was a big fan of never being so comfortable with someone that it was okay to leave the bathroom door open. After all, if she was to put her mouth anywhere, she didn't want to see—

She decided not to pursue that thought.

When everything was finished, she found herself back on the bed underneath Caspian, just as she'd left him.

"You really have to stop that."

Caspian didn't say anything, just crushed his mouth to hers. Grace was immediately on fire. His talented tongue ignited sensations in her akin to dropping a blowtorch in a drum of gasoline. She needed him in a way that was previously unknown to her, which was totally unacceptable. This was *business*. She had to get rid of him fast—and yet the bad-sex idea was still at the very bottom of her list of plausible courses of action.

She broke away. "Wait." She was going to ask him what he was thinking about right now. She was going to be disgustingly cute about it, too. He was male, so this had to work. Of course, she'd said that before.

"For what?" His hand slid to her breast, and his thumb across her nipple caused it to peak. Sensations shot from the sensitive bud deep into her belly.

"I want to know what you're thinking about." The words tumbled out of her mouth in a rush. Damn it! She must really want to know what he was thinking. That couldn't be good. Why did he have to think at all? He was eye candy. Who cared what he thought?

Apparently, she did.

His brow furrowed and he seemed confused. "What do you think I'm thinking about? You."

Oh! That warmed her insides, but the warmth was far from comfortable. It began a wildfire, knowing that Caspian was concentrating on nothing but her. But what had she expected? Did she picture him pondering the exchange rate of the zloty against the U.S. dollar? Maybe the plight of the Galapagos booby? She was repeatedly amazed by her own naïveté.

"Well, what *about* me?" she demurred, her hand on his chest, his deliciously wide expanse of chest. Oh, this was hard. And so was that rock of manhood seeking entry between her thighs, making her all wet and slippery. How could she tell him that the club was closed, its velvet rope drawn shut, when her body was being so traitorous? She was standing there holding the doors wide open and bringing him in for a landing like a 747. She was even holding glow sticks.

"Caspian—" she began.

He closed his mouth over that same nipple and looked up at her.

"I'm serious," she managed.

"Balls deep, baby doll. That's what I'm thinking about." His mouth was poised over her breast, his breath doing damnable things to that responsive flesh.

"That's it?" she prevaricated.

"What do you want me to be thinking about? The gestation of a Galapagos turtle?"

Grace scowled. She'd just been thinking that word, "Galapagos." Was he in her head again?

He laughed. "Oh, come now."

Come? Yes! Right now. Oh, please.

But Grace didn't listen to her body.

"You know you'd be angry if I was thinking about anything but being with you. What's with all this conversation stuff anyway? We speak an older language. A more primal dialect." He licked his lips before flashing his pearly whites and dipping his mouth back to its task.

Grace hated herself for a moment, but luxuriated in sensation. Then, she didn't know where or how, but she found the strength to move her hand up to palm his face and stopped him mid-delight.

Caspian sighed. "What now? I can't give you mind-numbing, earth-shattering, clit-wrecking pleasure if you keep interrupting me."

"Maybe I don't want mind-numbing, earth-shattering, clit-wrecking pleasure. Did you ever think about that? Hmm? I bet not."

Right. Because it was so horrible and awful, and not at all what a sane woman would be after. Not that she had all of the sandwiches in her picnic basket. Grace wanted to shake herself, to rattle her teeth out of her head like pennies from a piggy bank for being so stupid. Talk about cutting off her nose to spite her face. She shouldn't desire him as much as she did.

"Uh, no, Grace. I actually never did think about that. I thought we were past it."

"What's that supposed mean?"

"You know very well what it means," he replied.

"You mean, when I first summoned you and you did that female change-y thing? Just because I said okay then? Well, a onetime 'yes' isn't good for eternity. It's not like Open Admission Day at Yankee Stadium."

"Your hand is still on my face."

"Sorry." Grace moved her hand but didn't put it down. She knew the minute she did, Operation Talk Him Out of Your Knickers was a bust, because he would be in them and she would be out.

"Do you want to do that again? Is that what this is about? Fine. We can experiment. I can change form—"

"Caspian!"

"That's not the right answer either?" His brow furrowed, and she could see his mental wheels spinning fast and furious, clearly seeking the correct response. "I wasn't kidding when I said I've never worked this hard to please a woman. Mortal or no."

He looked so genuinely confused that Grace actually felt sorry for him—until she imagined him pleasing other women. Immortal women with voodoo punani. All of whom she hated instantly on principle.

Hated? It couldn't be jealousy. No, never that. She scowled at the thought. But it wasn't written anywhere that she couldn't lie to herself. She could tell herself any little thing she pleased. Thank God. Sometimes self-delusion was just what the doctor ordered.

"So, are you going to tell me the right answer or not? Usually that's what you women do when you start having feelings or . . ." He trailed off, glancing around like a kid caught up to his elbow in the Christmas cookies.

Grace growled. "I'm not having . . . any kind of feelings. What's wrong with you? Just because I'm female and you give great orgasms doesn't mean I'm going to get all anime-eyed, a baby seal awaiting your attentions. I'd have to be sixty-three kinds of coconut-flavored dumbass to fall for a demon. Your kind has the attention span of a goldfish."

"Whoa! I never said you were doing anything of the sort," Caspian replied.

Grace cursed her idiot tongue and wondered where its filter had gone. She was sure there'd been one installed at birth, right there between her brain and mouth. Apparently, it was on the fritz, or it caught some sort of virus that had eaten its operating system. She would never have vented that little bit of information otherwise.

Of course, even to her own ears her protests were a little too hot. And she knew she sounded petulant, but she couldn't help it. Or she didn't want to. Who cared, really? Of all the ways that this could end, none of them was good. Not for her, at least. Caspian wouldn't be hurt. He would just go on with his demonic business.

"You're upset about something," he said.

You think?

"What's wrong, Grace? I can't fix it unless you tell me." Caspian rolled to the side and with gentle fingers pushed errant strands of hair from her forehead. "This isn't like you."

What was this pile of horse apples? She'd just had a tantrum and he was indulging her? He was asking her what was wrong? Why wasn't he just washing his hands of her? And, how would he know what was "like her" or not? She could be a Bitch Kitty Deluxe on a red wagon for all he knew.

A faint and silly hope sparked to life in her breast: He *cared* for her. He had to! Joy burst through her limbs in a molten rush, but it congealed like cold lead when she realized that Caspian still had to go. There was Nikoli. Even if they managed to save him, she couldn't very well raise her son with a demon. And she couldn't forget what would happen when she got old. She would still age, still die. It was inevitable. Her life functions would cease, while Caspian was eternal. Why would he want to court that? And what about when her beauty was gone, when her "velvet-walled Heaven" was more like an abandoned cabin built of poison oak? Would he stay with her then? Could she even ask him to?

No. It was better to make him go away before he realized he cared. Caspian was a glutton, devouring any sensation he could experience. He'd suck the marrow out of her until there was nothing left. Even knowing the impossibility of their relationship, that's what he would do when he realized he had feelings. He'd glut on them—on the sensations, at least. She'd be left with nothing. Not her heart, not her soul. He'd take those both away.

No. Actually, Grace knew better. He wouldn't take her heart and soul; she'd give them away free and clear. She could already see it on the horizon, like a thunderstorm rolling across a prairie. And here she was, galloping forward at a hundred miles an hour.

What was she going to do? Should she really tell him what was wrong? Images flashed through her mind of Caspian in all his fiendish glory. While the sight was beautiful, it was also terrifying. She believed that he would never hurt her on purpose, but what if she made him angry, called forth the kind of rage that sometimes masked pain? Grace had really stepped in it this time, stepped in it with bare feet. With every second that passed she could feel badness oozing through her toes.

"Why do we have to rut like dogs in heat every time we're together?" she accused. Great. Perfect way to drive home the fact that she wasn't having feelings, pushing him away like this.

Goddess, though, she sounded like an Olympic champion nagger. Her voice was shrill and irritating, and she didn't like herself, not talking like this. She didn't know how Caspian put up with it. Or maybe he was just acting the way she'd expected, his attention like a crow's: on her until something better and shinier distracted him.

"Because you like it?" he said.

Part of her wanted to say that she didn't, but that would have been a big fat lie. There was no amount of language tampering that could make that statement true. She'd just end up choking on her words.

"I didn't say I didn't like it, but I . . . want to do something else." She almost hadn't been able to get that one out, because all she wanted was to feel his body working hers in that primal rhythm, slick and hot and hard. She imagined his hands, his mouth—oh, his mouth!

His lip curled in distaste. "What else is there?"

"I don't know. You could take me out to dinner."

He sounded hopeful. "Afterward, as you so eloquently put it, can we come back here and 'rut like dogs'?"

"No, I don't think so."

He sighed. "Grace. I hate to remind you, but . . . I, uh, already paid for it," he said.

"Really." Apparently Grace was also one of those people for whom the word was also a warning. This wasn't a question. It wasn't a declarative, either. It was filler. It was a placeholder to prevent her rage from spewing forth in a tsunami. For he'd just given her what she needed to escape him.

Caspian must have realized his mistake. "I didn't mean that how it sounded."

"How did you mean it?" Grace's mouth was a thin slash that barely concealed her teeth. She felt her face pinch with displeasure.

Caspian was backing slowly away, as if she were a lioness with a paw caught in a steel trap. He was clearly smart enough to know dealing with a woman's sensitivities was a brutal business, even if he was contractually in the right. "I just meant that we'd traded. That we're still trading. That . . ."

"That I'm just some whore. Your Mephisophelean contract binds me for fucking and suddenly I'm your property?" The last of it was half a question because her voice broke off at a higher pitch. Grace was angry, but her heart was also falling to pieces along with Caspian's dark but shining armor. She'd always assumed it would.

"I see that you're upset," he began.

Upset didn't even begin to describe this, but the situation was ultimately a good one. It was a good thing that her silly dreams and impossible hopes were shattered like spun glass on the concrete of reality. It would make the future easier. It would make what she had to do easier.

"I don't want this anymore," she said. And what do you know, it was the truth. It wasn't a half-truth or even a convenient stretch; she really didn't want this. She didn't want the pain, the complication, or the abject despair when he left her.

He moved away from her, making a show of getting up off the bed, though he could have just teleported himself away. Despite the fact that she had no patience for women who wouldn't say what they were thinking and expected their men to simply know, part of her was still hoping that he'd argue. It had been so easy to cast the first stone before she'd moved into this glass palace. But he didn't oblige. She wondered if he knew more than he said.

He flashed her a devastating smile and turned to leave. "Whatever you want, Grace." He paused by the dresser and turned to eye her once more. "If you change your mind, I'll be around." Then he was gone.

"*I* won't," she declared, needing the last word. Also, speaking aloud made her intention more real, cemented her resolve. It would be so very easy to call his name and bring him back, to forget everything but the heat between them, his cock pounding into her, filling not just her body but those dark, despairing places of her soul that would still be empty when they finished.

A sudden ache between her thighs drowned out all else. She remembered Caspian's demonic tongue teasing her clit while stroking the inside of her, his hands all over her body. How did she get herself into these messes? This infernal sex drive was like an STD. She hoped there was a cure, because she needed it now. In an attempt to find relief, her fingers traced her body, following the same paths, invoking memories of Caspian. They slid inside her very wet passage, and her thumb worked her clit.

It wasn't the same. She gave up and went to the dresser. Ha! No demon appendage could match her secret weapon.

This miracle of modern science was purple and glittery, and it had a rotating head and another piece that snuggled against her anus, and still another that vibrated her clit. Of course, she hadn't asked Caspian to try. Who knew what forms he could—

Enough! No more Caspian. She would use the Rabbit. There was no way the batteries would die, because this bad boy plugged into the wall and had more get-up-and-go than a Smart car—which was a good thing, because she had miles to go before she slept. The wicked always did.

Grace pulled open the drawer with expectant joy only to gasp and cover her mouth in horror. This was why the demon had stopped at her dresser before departing. Her Rabbit had been brutally murdered, an untimely death to be sure. Its murderer had taken a trophy, too. The rotating clit-hugger had been amputated and the device had been fried like bacon. There was still smoke coming off the molded plastic gel head.

Before her eyes, the thick, imitation man-sword wilted like a dead flower, sagging sadly in a parody of its former erect glory; this was how she imagined John Holmes on his one hundred and tenth birthday.

"Caspian, I'm going to kill you," she vowed, pushing the drawer shut with reverence while at the same time raising the maimed appliance. Grace shook her fist in the air as if she were Scarlett O'Hara and her Rabbit a turnip, declaring she would never be hungry again. The corpse of the Rabbit flopped in phallic punctuation.

To Caspian, watching from the shadows, it would have been the funniest thing he'd ever seen . . . if his previous words about scorned women weren't ringing in his ears like a fire alarm.

CHAPTER SIXTEEN
A Sacrifice

Sasha Dubenko was a man of few words, a predilection that had served him well in his career as a confidence man and consultant for the Vasilyev family. It was for that reason he knew where so many dark secrets were buried, including Nadja Grigorovich.

He'd outright lied to Michael when asked if he knew where Nadja was hidden. Sasha had witnessed the last battle between her and Seraphim firsthand. He'd been with Nadja as her living flesh hardened to stone, and he'd promised he'd take care of her. Nadja's magick even kept him young and fit, well enough to do her bidding, if not so much it was overtly noticed.

His appearance was unassuming. He could have passed for any of the mourners that miserable day: white, middle-class, and American. He was a forgettable backdrop in his camel-colored trench coat and dress shoes, and he was wearing a matching hat to keep the rain off his black-framed glasses. He was completely nondescript.

It was bad luck in the village where he'd been born to step on new earth in a cemetery, so he kept to the manicured walkways, careful not to tread on any of the freshly turned dirt. Sasha believed in things like the evil eye, throwing salt over his shoulder just in case the Devil perched there, and the witch eternal known as the Baba

Yaga. He wore a pewter charm shaped like a three-petal flower with intricate knot-work designs to repel all of these evils.

His fingers sought the charm and rubbed it absently. Nadja had made it with her own hands, infused it with her power, charged it with her own blood, and there was a smoothness that wasn't quite an indentation but was what his mother would call a worry spot. He often sought out the comfort provided by the remnants of Nadja's magick. Touching the amulet was as close as he could get to touching her. But today was different. He was going to see his beloved, was going to make a desperate offering. He was going to see if he could break the curse that held her in living death. He was going to break her suspended animation.

If only she'd agreed to relinquish her powers. If Nadja hadn't tried to steal the magick of the Baba Yaga from Seraphim Stregaria, she would have been able to keep them. But no, she'd been as hungry for power as some others were for bread or meat. The battle with the other witch had left her all but dead.

Seraphim had been within her rights to take Nadja's life. For some reason she had not. The woman was powerful, the most potent witch the world had seen in an age. She'd endured human trials, suffered the most horrific tortures that humans could inflict on one another. In the concentration camps such evil had been done to her, so it was a miracle she hadn't burned the world out of vengeance. Nadja would have. Seraphim had not. Therein was the only reason Sasha wanted to help Grace Stregaria defeat Michael. As much as he'd loved Nadja Grigorovich, he'd known she could never be allowed to claim the power of the Baba Yaga. Michael had been born with that same hunger. Mated with Ivan Vasilyev's evil, he was a destructive force. Too destructive.

Sasha hoped the sacrifice he'd brought earlier was still

asleep; it would be easier for all parties if she slept through what was to come. He imagined how awful it would be, to feel your conscious mind slipping away into nothingness while knowing your body would belong to someone else. A horrible thing, yes. But necessary. The woman had to die so that his Nadja could live. It was a trade that he was willing to make. Sasha would do anything for Nadja—well, anything but see her become the Baba Yaga.

He pushed open the wrought-iron gate and produced a large brass key from his pocket. It fit the heavy lock on the crypt, turned with no resistance, and Sasha gave a perfunctory glance at his surroundings for witnesses or anything out of the ordinary. A moment later he slipped inside.

He saw nothing suspicious but cast a ward on the door nonetheless. Michael had been searching for this tomb for a long time, mostly because he was the one with the power now and wanted to make sure that his mother understood. He wanted to give her an irrevocable demonstration. But Sasha wasn't ready to be parted from her simply to satisfy Michael's infantile ideals about revenge.

The vessel was still slumbering where he'd left her, at Nadja's feet. Her arms were bound in front of her, her ankle shackled by a chain embedded in the far wall. If by chance she happened to get free of her ropes, she still wouldn't be able to escape the crypt. It would have been easier to secure her arms behind her back, but Sasha didn't want to cause Nadja any discomfort when she pushed the girl's soul out of her body. All of the sensations that the shell experienced would become hers. It wasn't as if his reluctance to tie her had something to do with him being a kind man.

This girl was a virgin; he'd made sure of that. She had nice childbearing hips, breasts that could feed a third-world nation, and a dainty waist. Just how Sasha liked them, just how Nadja had looked all those years ago. Her hair was an unfortunate mousy brown, but this had been the closest Sasha could come to a body that both he and Nadja would approve of. At least, he hoped she'd approve.

He approached the marble statue in the center of the room. Pulling a jar of fresh rose petals from a hidden pocket in his trench coat, he scattered them around the base. When he was finished, he bowed before approaching the statue, ever the supplicant.

His hand found the marble cheek of the carved goddess and its eyes opened, bright with madness. That moonlight gaze fell upon the form below, the figure in chains, the sacrificial vessel. When Sasha kissed the cold, frozen lips of the statue, the eyes closed again. This was a dangerous transference: If the host body died, Nadja would, too.

The first deed was tackled with the blade of his *athame*. Sasha tried to be quick and gentle; after all, his Nadja was going to feel the aftermath. But virgin blood was necessary to begin the transfer of souls.

Sasha next began the invocation, continuing the ritual Nadja had left written out for him before her battle with Seraphim, wanting to cover all of her bases. It had taken him many years to find all of the special ingredients she'd listed, as well as the woman who would suit their needs. Michael had finally purchased her through his special channels. Sasha had never asked Vasilyev's kid for anything before, so Michael had been happy to oblige. Sasha was glad he hadn't asked any questions, though. Still, if he had, Sasha would have said anything to accomplish his mission.

Yes, virgins were highly priced commodities in these precarious times. American girls traded their virginity to hang with the popular crowd; Eastern Bloc women traded theirs for food. The choices kept getting younger and younger, and Sasha had had no desire for a child. He'd been specific that she be in her twenties. This one had been kidnapped from her doting papa—her doting, rich, and royal father who would do anything to get her back. Which meant Nadja would have the money she'd always wanted. Sasha would become her new bodyguard. It was the perfect plan.

He finished the incantation, mixing the vessel's blood with diamond dust ground up in the incarnadine light of the harvest moon.

Sasha lit a white candle, then a black one. Both were for protection. Then he pulled out a lump of red wax that he melted between the two flames and dripped down into the mortar with the blood and diamond paste.

There were other ingredients, too, secret ingredients that he dared not call by name. If he thought of them for too long, they would brand his aura; he'd be marked to anyone who had the power to see. He couldn't have that. Especially not with the Baba Yaga snooping about. She was bound to reveal herself soon. She'd never let this charade with Nikoli continue, which was another reason he'd tried to tell Grace the truth.

He smeared the mixture on the forehead of the vessel, then lovingly on his beloved's cool marble cheek. His hands traced the contours of the statue, gently, and with a reverence imbued with his love for her. The marble cracked, emitting a distinct sound like pottery knocked from a shelf. Bits of alabaster began molting from Nadja, and then the falling rock *was* Nadja. She was shattering, breaking apart.

The bound woman on the floor began to writhe and struggle. Her eyes were wide and her mouth opened to scream, but no intelligible sound came out, nothing but the struggle to force air into her rebelling lungs. There was no more blood, apart from what had been mixed to begin the process, but the host attempted to reject the parasite soul.

It didn't last; Nadja was too strong. She snuffed the virgin's light with ease, pushed her into the fringe darkness, and bound her there with the power of her will. Invading the younger body, Nadja's essence took root like a weed and blossomed. The shards of her statue began to disappear like melting ice, leaving no trace of their existence.

Sasha removed the chain from her ankle and sank to the hard floor of the crypt. "My love," he said, gathering her near, his fingers tangling in her hair. He noticed that the virgin's scent had changed, smelled now like freesia and honey, a scent that followed Nadja wherever she went.

She touched his face, his cheek; her thumb grazed his lips before she met them with her own in a hard kiss. She broke free and reached around him while he murmured endearments into her ear.

"I've missed you, *golubuska*."

"Do you love me, Sasha?" Nadja whispered against his cheek.

"More than breath." He didn't hesitate, for he felt the answer to the very core of his soul.

"Would you die for me?" she asked.

"I've said as much—my very last breath for you."

Sasha claimed her mouth again in a searing kiss, and Nadja echoed his passion, pressing herself into him, returning endearments in the language of their homeland. She pulled back, looked into his eyes, and smiled, and in that moment Sasha Dubenko thought her a goddess, the most radiant woman in the universe. He thought his heart would burst from love.

And then it did. An impossible pain shot through him, like his chest was ripping apart, like the concurrent spontaneous combustion of all his internal organs. It registered in his brain that this must be death, but Nadja was still smiling. She was gazing at him with so much love in her eyes.

His fingers flew to his chest and found Nadja's dainty, perfect ones wrapped around his mother's *athame*. She pulled his hands away, twining their fingers and using her magick to push the blade ever deeper.

"Thank you, Sasha," she whispered.

Nadja looked down at the man she'd loved and smiled again. She would miss his ardent embrace, his passion. She'd miss knowing that he'd always be there for her, and she was grateful for all he'd done. But she couldn't trust anyone else to complete this transference ceremony, and the rite required the physical death of a body to keep her soul anchored.

She again pressed her mouth to his lips, a sweet lingering kiss that would be their last. Using her magick, she sapped the last of Sasha's strength and turned it against him. She used that borrowed force to move the *athame* up through his body and then down again, gutting him like an animal.

It was what he would have wanted. After all, she'd asked him if he would die for her and he'd agreed.

She raised her arms and called a storm. Thunder crackled outside, and clouds covered the daytime sky with inky black depths. The tender rain that had been like tears from Heaven became torrential, crashing down into the soft earth, the drops like bombs, slamming into the landscape and crushing flora and fauna alike. Lightning ripped the atmosphere, tearing asunder the very fabric of reality.

Inside the crypt, another bolt struck. It incinerated Sasha's body, reducing it to ash. Nadja spoke more words, and that ash merged with the blood and diamond paste to become a whole stone. It burned red with the love that Sasha had held for her.

When the smoke cleared, Nadja picked up the stone. It was warm. She pressed it to her chest and the stone fused there, its power keeping her soul bound to the mortal realm and also feeding her energy from the endless strength of Sasha's love. He'd always be with her. She caressed the rock, enjoying the incongruent texture with the softness of her new skin, and she smiled some more.

But the time for woolgathering was past. She needed to find a mirror and see what Sasha had given her to work with. Then she had to find her idiot son and bring that self-righteous bitch Grace to heel. The latter would destroy Seraphim Stregaria, which was something Nadja had been looking forward to for a very long time.

CHAPTER SEVENTEEN
Hot Dog Down a Hallway

Michael Grigorovich was balls deep, as Caspian was wont to describe it, but he wasn't happy about the fact. To be honest, he was getting as much pleasure from being with Dina as screwing a wet paper bag. Not at all a good time. Some of his men had once described doing certain women to be like throwing a hot dog down a hallway. He now understood. Dina just lay there; her pussy was lax and wide. The least she could do was clench her interior walls so he could feel them. Otherwise, it was just like a hot-dog toss: nothing but open space for miles and miles.

Her passivity made him want to hurt her—anything to get some sort of reaction. Well, he also just liked hurting women. It made him hard to see their faces twisted in pain, to hear their high-pitched pleading for him to stop, to feel the way their bodies contorted when they tried to fight. It was nothing short of divine.

Dina was so skinny that her hips were digging into his. When he looked down, he could see her ribs jutting out more prominently than her breasts. Her bra would have fit better backward. She did have a great ass, though. She'd have to starve herself with a little more discipline to get rid of that.

Michael pulled out and turned her over. She didn't protest because she thought he was going to enter her from behind. And he was. But his idea of rear entry was some-what different.

When she felt his intent, she tried to say no, but he pushed her face down into the pillow.

"Try it." It wasn't a request.

His cock was slick from being inside her and he pushed himself past the tight ring of muscles. Now *this*, Michael decided, this was good. It was tight and hot, and she was crying. The fast track to multiple orgasms. For him.

That is, until he felt a stabbing pain in his ass. He cried out and started to withdraw and immediately the pain less-ened. Deciding it must be over, he entered her again—and the pain came back. A red-hot poker was being shoved into his nethers.

He wanted to scream, but he was no woman. Instead, he pushed harder on the back of Dina's neck. This was her fault, somehow, a theory confirmed when he felt himself begin to lose air as she struggled for breath.

Bitch! Fucking bitch! He'd *kill* her. He used his free hand, closing it around her throat to snap her neck, but immediately felt pressure on his own throat. He tried to en-ter her again, but felt the same horrible pain as he had be-fore.

"I'd think you'd have figured it out by now," a voice said behind him. He turned and saw Ethelred leaning against the doorway, watching.

Dina shrieked at the intrusion. Michael slapped the back of her head. "Shut up, bitch." He resisted the urge to flinch when he felt the slap against his own head. "Figured what out?"

"Remember that little bit of Latin Gracie whispered at you in your bar?"

"Not really, no. It didn't seem important at the time." He rolled off Dina and shoved her out of the way, sprawling out angrily on the bed as she crashed to the floor.

"Well, you're feeling the effects of the spell right now. Everything you do will come back to you."

Dina tried to pull the sheet down to cover her nakedness, but Michael refused to let her have it. She'd have to walk by Ethelred to get to the bathroom and retrieve her clothes; it was either that or sit on the floor naked.

She stood and lifted her head, tossing her blond hair over her shoulders. Ethelred gave her an appreciative swat on the ass, and she grimaced. "Proof I'm not a total cad," he said. Her expression relaxed.

Michael scowled. "What did you do?"

"Do I answer to you?" Ethelred swung his head around like a lion that had just caught the scent of blood.

"I summoned you," Michael said petulantly.

"Yes, you did, and you let me out of the circle, too. Didn't you? Your soul is mine, Michael Ivan Grigorovich. You've signed in blood my book of debts. You owe me a thousand years of servitude." Ethelred's irises burned as he spoke of the contract. "And you bear your mother's debt as well."

"It won't matter when you have Grace," Michael said with confidence.

Ethelred smiled, baring sharp teeth. "You are correct."

"So, what did she do to me and how do I break it?"

"She cast a Karma spell on you. Your Karma is immediate, however. Your bad acts register instantly, the sensation of whatever you do to another person replicated against you."

"She has the power for something like that?"

"Oh, yes. Grace is powerful beyond her ken. She even managed to bleach Caspian's hair with a banishing potion."

"Big deal." Michael snorted.

"It is indeed, little man. It is indeed. No mortal magick can touch a Crown Prince of Hell."

Michael shrugged. "I told her she has ten days to get rid of the bastard or I'll kill Nikoli."

"That doesn't seem to have stopped them from enjoying your hot tub."

"What do you mean?" Michael asked as he pulled his pants on.

"He was right here shagging her two shades of blue the night of the opera. Had her in your hot tub. Made her scream his name really loud, too." Ethelred looked gleeful as he relayed this information.

"I'm going to kill her."

"I wouldn't. Not while you're under her Karma spell. Well, I suppose if you're ready to begin serving your time in Hell as my bitch . . ."

Michael curled his fists and slammed them into the bed, growling through his clenched teeth. "Damn it. God. Damn. It." He looked for a moment as if he would start chewing on the coverlet. "What do I do?"

A large, leather-bound tome appeared. It looked longer than *The Odyssey* and heavier than a block of cement.

"Ah, Michael, my lad, you know nothing is free." Ethelred winked. "Sign on the dotted line and I will map out a plan."

CHAPTER EIGHTEEN
More Rabbits

It was a neon Sodom and Gomorrah, a modern-day pleasure palace, a carnal candy store. The lights were extremely bright, and as she stood next to the building Grace Stregaria felt as obvious as a swollen and red baboon butt during mating season. It had taken her a day and a tank of gas to even pull into the parking lot.

The remedy would be to go inside, but she wasn't quite ready to do that. She was embarrassed, even though there were sunglasses perched on the end of her nose tinted like something you'd see on a highway patrolman and her hair was covered by an old scarf that was Hollywood couture. To be honest, she was right to be nervous. Her outfit only made her stand out more.

Grace prided herself on being a modern woman with modern ideas. She'd told herself that she was comfortable with her needs, that they were nothing to be ashamed of. But it was different logging in to a Web site, browsing whatever struck her fancy and examining it in as much detail as she liked, compared to actually asking a real person, to his or her face, if an item could make her scream in tongues and change her religion. It was a hoarse cry of a different color. And her packages always arrived in discreet brown wrappers with banal if neatly printed labels like Jane & Dick Distribution. Not bright red bags that screamed Plastic Cock.

Then, of course, there was the manner of item she was buying. Grace had broken several clit snugglers, dildos, and other toys designed to bring a woman to orgasm. The only thing that never broke was her Rabbit—well, until Caspian broke it. The Rabbit had gone until she couldn't, and then some. There was never any choking to death for the poor creature, its batteries sputtering to a miserable end just before she got off. It was industrial strength, had a cable for a wall socket, and was a true *power* tool.

Yup, even if it was pretty—a glittery, unicorn purple—it was still what you would call a bad motherfucker. That was why she was so embarrassed. Guys seeing her carrying it out of here would think she gave velvet cave tours complete with men in lighted hats and trolleys where they could get out and take pictures. Guided spelunking expeditions. It wasn't really the sort of reputation she wanted, even if she didn't know these people, probably would never know them, and knew rationally that they didn't give three buffalo cakes about what she did with her hoo-ha or what she shoved inside it. After all, if the thing didn't sell, they wouldn't carry it. Therefore, more than one hoo-ha in the world had to be partial to a plastic purple penis able to violate its owner in many different ways.

She took a deep breath and pushed the door open. Correction: She tried to push the door open. And Grace was so nervous that her feet didn't notice as the rest of her stopped moving. Her head made a distinct *thunk* as it hit the glass.

Damn security. Her face flamed a bright, candy apple red. Even if she was a modern girl with no hang-ups whatsoever, how the hell was she supposed to get into the establishment if the door was locked? Were they closed?

As she searched for a sign with listed hours, a voice informed her, "There's a bell."

Grace looked up through the window to see possibly the most beautiful woman she'd ever laid eyes on. Ringlets of long hair spilled down that could only be described as crimson. It was the deepest, most fiery red Grace had ever seen, more so even than her cheeks after walking into the locked door.

She tried to glance away, but the woman had an aura that was irresistible. Grace managed to drop her gaze to the redhead's feet, but the woman's vinyl fuck-me boots led up perfect legs to black patent-leather hot pants and a green angora sweater that covered a bosom bigger even than her own. Maybe. Her green eyes were bright and friendly, and her mouth curved into a smile with perfect white teeth.

She was probably a demon; Grace consoled herself with that fact. A person would have to sell their soul to get teeth that straight and white. All of the demons she'd met had lovely smiles, Caspian included, and he'd been born back when mortals still chewed on leaves to clean their teeth.

Grace realized that she hadn't replied. "Oh." It was all she could get out.

"Is this your first time here, honey?" the redhead asked.

Grace nodded.

"I'm Jill." The woman reached over and pushed a button. A bell rang, and the distinct sound of a disengaging latch echoed outward. Jill pushed the door open.

"I'm Grace."

"I know," the redhead said with a smile.

She knew? Grace was rooted to the spot by a sense of overwhelming dread. How did this creature know who she was? "Creature" was the perfect description, too. She had to be a demon.

"Don't be afraid, dearie. I'm your . . . demon godmother, so to speak."

"You look familiar."

"I should. Last time you saw me, I was wrapped in plastic and that douche bag Petru was stuffing me into a Dumpster."

"You were *dead*." Grace managed to keep her voice calm.

Reanimated corpses were dangerous things, not something that she wanted any part of. Though, this Jill didn't stink like rotten eggs and mildew. No, she smelled more like roses. Michael's favorite scent.

"Sure was," Jill agreed, dragging her over to a display.

"It begs the question . . ." Grace let the question hang.

Jill began shoving jelly cock after hard-molded phallus into Grace's arms, something shaped like a butterfly, a bullet, a device with a remote control that looked like it needed a bomb squad, a clit clamp—something Grace was *sure* she wouldn't be interested in—something else like a nipple vacuum, and finally a ball gag. Grace felt every eye in the shop train on her like snipers, but Jill was oblivious. The redhead eyed her critically and seemed not quite satisfied.

The once-dead beauty held up a traditional set of handcuffs and a pink fur-lined pair. "The question would be: fur, or no fur?"

"No fur. I mean, if you're going to have the experience, you might as well go all out."

Jill tossed the package on top of what Grace already held. "That-a-girl!"

"But I really can't very well handcuff myself," Grace pointed out.

The redhead snorted. "Of course, you can. You're a witch."

Grace paused. She had to admit she was kind of disappointed that Caspian hadn't miracled himself into the middle of the conversation and offered to do it for her. In fact, she'd kind of expected that. She had to remind herself that it was a good thing he hadn't. She'd told him to go away, and he had. He wasn't forcing his rights, the rights she'd given him by contract. She sighed aloud as Jill dragged her forcibly through the store.

"If you want him back, just say so. He'll come."

"I don't." She didn't bother asking how Jill knew her reason for acting like a middle-schooler.

"Then why are you sighing, all morose and bereft? It certainly can't be from the loss of Michael." Jill rolled her eyes, then paused in front of another display. "Oh, sweet bleeding hell, that's not it, is it? You're not one of those who likes abusive shit bags?"

"Oh, no. *No.* Fuck him with a rusty potato peeler. I don't care about him at all. The only thing that concerns me is my son."

Jill smiled with diabolical intent. "I just might."

"Might? What?"

"Oh, nothing." The redhead tossed a whip onto Grace's pile.

"Hold on," Grace said.

"That's for me, sweetie," Jill promised.

"Oh. Uh, the rest is for me? I really think this is plenty. I just wanted a new Rabbit."

"The plug-in one, right? God. Yum."

Grace found herself liking the other woman, even though the jealousy bug had taken a big old bite out of her hindquarters. There was something real about her, honest and open. It seemed to say she took the world for what it was and it didn't scare her; it just made her hungry for more. She was alive—more so than anyone else Grace had met—and this gave her a certain charisma. She decided to say, "So, you didn't answer me. How did you come to be what you are?"

"Your grandma. She's a class act, that one."

"She'd dead," Grace pointed out, as if this would be a startling surprise.

"So was I. Anything is possible. She brought me back to do the one thing that I need to do. She gave me demonhood. Michael is . . ." She trailed off.

"Michael is what?"

"Can't tell you, honey. I'm sorry. But I figured I'd come help you since she can't. You seem . . . kind of awkward. Plus, I like you."

"I like you, too," Grace replied, "but my arms are starting to hurt."

Jill laughed. "Oh, sure. Let's go pay. I have demon credit." She flashed an odd-looking piece of plastic.

Grace grinned. "Actually, if you'll let me get my purse, I have a credit card in Michael's name."

"Oh, well, in *that* case." Jill dashed to a wall, and just as quickly the entire contents of the display were piled on the counter.

So much for being inconspicuous. This did indeed cause every eye in the store to focus on them. Two hot women with an end-of-the-world supply of sex toys? Yeah. They all thought that she and Jill were going to be elbow deep in each other before they got home.

Grace's face flamed again, but she bit down on her lip to keep her mouth shut. If she tried to deny they were together, it would just be worse. Besides, why couldn't a witch and her demonic godmother go rubber-dick shopping together?

"I think I have a box in the back. Let me go get it," the cashier said, sauntering off with a happy hitch to his step, something not altogether at home on his bent form.

Jesus Harold with a riding crop! They needed a box?

Jill was standing there, a smug queen of debauchery and happy about it. She met every turned eye with a brazen shamelessness that Grace admired. She wanted the same for herself. She wished she felt just as devil-may-care.

Thinking about it, Grace made up her mind. These people could all think what they liked. So *what* if they knew she was going home to . . . she'd been about to say "jill-off," but the terminology seemed unfairly personal somehow, considering her new friend's name. Anyway, she could start a fire by rubbing her bean if she wanted and it was her business and hers alone. The haters were all cordially invited to shove a—

Jill interrupted her thoughts. "I have to go. I'll pick up my loot from your place later, okay?"

"Why?" Grace asked. Then, "Oh, no. You're not leaving me with this pile of perversions to lug home all on my own."

"I'm outranked," Jill whispered. "It seems that there are princely powers that have plans for your sweet self." Then Jill hugged her, hard and fast, and scurried out the door.

Grace's eyes ignored the commands of her brain and scanned the room for those "princely powers." Scanned it hopefully, feeling a rush. She didn't see any, however, so she in turn ignored her stomach, pretending those slam-dancing butterflies hadn't turned to bricks. If it was Caspian, where exactly was he?

She turned back to the cashier, who was eyeing her lasciviously.

"Where did your friend go?" he asked, ringing up each item and stuffing it into the large cardboard box he'd brought from the back.

"She was late for an appointment."

"I see." The cashier held up the ball gag. "Interesting. I didn't know you were into this."

A couple of customers were once again intrigued by what was going on at the register. Grace just blushed and looked at her feet, but a moment later she realized that the cashier shouldn't know anything about what she was into. Which meant . . . this homely little troll was Caspian! The sneaky bastard. He wanted to play with and taunt her? He wanted to play up her embarrassment here? Oh, and he still had it coming for the murder most foul he'd committed earlier.

She smiled lasciviously at the little man. "Yeah, I'm a total freak. What can I say?" Later she would contemplate why that statement had rolled off her tongue like honey. The implication would haunt her. Was she indeed a freak?

He chortled a bit and inspected the next item. It was a cock corset. "Who's *this* for?"

"Not sure. You maybe. If you play your cards right." Grace smiled.

The cashier narrowed his eyes, his brow furrowed. "Really? That desperate for cock, are you?"

"Insatiable, really." Another embarrassing truth, at the moment. But to hell with it. This was all Caspian's fault. Let him deal with the consequences.

"Why do you need all this stuff? Don't you have a boyfriend?"

"Nope," she replied. "Had somebody I was fucking, but you know, he didn't want anything deeper. Wouldn't take me to dinner. Wouldn't do *any*thing. Doomed relationship, really."

The little guy was still ringing up items and shoving them into the cardboard box. He'd apparently given up on trying to embarrass her. "You couldn't just, you know, shag him because it's fun?"

"It's not fun anymore. See, there are things called feelings. They're like roaches. Once you have them, you can't get rid of them. So I'm just trying to keep the dishes clean and tidy and the food put away so they don't see anything they think they want."

"Ah." The man eyed her, then spat a big wad of chaw into a spit cup. Grace almost threw up.

With a loud smack, she slapped her credit card down on the counter in front of her. "So. How much is it for this behemoth box of bang?"

"One thousand eight hundred forty-two dollars and ninety-seven cents."

Grace shrugged and pushed the card forward.

"This says 'Michael Grigorovich.' "

"It does, doesn't it?" She didn't sound the least bit surprised.

"I don't think that's you."

"Nope, it's not."

"Do have another form of payment?"

"Don't need one. Look again." Grace used her magick to change the name on the card.

"Grace, if you think for one minute," the man said, his form already changing, "that I'm going to let you go without a fight, surrender you to the delights of silicone sex, you have another think coming."

Grace laughed, but this time none of the shop's other patrons turned to look. Instead, they melted away into a waterfall of fire. Unfortunately, so did her new Rabbit. What did the demon have against those poor little creatures?

"Grace, I can be anything you desire," Caspian said. He wore his normal shape. "Anything. All you have to do is tell me your fantasies. I can make them happen. Every damn one."

Suddenly they were on a ship and she was dressed like a wench, her bosoms heaving like great barrels of ale over her cincher. Caspian was dressed as a sea captain—no, not just a captain, but a *pirate* captain. He stood at the helm, breeches tighter than sin and Hessian boots up to his knees. A fine lawn shirt hung open, revealing the wide, tan expanse of his chest. A gold hoop adorned his ear and he even wore an eye patch. A slightly intimidating scar marred perfect features, which made him look even more delicious. In fact, he looked just how she'd envisioned the dashing pirate/disinherited lord in the first romance novel she ever read.

Her resolve died a quiet, lonely death. The rest of her was too busy eye-humping the pirate about to plunder her booty.

"Like this, Grace. Is this what you want?"

Caspian yanked her to him with little care for tenderness, crushing his mouth to hers in blatant and absolute owner-ship. She melted into him, the familiar heat a delicious jux-taposition against the salty sea spray, the—

No, no. She mustn't.

She drew away from him. "You can't just kidnap me on your supposed pirate ship and treat me like a . . ."

She didn't get to finish. Caspian was blond again, and they were surrounded by fog. Screams of terror tore through the darkness, and heady blazes sprang to life on the surround-ing huts.

She looked down and saw she was wearing nothing but a wool shift, her hair now long and falling past her waist. She was freezing her tits off. About to tell him so, she sud-denly zeroed in on the fur loincloth he wore. There were gold bands at his wrists and biceps, and he was resplendent in Viking glory. The sword hanging down his back wasn't the only one vying for attention, either. She could see the outline of a different weapon lurching against that oh-so-small loincloth, and was tormented by visions of him pillag-ing her right there, of him carrying her off to his longboat and giving a thorough demonstration of his oar.

"No?" he asked, his mouth next to hers, his hands burning her flesh through her threadbare garment. "What about this?"

She was in a damned corset again, and all she could think about was his hands getting her out of it, freeing her breasts for his mouth, his tongue and talented fingers. But while she couldn't breathe, it wasn't from the growing heat be-tween her thighs. It was from the rocking of the blasted car-riage. Each bump pushed her cleavage against her throat.

"Stand and deliver!"

The door opened, and Caspian stood there wearing a mask that covered only his eyes. It lent exquisite focus to the perfect lines of his jaw, the sensual curve to his mouth. "Your jewels, my lady . . . or mine!"

Sweet hell, Grace was done for. The Highwayman Fantasy had been in the spank bank forever. When she watched old episodes of *Star Trek,* she'd wished for the holo-deck to be real so she could be held up and accosted by a handsome highwayman who was really a disinherited duke trying to right some horrible wrong, the gentleman Jack whose touch ignited ignoble fires and . . .

Grace could easily see riding Caspian in this carriage, the uneven road helping her bounce up and down on his cock like a pogo stick, but she could only come to the conclusion that he was trying to kill her. Her Kegel muscles couldn't clench any more, and one of them was about to snap and cause an aneurysm in her brain.

He grinned wickedly, and she found that her breath was even harder to catch. "So you like this one, do you?"

Anything to make this torture stop.

He climbed inside the carriage and knelt before her, shoving her skirts up around her waist. Her pantalets came down, and he pushed his palm against her mound to send frissons of hyperawareness through her entire body.

"I like it but—"

"There is no 'but.' Just sensation. Just let me pleasure you, Grace," Caspian whispered, removing his tricorn hat and dipping his head down between her thighs.

The first touch of his tongue sent shudders of delight through her. Grace got a handful of his hair and pushed him closer, harder, wanting more. She'd known she would. He made a sound in the back of his throat that was almost like a growl, and she felt his tongue do what only it could, gliding into her hot channel while also laving her clit. The imagery this evoked was nothing short of disturbing, but she'd never been able to hold it in her head long enough to let it bother her; the sensation was too delicious to give a damn what exactly was going on.

Grace spread her legs wider and found that she kind of

liked being forced by the corset to control her breathing. It would prolong the pleasure. The great thing about demon sport was that they didn't have to breathe, so she hoped Caspian knew he was in for a long haul.

He tongued her honeyed lips, tasting her ever more deeply, echoing her cries as if her pleasure was his as well. Fingers replaced that tongue as he moved up her body to kiss her mouth again.

Grace could taste the evidence of her pleasure on his lips, and it caused something new to curl inside her. She carefully ran her tongue across Caspian's upper lip, then tangled it with his as he allowed her to take control. In that moment, she knew what she wanted.

"Tell me what you want and I'll give it to you," Caspian growled. "The world, Grace. I'll give you anything."

She was tempted to ask for his soul. He'd said she could have anything.

But that was unlikely. Instead, Grace chose something else. She was tired of being whisked away to scenic unknowns, bound to walls for this demon's pleasure. She wanted him to await *her* pleasure. "I want the power, Caspian," she said softly, as she broke their kiss. "I want to be in control. I want you at my mercy."

"I am, witch. Completely."

He silenced her with his mouth and also worked his magick. Her need grew to get closer to him, to make slick contact of heated skin on skin. Except, he'd left her corset on. It held up her breasts and still managed to keep her from breathing.

With deft fingers, he undid the top laces. He moved to pull away, but she dug her nails into his shoulders to keep him from teasing her more. She knew what she needed.

She raised her eyes to his and whispered, "You can't deny me this. How am I in control? Please, Caspian."

He watched her for a moment, and then he nodded. The

head of his cock slipped between her legs, slipped across her slick folds, through, atop. Slowly. She bucked her hips to force his entry, crying out with need, but he was immutable.

"You're beautiful, Grace." He brushed the pad of a fingertip across her lips, which were swollen from his kisses. "You're flushed with desire for me and it makes me *ache*. Your hair is spread as if you were posed, but I know you were not. Your mouth is ripe like summer peaches. You are all I want. I *ache* for you," he added, this last coming as if it were a revelation even to himself.

"Then why don't you take me?" Grace knew she sounded desperate, that she was reinforcing their tendency to spend all their time rutting like beasts, but it didn't matter. Not when he was looking at her like that. "I'm yours."

His eyes burned with dark flame. That hellfire didn't frighten her in the least, however; now it spurred her desire. Grace pushed herself up on her elbows and arched her hips, rocked back and sheathed his cock. After a moment, she pulled herself free. She repeated the process, quickly, deftly, dangerously.

The leather seat where Caspian braced himself began to smoke, little halos rising around his fingers, and he cried out as if in pure bliss. *I'm yours.* Both of them felt it. Her casual vow burned between them. Her words were inside him like he was inside her, filling her to bursting with his demon cock.

Grace met his sudden intensity thrust for thrust, and he moved his forearm behind her for support—a move she was coming to love. It helped her arch her body just so, and he always hit a spot that sent waves of pleasure so powerful it was almost pain that spiraled through her. And he never let go until she came.

She felt herself on the edge of a precipice and realized she was about to do just that. And as usual, this was no "that was nice" type of experience. In fact, this was a "screaming, crying, stars shooting across the sky, I've touched the universe and know the meaning of life and this is it" clitoral orgasm that she'd never achieved.

Grace heard shrieking and realized it was her own voice. She was clinging to Caspian as her body rocked against his, and when she opened her eyes found him watching her with unbreakable intent. He didn't stop fucking her, though. His movements were slow and in time with the shudders powering through her like aftershocks from an earthquake. And she was still coming. Grace didn't know how it was possible, but languorous pleasure wrapped tendrils around every one of her limbs and her enjoyment only seemed to be increasing.

"What are you *doing*?" she gasped, fighting to keep her eyes open.

"Sharing my pleasure with you. You're feeling what I feel." His gaze was dark and deep now, those irises endless pools that had no color, no place in or out of time. He poured his awareness into her: what it was like to want her, what it was like to be inside her, how she looked to him when she declared his ownership of her.

Grace's eyes closed once more and she tossed back her head, biting down on her bottom lip as she rode the new sensation with even wilder abandon. It was more than he could take. He spilled the essence of himself, his demon seed rushing forth. The stars exploded inside her.

Her eyes opened, and Grace stared at her lover. She felt her eyes blazing, and something equally fiery erupted from her back. It bent the doors off the carriage.

Seeing the fire in her eyes and her new-formed lavender wings, Caspian seemed to be at a loss. "Well, hell."

Chapter Nineteen
A Disturbance in the Force

Seraphim knew something wasn't right. She felt it in her bones.

Well, she felt something wasn't right in addition to the fact that she looked like a twenty-two-year-old showgirl from Vegas but in reality was a withered old crone who liked hot tea and stories. Though, her stories were a bit different from those of most old ladies. And it wasn't like she was normally a stick in the mud. She refused to get her hair cut short and curled, sit around in a knit pantsuit, and play Yahtzee. If she was acting her age, she would keep her hair long if in a tidy bun, and she would wear Dolce & Gabbana while watching *Supernatural* and *Being Human*. She'd really enjoyed *Hexed* and was heartbroken when it got canceled. It had been very tempting—very tempting, indeed—to work a little gris-gris to get it back into production. She'd consoled herself with *True Blood*. That Eric Northman tied her knickers in two kinds of knots. That face! Sometime when she was next dream-walking she would—

A voluptuous redhead bounded through the door like a Newfoundland puppy and interrupted the lascivious journey of her thoughts. She'd have to get back to her Viking dreamboat later.

"I take it you accomplished Operation Get Grace a—"

Seraphim couldn't bring herself to finish the sentence. Not when it pertained to her granddaughter. She could set a plan in motion, knew what was going on, but she just couldn't articulate it. There were some things that were simply beyond the realm of acceptable, even if she'd seen similar things going on in her crystal ball. It was just as well that Jill cut her off.

"No, I did something better."

"You got her a man?"

"Sure did."

"Lovely. Now she won't be pining for that demon."

Jill raised an eyebrow and pursed her lips. A second later, she looked away.

"Balls," Seraphim swore.

"It was so *cute*. Really," Jill assured her.

"That's the problem. It's cute. He's a demon. She's a . . ." Seraphim trailed off and gazed into her cauldron. "Are you shitting me?"

"Uh . . ." Jill was unsure of what she was being asked. Being a demon, she saw nothing in the cauldron but boiling water and odd bits floating in the foam.

"By the Sulfuric Rod!" Seraphim said.

"You rang?" Hades was suddenly sprawled on her four-poster bed eating grapes. A strategically placed fig leaf was his only attire.

Seraphim shook her head. "This is no time for fuckery, Hades. Get over here and look at your granddaughter."

The Devil chuckled. "Seraphim, my love, I'm looking at you and envisioning scenarios that have nothing to do with her—except that they might give her an uncle."

"You and your quest for a son! You didn't get one off Persephone, and you're not planting any more seed in this field. You're a lousy father. But get over here and survey the predicament of the spawn that we did make."

Hades saw Jill and made a big show of sniffing the air around her. "You smell like one of mine, and yet I don't know you."

Seraphim spoke up. "That's Jill. You gave her to me, remember? I made her."

Hades gave the redhead a second glance, then shrugged. "You do good work."

"I know that! Now grab your Sulfuric—"

Hades was at her side in an instant, for he could tell she was really done messing around. He peered over her shoulder and saw his granddaughter in flagrante delicto with the Crown Prince Caspian. It didn't bother him like he supposed it should. Grandfathers probably weren't supposed to approve of such actions.

He said, "Look, I was the first one with my jock in a knot, but I took care of the whole imp problem. We knew Grace would have to summon a demon, you saw it written in her fate. I had a discussion with a certain angel who didn't want to see our girl baking an infernal bun in the old Eve-oven either. She's walking a fine line between worlds, but when is love wrong? And she looks happy. *Really* happy, actually. What are you so upset about?"

"The wings, Hades. Look at her wings. My mostly human granddaughter has sprouted wings like a goddamn fairy," Seraphim snapped.

"Or a Crown Princess of Hell," Hades offered.

Jill sighed. "I can't see."

Hades puffed his chest out like a cockatiel. "They're very pretty, of course. They would be. She's my granddaughter." He seemed very pleased with himself, as if he wanted to share his accomplishment with everyone. As if he'd done anything but give her grandmother the old in-and-out.

"Here." He gave Jill the gift of magick sight so she could see.

"Ooh, lovely," the redhead cooed.

Seraphim slapped his hand. "Stop that. You can't just go around gifting any demon you please with whatever you—"

"Why not? I'm the Devil!"

"Stop interrupting me," she snapped. "You just can't."

"Again: why not, Seraphim?"

She sighed; a great, put-upon sound. "Because I said so. That's why," she answered, just to be done with it.

He smirked. The smirk blossomed into an honest grin, which was rather frightening on his particular countenance. And then Seraphim realized that she was caught.

"Never make a deal with the Devil," she grumbled.

Jill was at a loss, though she wasn't sure she wanted to know what was going on. "I don't understand."

"I made a bet with this arsebag a long time ago that I would never say that. It was in reference to our daughter, but I didn't specify who I'd never say it to. He bet me I would, and . . ."

"So, what do you have to do?"

Hades answered. "She has to marry me."

"The Devil can get married?"

"Why not? She'll be my consort."

"Which I don't want. I'm the Baba Yaga. I have my own job. I'm busy here." Seraphim turned back to her cauldron.

"With what?" Hades asked. "Meddling in our grand-daughter's life? She thinks you're dead, old woman. Let it go."

"And leave her all alone in the world? Have you lost your mind?"

"She's not alone. She has Caspian. He'll take care of her. You'll see."

Seraphim sneered. The Devil he certainly was—full of trickery and empty promises. He was predicting this as if he had some control over the outcome. "Just the other day you were shitting blue kittens because Caspian demanded sex in payment from Grace. Now you're farting sunshine?"

Suddenly suspicious, she turned her attention back to him. "What did you do?"

"Caspian has grown a heart, my love. He'll be fine. Grace will be fine. They will be fine together, and we can get on about our business."

"What about Michael?" Seraphim asked.

"I've got that covered," Jill spoke up. "I won't disappoint you." A whip appeared, and she cracked it with vicious precision. Hades flinched, but it would only be visible to someone watching a slow-motion instant replay.

"Okay, but there's still the problem of the jetliner wings hanging off of my granddaughter's back. Not to mention that they're lavender. How did *that* happen?"

Hades shrugged.

"Oh, and you say this demon grew a heart? Well, what's he going to do with it—eat it? The thing's not going to last long. He'll have to become a human. And when, *when* is Grace going to come to her senses about Michael's curse making her think she has a son? How will—"

"Look, I told you. It's already taken care of. You're such a doubting Dolly. Caspian will earn his humanity. He chose demonhood, but his heart will choose humanity."

"Like I already said, what's he going to do with it?"

"Trade it, of course."

"I still don't understand."

"Woman, you've seen *The Godfather*, right? Don't ask me about my work," he replied, a smug look on his face.

Hades bent her back over the cauldron before she could say anything else and kissed her desperately. Or at least it seemed desperate to Jill. He was the Devil, though. Maybe he was just desperate to shut her up.

"Woman, will you just trust me? It's handled."

"Never trust a man who—"

Seraphim's mouth was once again occupied. The Devil quite literally had her tongue.

★ ★ ★

Petru was lost. He hadn't seen Sasha in two days, and he wasn't quite sure what to do. Sasha had claimed he was going to see the woman of his heart, that she was in trouble and needed Sasha to save her, but he'd promised to be back that night. He hadn't come back. Grigorovich hadn't seemed to notice and had asked nothing about the other man's whereabouts.

At first it had been okay. Petru had used the microwave, even though Sasha didn't like him to use it by himself, but he'd been so hungry. He'd warmed up some chicken stew that the nice neighbor woman brought over from next door. She was a nice girl. It was true, she was a witch like Nadja Grigorovich, but she didn't do bad things. She didn't hurt people. And any woman who could cook like his mother had to be touched with something divine.

Her husband had died in service to the Vasilyevs, taking bullets for Ivan, who allowed her to keep the apartment because of that. Otherwise, she'd now be working off debts on her back with clients of Michael Grigorovich's choice, rather than the ones she currently served to keep food on the table. Petru wasn't smart, but he knew how the world worked. He also knew that Sasha gave her things from time to time, and in return she brought them pies and cookies, roasts and casseroles.

He'd thought for a while that Sasha would make her his girlfriend, but the girl didn't exactly seem up for it. Petru would have been glad to have such a wonderful lady. She was pretty and a fantastic cook. Her apartment was always warm and smelled a bit like home. But while Petru did whatever he was told around her, he feigned disinterest because he didn't want her to feel forced into anything she didn't want. She seemed to have been truly in love with her husband.

Petru knew he wasn't handsome or smart. He didn't have

much to offer a woman—nothing besides the security of having a man who wasn't afraid to work. But he would have been good to her. He kept the values and traditions of his family. He demanded respect and fidelity. Women were respected, cared for. They didn't go out and work, they worked in the home. Unless they had no other options.

He thought about Katerina's pretty face and his shoulders slumped. He had nothing to offer her that she couldn't get somewhere else. So, no, he wouldn't try to make the pretty one his girlfriend. Even if Sasha would be gone for a little while longer, likely wanting some alone time with his lady after helping her.

He was hungry again. He'd eaten the stew yesterday but had found nothing else. For that reason, Petru thought perhaps it would be okay if he knocked on Katerina's door. He didn't have anything to take her, like a gift, so he hoped that cash would be okay.

He straightened his clothes and used his palms to smooth his hair before knocking on her door. Then he realized he could taste his own breath. He hurried back to the small apartment and gargled with vodka. Petru thought that was much better, but it occurred to him Miss Katerina would think he was sloppy with drink. Petru rummaged around for a toothbrush and toothpaste and made quick work of his mouth before rushing back to the woman's door.

"Miss Katerina, it's Petru."

The lock clicked and she opened the door. She was wearing a yellow day dress and an apron. Her butter-blond hair was piled in a bun on the crown of her head, and her smile was bright when she saw him. He couldn't help but feel warm inside when she smiled like that.

"Come in, Petru," she said. The door opened a little wider as she made room for him to enter. He was a bulky man. It was a squeeze, his shoulders completely filling the doorway. He had to turn sideways to get inside.

The kitchen smelled of homemade bread and dumplings. More chicken. Sasha must have given her a large chicken.

"Where are the little ones?" he asked.

"At a friend's."

Petru wasn't sure how to ask for some of what she was making, so he shoved a wad of twenties into her hand and took a deep breath, hoping she would share. A moment later, he became aware that he had done something very wrong. Her radiant smile lost all warmth. She nodded her head but didn't say anything. Then she pulled off her apron, very slowly, as if the action hurt her.

Her fingers moved to the buttons on her dress, which were in the shape of butterflies. He loved how she painted shaped enamel covers like that for her buttons: butterflies, bumblebees, ladybugs. He especially liked the ladybugs, their bright red and black colors contrasting with the green of the dress she'd sewn them on; they always caught his attention. He wished she'd wear that outfit more.

Her yellow dress gaped open and revealed small, pert breasts. He couldn't help his eyes traveling lower—and she wasn't wearing anything down there either. She was beautiful. He wanted to touch her, but . . . she was crying. Why would she take her clothes off and cry? He was her good friend. Then Petru remembered the money he'd handed her. It must have been a lot. He'd never been good with such things. Sasha handled the money always. Now Katerina thought he wanted to have sex.

Well, of course, he did, but not if she was crying. Petru knew it was wrong if she didn't want it, too. So when her dress slipped to the ground, he bent to pick it up.

"No, no, Miss Katerina. No."

She looked confused. "Am I not pretty to you, Petru? Is it my scars? Did you think you wanted this, and now, after seeing me . . ." She looked away.

He hadn't noticed them before, but there were burn

marks on her belly. They looked like they'd been caused by the end of a cigar, and there were others, a crisscrossed web of some other trauma running from her navel all the way over to her side and up under her arm. These seemed to be some kind of burns, too.

Petru shook his head and handed her the dress. "You are *very* beautiful to me."

"I don't understand," she said softly, trying to hand his money back.

"I didn't know how to ask, but I was hoping you would share your food with me again. I wanted to pay for it. I know you have little ones to feed, and I . . . I eat a lot." Petru felt stupider than usual.

"Oh." Katerina's cheeks flamed. "I don't know what to say."

Petru shrugged miserably. "I am a stupid man, Miss Katerina. A stupid man."

The woman hung her head, ashamed. "Now you know what I do."

Petru sighed. "To live. To clothe your children. As a mother, you do as you must." He'd seen such a predicament many times, and he couldn't blame her. Sometimes there were no other options for a woman.

He couldn't deny that he wanted her as a woman. He'd had sex before, had even paid for it, but he wanted Katerina in a different way. He felt something odd when she smiled at him like that. But that was a silly notion. He knew that, too.

"You don't think poorly of me? I'm still 'Miss Katerina' to you?" She asked it softly, as if she dared not believe it could be true.

Petru sat down at the small table in the kitchen. "Woman, you will *always* be my Miss Katerina."

Katerina beamed. "I have chicken and dumplings, hon-eyed carrots, and a raspberry tart. Does any of that sound good?" She brought him a plate heaped with food before he could answer, but she still didn't look at him. She also brought a tall pitcher of sweet tea. Knowing he'd drink the whole thing, she didn't bother to get him a glass.

"Will you sit with me?" Petru asked before shoving the first bite in his mouth.

The woman looked at the floor. "I'm . . . I'm still a little ashamed, Petru."

"Miss Katerina." He grabbed her wrist as she tried to walk away—gently, though, so he wouldn't hurt her. "You are beautiful to me, even more so because of the sacrifices you make for your children. My mother sold her body when that was all she had left, did it to care for me and my sisters. She hasn't had to do that since I could work, though. No, Miss Katerina, I only have respect for you. "

"Then why don't you want me?" The blond woman spoke so softly that it was hard for him to hear.

He pulled her into his lap. "I do. But I would want you to want me because you feel something more than obligation."

She pressed her lips against his cheek. "I do."

"Then, why did you cry?" It didn't make sense.

"I thought you meant to pay me for it, not to . . . well, not in the way I wanted. I've dreamt of you, Petru. I dreamt that you would realize your love and come to me, not use me but *make love* to me. I dreamt you would take care of me and my children. That you would love them, too. You are a good man and would be a strong father."

Petru was embarrassed. "I kill people, Miss Katerina. I am not a good man. I do the work that I can, but I would not be a good father."

"And I am a witch. I've done things I'm not proud of, more than just selling my body. If it doesn't matter to you, why should it matter to me?"

"Anything you've done I know is from the goodness of

your heart to help others or to survive. You are a good witch, Katerina. Not dark like Nadja."

"And you are the best man I have ever known. I love you."

That declaration was enough. Petru made love to his Miss Katerina there in the kitchen, the sunlight streaming through the little window by the table. He promised her many things. Unlike most men and women in the throes of passion, he meant every word.

CHAPTER TWENTY
Hell's Bells

Grace wasn't sure what to think about the new appendages sticking out through the place where the carriage doors used to be. She was trying very hard not to get upset, though she was aware that Hysterical City was the next exit ramp off this particular emotional highway.

There was no reason to explode like an overheated Jiffy Pop bag. She was sure wings came with advantages—advantages that she would be more than excited to explore with Caspian. She just needed to figure out if she could put them away, or if she was stuck looking like a freak show. This would teach her to play in the toy aisle.

They were really lovely, though. Straight out of Barbie Fairytopia.

Caspian reached out and touched them, his warm fingers sliding down their gossamer surface. This sent a shiver through Grace that was new, unknown, but completely decadent. His touch traveled the length of her wings, and her lips parted and her eyes closed in pleasure.

"Does it hurt?" he asked, pausing midstroke.

"Oh, no. Keep doing it. It's . . . I can't even explain what it feels like. Is it the same with your wings?"

"My wings are kind of like my hair. If you pull them, I'll feel it, but just a touch? No."

"I would really like to know how to make them go

away." She turned her head and caressed the arch of one wing herself. Unfortunately, she didn't get the same pleasure as when Caspian did it. Still, they were nice to touch. Like cotton candy, only they didn't stick to her fingers.

"I don't know how to make them go away." He shook his head. "I'm sorry, Grace."

"How do you make yours go away? I'm trying really hard here not to start screaming. Every minute that passes pushes me a little closer to the edge, and I didn't have much clearance to start with."

"I know. I mean, I know you're upset. I guess it wouldn't help if you knew your eyes were blazing hellfire like mine, would it?"

"No, that would be absolutely no help at all." Grace took a big, shaky breath. "What does it all mean?"

Caspian smiled. "It means you've chosen not to be human. You've chosen to be with me."

"I did no such thing! I'd have to sell my soul!"

Caspian eyed her questioningly but didn't stop petting her wings. He had a feeling that if he did, she would lose what little control she maintained. "Didn't your grandmother tell you?"

"Didn't she tell me what, exactly?"

"About your mother, your heritage?" Caspian was using both hands now.

"My mother died. I don't know much else about her. It was hard for Gran to talk about her—too painful. But I still don't understand what this has to do with the price of goat meat."

Suddenly Grace found herself in pigtails wearing her favorite dress from when she was five; it had bells in the crinoline. Thankfully, her wings had disappeared, but so had Caspian. Uncool, leaving her wherever he'd zapped her. That was a strike against letting him take her on another date. Maybe two strikes, but definitely a foul ball.

A man sat across from her—a handsome man, but he wasn't Caspian. He was wearing jeans and a Ralph Lauren shirt. He looked very Nordstrom. But he did have a goatee that looked decidedly devilish.

"Hi, sweetie. Looks like we need to have a talk before your grandmother has a stroke."

Grace had said she would scream if just one more thing fucked with her chi. Why wasn't she screaming? "Who are you?" she asked. "Where the hell did you come from?"

"Exactly." The newcomer looked pleased with himself.

"Another demon? I've got demons flying out of my ass here. I don't need another."

"Really? Where?" The man peered around her.

"It's an *expression,*" she sighed. "Where's Caspian? And what do you want?"

"Don't scream, okay?" The newcomer held up his hands as if showing her he was unarmed.

"I'm going to scream if you don't get off *Dancing with the Stars* and stop tap-dancing around all of my questions. And just what does my dead grandmother have to do with anything?"

"Hmm. Which question should I answer first?" he asked, smiling as if she were the cutest little thing he'd ever seen.

A low, irritated noise erupted from Grace and her wings emerged again, spreading from her back like a lavender explosion. Magick gathered in white-hot nimbuses around her balled-up fists, and as the newcomer reached to touch one of her wings, she slapped his hand. Only Caspian would be touching those!

"You are so much like Seraphim." He sighed, and it sounded very much like a man in love—not with Grace, but with her grandmother.

"Your name," was all she could manage.

"Hades, but don't scream."

"Why would I scream? You keep saying that. So, your

name is Hades. Who gives a furry rat's ass? Big deal. It's not like you're the Devil."

"Well, actually . . ."

She did scream this time, and for good measure she blasted him with two comets of pure energy from her fingers. Hades just smiled and produced a box of Godiva chocolates as a reward. She hadn't even so much as singed that evil little curl on the end of his goatee.

"Good job! I'm very proud. But I guess I need a new publicist. Why do I always get the screaming?"

Why was he proud? How did he know her grandmother, and why . . . ? Oh sweet Circe, her wings. What Ethelred had said about her "gramps"? Everything was starting to make sense, but she didn't like where Occam's razor led. Didn't like it one bit.

"You're pulling my leg, right?"

"Nope." He was still smiling like the cat that ate four canaries.

"No?" It was a hopeful sound, almost a squeak really. As if the higher the note she hit, the more likely his answer would change.

"Yes," he corrected.

"What's with the dress?"

"So inquisitive! I love that about humans." Hades flashed his white teeth again in an indulgent smile. "Remember Lucy?"

She snorted. "My imaginary pet dragon when I was five?"

"That was me."

"Bullshit." Then she thought about it. "Uh, why?"

"Seraphim wouldn't let me see you. What grandfather doesn't dote on his granddaughter? Remember all of those treasures we found together?"

Suddenly it all came rushing back, things that she'd forgotten. The strange magickal items she'd brought to her grandmother after digging in the garden. The surreal adventures through space and time in her tree house, the swing on the tree in the front yard that would take her anywhere she wanted to go if she swung high enough. The candy apples that fell from that same tree that no one else could see. She'd never been afraid of the closet, the basement, or the monster under the bed because Lucy was always there, keeping her imagination alive and all of the bad things away.

Grace also remembered the time she'd gotten separated from Seraphim at the market; she'd wandered too far and a strange man had tried to hold her hand. Said he would take her back to her mother, but there'd been something about him that frightened her. She'd tried to run away, but he'd gotten such a tight grip. What she didn't remember was how she got away. All she knew was that later that day he'd been on the news. He'd set himself on fire, and the police had found remains of other children buried in the cellar, just where he'd described in his suicide note.

She also remembered getting in trouble with her grandmother for using magick to put bells on all of the crinolines of her dresses. But she hadn't. Lucy had done it to make her happy after she saw a similar fashion in a store window. The dress had been very expensive, too expensive for her grandmother to buy. That day had been the last time she'd seen Lucy.

So, he wasn't the big, scary Devil. He was Lucy, her friend. He was her grandfather. She used magick to quickly change her clothes—jeans seemed a bit more appropriate—and propelled herself into his arms for a tight hug.

"If only you could talk Seraphim into that kind of welcome," he said over the top of her head as he hugged her back.

"So, Lucy for Lucifer? Should I call you 'Grandfather'?"

"Call me whatever you like, little Grace. My name is Hades. Lucifer is more of an office title. 'Lucy' seemed innocuous enough not to clue your grandmother in to my plans, and close enough to my title so you could summon me if you needed."

"Why did you leave?"

"After the bells? Seraphim is one scary creature when she's angry. She was bound to figure out it was me if I stayed. I still watched over you, though. Well, when I could."

"The Devil is afraid of my grandmother? Now that's something."

"Ah, kiddo, any man who has the sense God gave a goose is afraid of the woman he loves."

"Uh, can I see my grandmother?"

"I'm afraid not right now. She can't interfere in the path of your life unless you invoke her, and you can do that just once. I'm really not supposed to be here, either, but you know rules were made for me to break them."

"I miss her so much," Grace said.

"She misses you, too. She's been watching over you."

Grace was up like a shot. "Watching? What can she see?"

"Everything."

"Everything?" Grace squeaked. "Does she know I've been . . . uh . . . consorting?"

"Everything, Grace. She sees everything."

"Oh, hell. I'm never getting laid again."

Hades was tempted to plug his ears and scream, "La-la-la-la" to block out the words escaping Grace's mouth. For some reason he was quite unnerved. It was one thing to know intellectually that his granddaughter was getting laid, quite another to hear it from her own mouth.

"She was more displeased seeing you moon like a sick cow. Over a demon!"

"I didn't moon!"

"Oh, yes you did. You're completely retarded for that guy. It's kind of cute, actually."

And suddenly that was the end of the conversation. He winked at her and she was teleported back to her apartment, where Caspian was waiting with Thai takeout.

"I hate that! Knock it off!" she shouted at no one in particular.

Caspian frowned. "I see what you mean, Grace. He just poofed me here to wait for you. I find that unpleasant in the extreme."

"The pitchfork is poking the other cheek now, huh?"

"Yeah. But the bigger question would be"—he handed her a plate—"if you are okay."

"Actually, considering I just found out that I'm part demon and my grandfather is the Devil, my dead grandmother is alive somewhere and watching me have sex, I think I'm quite well. Oh, not to mention the part that when I get upset wings explode out of my back, wings that are more obvious than a fart at a funeral. Yeah, considering all that, I'm doing great."

"So, I put Jill's purchases in a bag by the door," Caspian said casually, taking a bite of pad thai. "You know. From that store."

Grace eyed him warily. "That was nice of you. What did you do with mine?"

"Yours? You don't need any." Caspian shoveled more food into his mouth and sighed. "I love eating. The best part about being topside is food. Oh, and sex, of course."

Grace wouldn't be distracted. "I paid for them and I want them."

Caspian shook his head. "No, you didn't pay for them. Michael did. So every time you use one, it's like letting Michael in your pants all over again."

"That's the most ridiculous thing I've ever heard."

"Is it? What about using an imitation cock when you can have the real thing? *That*'s the stupidest thing I've ever heard. I mean, what can this"—he magicked one of the toys into his hand and shook it at her—"do for you that I can't?"

Grace had to bite her lip to keep from laughing. He looked so funny, shaking that rubber dick at her with such a serious look on his face. "Caspian, you're jealous!"

"I am not." Then: "So what?"

"At least you admit it."

"Okay, I admit it." He shrugged. "Now answer the question, Grace. What can this sad thing do that I can't?"

"Nothing," she admitted.

"Then why do you need it?"

"Because I don't want to be dependent on a man for my needs. Especially when he will pop in and out of my life as he chooses."

"What if I promise to stay until you don't want me anymore?" he asked. His voice was quiet, as if he wasn't quite sure what he was suggesting.

"Men promise things to women all the time."

"Well, I'm not just a man. I'm a demon, bound to my word."

"Why would you do that?" Grace asked.

"Because I like you."

She shook her head. "I like you, too, Caspian. But this isn't a good idea."

"Why not?" Caspian looked annoyed.

"You know why not." Then Grace shoved another bite of peanut noodles into her mouth so she didn't have to say anything else. But he didn't speak, either.

"Caspian," she began.

"I don't like the sound of that."

"All I said was your name," she said.

"Yeah, but you said it all put upon and miserable like. As if we need to, you know, talk or something. There's no need for any of that."

"No? So, what is there a need for?"

"I think you know," he said, and arched a deliciously devilish brow.

Grace gulped audibly. All this guy did was eat, screw, and tamper with her peace of mind. Didn't he have other goals? Like, didn't he have to recruit contractees for his evil schemes? Didn't he have to tend the fires of Hell? Didn't he have *something* to do other than her?

It seemed not. This was really going to suck, being at the bottom of her options list. Grace was going to be forced to have bad sex. Not only bad sex, but really bad, horrible, no-good sex. Sex that would make Caspian cringe like he'd just had fourteen fillings and was required by law to chew on tinfoil.

Yup, she had no other choice. She'd tried banishing him, had tried talking about her feelings, made him jealous as all hell with sex toys, but none of it had made him go away. Grace had even asked him to leave, and she'd just ended up getting one of her private fantasies fulfilled in a carriage barreling down a country road. So now she was going to have to be a bad lay.

Her ego would take a blow. She was going to have to do something awful, something so that there would be no coming back. She was going to have to be so bad that in a hundred years Caspian would still think of her and cringe. And it wasn't something she could apologize for or even explain. He was just going to have to think it was what she'd wanted and intended.

She was sorely tempted to let this time be one last good one. After all, she'd seen Caspian in all of his Viking/pirate/highwayman glory. Just one more time! But that was being selfish. While she was a reasonable red-blooded witch, she just couldn't ask for true love and fidelity. Not marriage. Not fatherhood. None of these were possible where demons were concerned, and she wanted and needed all of them. Having great sex one more time would just draw things out.

So, how to start? She didn't ponder long before blessed— or cursed, depending on how you wanted to see it—inspiration struck. She knew just want to do. Caspian would want to get his cock at least three states away after she launched this next stunt.

Grace smiled docilely, which should have been his first clue that not all was hunky in Doryville. She crawled onto his lap and kissed his mouth, his chin, his cheek. They were sweet kisses, lingering and soft, until she scraped her teeth along the edge of his jaw. He made a pleased sound low in his throat and filled his hands with the firm globes of her bottom, positioning her to rub together their appropriate anatomies. It felt like heaven. It was so good that she didn't want it to end.

But it had to. This was where the Baloney Pony Express made its last stop.

She shifted and moved down his body, and freed his cock from his jeans and took it into her mouth. Grace loved how his clothes changed to suit his environment. She loved the flesh that was in her mouth, too. The only problem was the demon to which it was attached. The demon and her feelings for him. She could *do* this.

"Grace," he cried out. Grasping the back of her head, he pushed her down farther—which was just the motivation she needed. She hated when guys held her head, not letting her get away or move however she chose. Regardless of the fact that she herself had used his ears like handlebars, this was different. Caspian didn't have to breathe.

She tried to pull away, but he didn't seem inclined to let her. So she bit down. Not too hard, of course. Just enough to get his attention. And Grace would have to say that, yes, the move was definitely an attention getter. He popped her off him with a noise like champagne being uncorked.

Actually, she wasn't sure if there was an audible pop, because of the ringing in her ears from the swift movement of her head. Caspian hadn't hurt her, though, for which she was grateful. She couldn't imagine what Michael would have done. The bastard.

"Are you okay?" Caspian asked. "I'm sorry I pushed you, but that was rather unpleasant. Um, did you have to sneeze or something?"

"No."

"Oh," he said. He looked a bit disconcerted, but then ran his hand over her hair in an unquestionably tender way. Nimue's Buttery Butt! She'd just bit him in the worst place a woman could bite, and he was apologizing? He was just too good to be true. What did she have to do to make him not want her?

"I couldn't breathe," she admitted. "You wouldn't let go of my head. I didn't want to hurt you, but I didn't fancy choking, either. Not very high up on the list of cool ways to die."

He looked sheepish. "Sorry."

Grace was, too.

She supposed the key to her problem lay in finding out whatever it was that would make *her* not want *him* anymore, at least not as desperately as she did. But somehow she knew she'd have better luck finding a virgin after Beltane.

"Let's try this again," he said. Sweeping her into his arms, he bent her back for a soul-searing, knight-in-shining-armor kiss. She let him complete it, of course; as the heroine of the story it was sort of required.

Why couldn't she have sought a traditional form of revenge and just seduced one of Michael's rivals? Someone he couldn't kill. Why hadn't she thought of that? No, she'd had to jump feetfirst into demon-summoning. The water kept getting deeper, and she was about to drown. It wouldn't be wholly unpleasant, either.

Resting on the back of her couch for support, she found herself naked again and on her knees with her legs spread wide. He was underneath. His tongue was delving into her slick heat and she was begging for more. Again. How did he always do that? Last thing she knew, he was kissing her and doing the romance-novel backbend. Now she was naked and grinding herself against his talented mouth.

This couldn't go on. No. It just couldn't. And there was something she could do to end this, but it was too horrible to contemplate. It was something she wouldn't wish on anyone, but here she was with no other option. She tensed, preparing . . .

Just as she was about to do something she'd regret for the rest of her life, Caspian tapped her thigh. Grace realized then that she was very, very full. His tongue had stretched and filled her more than even his wonderful cock, and she had a momentary shiver of pleasure remembering everything he'd done with that. But from the frantic taps on her thigh, Grace didn't think this was something he'd done on purpose.

She tried to move, shifting her leg so that she was no longer riding his face like a competition pony, but she found that she couldn't; Caspian had somehow anchored her there with his tongue. There were sparks of magick swirling off his fingertips, but these didn't seem to be doing any good. He was still good and stuck.

Every shift was delicious. She felt just a little bit bad about enjoying his discomfort, but Goddess above, was he ever hitting her G-spot. She reluctantly twisted so that she was lying on her back and he was on his stomach on the couch, but he was still attached. Docked and locked in the station, as it were.

He mumbled something that sounded like *peanuts*. What in the name of all that was holy did peanuts have to do with anything? Maybe he was saying *penis*? That was possible. But then he repeated himself, and it was definitely what she'd first thought. Not penis.

"Peanuts? What about peanuts? The Thai you brought had peanut noodles."

Caspian muttered something unintelligible. His breath teasing across her clit made Grace shudder with desire, and her muscles contracted around his swollen tongue. He shook his head, which created an effect like he was giving her puss a raspberry. And while he seemed upset, Grace found the imagery hysterical.

She wanted him to keep moving. "Caspian, it's so good. Please," she begged.

She was so wet that his engorged oral member should have just fallen like candy out of a mangled piñata. After she thought about it, she discarded that image. She didn't care for the comparison. Not at all. Again he tried to speak, saying something else that sounded like peanuts. What was with this obsession? Why did he want peanuts when he was nose deep—

Oh! He couldn't be allergic, could he? Caspian didn't breathe unless he wanted to, so a tongue swollen from an allergic reaction shouldn't be a big deal. Should it? He seemed like he was in a lot of distress, but so did her clit. It was swollen, too, and he kept breathing on it like he was puffing life into a dying ember. His tongue was so distended, however, it probably felt like she was trying to pull it out of his mouth like a dandelion every time her body contracted.

"Caspian, are you allergic to peanuts?"

There came more mumbling from around her very wet and aching private parts.

"Look, sweetie, I can't understand you. Where is your magick?"

Caspian could bend space and time, but he was laid low by a peanut? Really? Grace shook her head. He'd been the one who'd ordered the food tonight, or so she'd thought. Why had he ordered something that was going to make him sick?

She tried to use her own magick, felt the familiar warmth swirling around her fingers and released it to do her bidding. She was thwarted, though, because it did nothing but tickle Caspian. In fact, her power made him giggle. At least, she thought he gave a giggle. He flinched, and small sounds came out of his throat unlike those of a man in pain.

It was a delicious sensation, rubbing against her clit in just the right way. She was just preparing to cast another spell when she heard a knock on her door. Great, just what she needed. Well, no way in hell she was going to answer.

"Grace?" Petru called, slamming his big fists on the door.

Oh, fantastic. Just when she was thinking her day couldn't possibly get any more complicated. But maybe she could convince Petru that she wasn't home. At least, she thought she had a chance before Caspian made a really loud sound like a startled pig. The Russian outside just started pounding harder.

"This isn't really a good time, Petru."

"Just open the door so I can see that you're okay."

He would choose today to grow a sense of chivalry. "I'm fine, really. I've got company, and we're . . . busy."

"Who is it?" Petru demanded.

"Mind your business," she called.

"You *are* my business, Grace. Sasha is busy, so I came to check on you. I won't leave until I see you're okay."

She tried to use her magick to open the door just a crack, but her spells weren't working. Whatever had zapped Caspian's power had zapped hers, too. This was turning out to be the perfect hemorrhoid on a big, fat hairy ass of a day.

"Petru, if you could please just come back later? My door can't handle any more of your visits."

He didn't answer. Instead, he sent the door flying off its beleaguered hinges with a well-placed kick and shoved his gargantuan frame through the newly made opening. It was barely big enough for him. So, for the second time in recent memory, Petru could see more of her flapping in the breeze than she wished. She didn't know whether to be insulted or flattered that he turned away.

His large jaw was flapping up and down like a seagull skimming the water for breakfast. "What the iced blue fuck . . ." He trailed off, clearly at a loss.

"He's stuck." Grace crinkled her toes up with every syllable. "We're not sure what to do."

"You can't just . . . ?" Petru waved his hands in the air.

"Caspian, I now understand," Grace said, remembering their earlier conversation about why he couldn't just use his magick to fix his banished hair color. "Yes, that's extremely annoying."

She exhaled heavily. "No, Petru. I can't 'just . . .'" She didn't bother to wave her arms. He knew what she meant.

"Why not?"

"It's like a magickal flu or something."

Petru shook his head and eyed the table. "Did you get the peanut noodles?"

More talk of peanuts! Yes, that could be what was wrong with Caspian, but what would it have to do with her magick? She didn't have a swollen tongue. She'd never had a peanut allergy in her life. "Yeah, so?"

"He's obviously allergic," Petru said, as if she were the dumbest of creatures—which was really ironic, considering his own placement on the brainpower pyramid. "So are most demons after spending too long topside."

Grace was taken aback. "And how do you know this?"

Petru dropped his voice an octave, as if he were sharing a great secret. "Everyone knows that, Grace."

"How come I can't use my magick?"

"I don't know." Petru shrugged. "It seems like you're stuck."

Caspian had lain serenely while they talked, but he was starting to struggle again.

Petru saw his discomfort. "Don't try to talk. That will just make it worse. I'll see if I can pull you out."

What? Oh, no! Grace opened her mouth to discourage them, but Petru threw a sheet over her head. She wasn't really sure how she felt about that.

Drawing the sheet down, she saw Petru wrapping his arms around Caspian's waist. The big Russian pulled, but it was like her demon lover's tongue had dropped anchor in her womb—or maybe grappling hooks. Petru huffed and puffed, heaved and hoved, but he got nowhere.

A new voice startled everyone. "I was going to knock, but the door was gone." Ethelred leaned against the door frame, blasé as usual. "If I'd known there was this much fun to be had, I would have arrived sooner."

He peered around Petru to meet Grace's eyes. "You know what this looks like from behind." Ethelred smirked.

Petru let go so fast that he tumbled backwards into Ethelred. The smart-alecky demon was knocked on his ass. "If you wanted me to join, all you had to do was ask." The demon grumbled, straightening his clothing as he stood. "Peanuts, huh?"

"Does everyone know this but me?" Grace shrieked.

"Yeah, sweetcakes. 'Fraid so."

Ethelred helped Petru up and tossed him a sheet to wrap around Caspian. Whether it was in the interests of grip or modesty, Petru didn't know, but he was thankful nonetheless.

"Okay, let's try this again."

Petru grabbed Caspian's waist, and Ethelred grabbed Petru's. Caspian braced his arms on the couch, and Grace said prayers to the Powers That Be. One tug. Two tugs. Three!

Still nothing. Grace's body was creeping toward numb from the waist down.

On the plus side, Caspian would be so traumatized after this that he'd never want to look at her again.

Grace wasn't sure that she cared for the party going on in her living room. She especially didn't care for it when Jill showed up.

"Hey, Grace! Your door's open . . . er, gone." The demonic ex-prostitute surveyed the scene much like her predecessor had, but she had more to say about it. "Shit on a shingle, girl. How *do* you get yourself into these things?"

Grace pursed her lips and wished she'd left the sheet over her head. "I don't know."

The men decided to try again. Without even being asked, Jill moved to stand behind Grace and got a good grip under her arms. Her hooker boots were braced against the couch, giving them some leverage as Jill pulled on Grace, Petru pulled on Caspian, and Ethelred brought up the rear. Though it would have been smarter to make Petru the anchor and have Ethelred in front, it had occurred to Ethelred that he preferred having his arms just where they were instead of pulled out of their sockets by the Russian mobster's brute strength.

How in the name of Hell was Caspian still rooted inside Grace? Tongue or twat, something should have given up.

"Damn it," Jill growled, huffing and puffing almost as much as Petru. "Seraphim protect us," she muttered wishfully, as if she were talking about a saint.

The Universe does not take such mutterings casually—not speaking the name of the Baba Yaga. To call her name is to invoke power, especially with an impassioned utterance such as "Protect us!" The atmosphere crackled with kinetic energy. Lamps and knickknacks levitated into the air, and the very foundations of the building shook. Grace's hair stood on end and so did Jill's. Her pots and pans flew out of the cupboards, glasses crashed to the floor, and the entire world seemed to shiver. Not even the Devil had made this much of an entrance!

Ethelred turned his head to see what was coming. "What the hell is that?"

"The Baba Yaga," Petru grunted, continuing to pull.

Jill stomped her foot. "I've done it now, haven't I? Sorry, love."

Grace was not happy with this new development, though she was excited at the most minimal prospect of seeing her grandmother again. The circumstances could have been better, of course. "Oh, what, like I'm going to be grounded or something? I'll believe it when I see it."

A woman appeared, rising up amid the horror show. But she was nothing like Grace's grandmother. This woman was young. Those hands couldn't possibly have made chocolate oat muffins. They couldn't be the same that put bandages on all of Grace's skinned knees. They certainly weren't the hands that had trained Grace in the art of herbs and poultices. No, this woman was not her grandmother.

"Why hast thou summoned me?"

Her voice echoed with power, and things continued to fall off the wall. Grace had to admit that her windowpane rattling was a bit more impressive than Caspian's. Then the Baba Yaga looked at her and winked.

Perfect. It *was* her grandmother. All it would take was one more person and her humiliation would be complete. Perhaps Hades—

Seraphim screeched like a hyena in labor. "Don't even think it! You already did, didn't you?" She glanced frantically around the apartment. "Don't you do it, Hades! I'm warning you!" The woman narrowed her eyes on a small statue of a dog that Grace hadn't known she owned. A moment later, it disappeared.

"Did she just punk out the Big Boss?" Ethelred asked, releasing Petru's bulk.

"I told you the Baba Yaga was nothing to mess with, but no one listens to poor, slow Petru, who still believes in children's tales." The Russian shrugged massive shoulders and sighed.

"Um," Grace said, in the sweetest voice she could manage. "Excuse me, but could you all please get the hell out? Hmm? I'm naked, and my boyfriend is suffocating in my . . . well, if he were human he would be. My grandmother is here to bear witness to my humiliation, and that's more than enough. She can help clean up the mess, so, thank you all for coming. Can I die now?" she added to Jill.

The redhead looked surprised. "Sorry?"

Grace shook her head. "Your bag of tricks is by the gaping hole in the wall that used to be my door."

"We'll go shoe shopping later this week." Jill patted her on the head, grabbed Ethelred's hand, even though he looked as if he had no intention of leaving, and headed for the door. He'd either go with her or have his fingers reset. He chose to leave with her.

Petru was tempted to beg Grace to remain silent regarding his mishap with Seraphim's picture, but he decided she already knew. He bowed and kissed her hand.

She eyed him kindly, pressing a small charm into his hand. "Petru, your Miss Katerina needs you. Now," she added. "But wear this. Nadja walks again."

Nadja? Such talk scared the faith and begorra right out of Grace. She'd heard Michael talk about his mother quite often; she'd been the one who shaped him into a monster.

Willingly, wantonly. Nadja was everything that went bump in the dark. She was evil through and through.

Her legs tensed, and Caspian had to put his elbows on her thighs to keep her from clamping them shut. "Sorry, Caspian." Grace's shoulders slumped unhappily.

A light came from Seraphim, and there was an audible exhalation from Caspian as his tongue shrank back down to a size that he could fit into his mouth.

"Feelths like iths wearing socks," he muttered, still trying to get the thing to lie properly in his mouth. The effort made him look a bit like a Saint Bernard who'd gotten into a vat of peanut butter.

"Okay, you two geniuses," Seraphim demanded, a hand on her hip. "What was with the peanuts?"

"I didn't know demons could have food allergies." Grace pulled her sheet up to her chin. "Next thing you know they'll be getting swine flu."

Caspian shook his head, clearly just as surprised.

Seraphim sighed. "Grace, no more peanut noodles for you. Since you've tapped into your demon heritage, you're susceptible, too. You'll have to pay more attention."

"No more peanut butter?" Grace asked, horrified.

"Nope. No more peanut butter cups, no more PB&J's, no more anything processed with the same machinery as nuts. It's all out. You're lucky that you just lost your powers. It could have been much worse."

"It gets worse than what just happened? I really don't see how it could."

Seraphim glanced at her, scandalized. "Merlin's Cookie Dough, child! Haven't you learned that lesson in an all of your years? Never, ever, should you challenge the Universe like that. It will always show you how it can get worse. I think it wants to make you thankful for the blessings you do have."

"Worse?" Grace was growling. "Name someone who's

had it worse—and no naming random starving kids in the Congo."

"I didn't say your life was sunshine and fairies, you little smarty bug. Maybe those *are* the only people who have it worse than you, but that still means things can get worse. Did you think of that?"

The woman definitely sounded like her grandmother, even if she didn't look like her. Grace studied her again.

"Looking for an old hag? Well, I've been wearing the maidenly form these past few days. Seems I can't let myself be old whenever Hades is around." She looked a bit embarrassed.

"Why didn't you tell me?"

"About which?"

In that smile, Grace saw a glimpse of the woman she'd known. "About all of it, but especially the part where, you know, you aren't really dead."

The maiden was suddenly gone. In her place stood Gran. There were apple cookies on a plate in her hands, and piping hot tea sat in familiar china atop what was left of Grace's table.

"Gran!" Grace wrapped her sheet around herself like a toga and hugged Seraphim tightly.

"Goodness, child. If I wasn't the Baba Yaga, you would have crushed these old bones like eggshells."

"I missed you!"

"I know, and I'm sorry I couldn't tell you before; it broke my heart to hear you crying for me. You had to grow on your own, however, or you never would have become strong."

Grace sniffled. "I thought Petru and Sasha had both lost their minds."

"You've had quite the day today, huh? There's still the final revelation, but that's the one you must figure out on your own. I can't help you, and neither can Hades."

"It's always cryptic answers with you." Grace hugged her grandmother again. "Is that something contagious from demonkind as well?"

Her gran smiled. "Eat your cookies and drink your tea, dear. Every last drop, if you please. It will help you heal. That goober sleeping on your couch, too." She indicated Caspian, who was very much dead to the world. "I think he's going to be very unhappy when he wakes up."

"Why?" Grace asked.

"He's fallen asleep with his cheek on his belt buckle. There will be an imprint in his cheek for days."

Grace shrugged. "He can just use his power. He'll be fine."

"No," her gran snapped, "and this is very important. Even though the tea will help, it will take a few days for his powers and yours to come back. You will be extremely vulnerable. Don't leave this apartment unless you absolutely must. And no takeout! Remember the peanut thing."

"Are you kidding me?" Grace pouted.

"See? I told you it could get worse. Now, I have to go. Be good, Gracie." And her grandmother was gone.

On the plus side, her door was fixed. In fact, it looked like a brand-new steel door. There were hex bags hanging at all of the entrances, and her apartment was completely clean. Her grandmother had handled everything—which was wonderful. Fine and dandy. Brilliant, of course, but the problem was: She and Caspian were trapped together in her apartment. And after what had just happened, she'd be surprised if he didn't run away screaming without giving a single fuck about his peanut-induced vulnerability.

Poor Caspian. Not even a demon deserved this, did he?

Poor her. Grace knew *she* didn't.

CHAPTER TWENTY-ONE
She Walks in Death

Nadja Grigorovich was not what you would call a happy camper. In fact, she was like the bear who couldn't quite figure out how to get that picnic basket without having Ranger Rick up her ass. Every act she could devise at this juncture destroyed the best thing she had in her arsenal: the element of surprise. If only Sasha were here, he'd know what to do.

None of this would be a problem without Seraphim Stregaria. Just thinking about the old witch made Nadja's knuckles swell, warping her fingers into twisted, useless, arthritic sausages. How she hated the woman! Seraphim didn't deserve what she had. What was the point of having power if you weren't going to wield it? Nadja would re-make the world in her image, and angels and demons alike would quake before her. Perhaps she would even unseat that bastard Hades while she was at it and take over Hell. Michael would certainly have his demonhood then, and he would be subservient to her forever.

Her son had other plans for her, of course. Less pleasant plans, if he found her before she came fully back into her power. She'd sown the seeds of depravity inside him, so she wasn't surprised. She knew what lurked in those dark little corners of his mind, and she could only be prouder if he'd actually gotten rid of Seraphim's brat of a granddaughter on schedule. But, Grace? That little witch was more irritating than poison ivy. If Nadja could strangle her and her grandmother together, at the same time, it might just be the happiest moment in all of her existence.

Well, that was her goal. And to achieve her goal, Nadja needed minions. And she knew just where to start: Katerina.

Having decided this was the best course of action, Nadja transported herself to Katerina's door. The act left her so winded that she almost threw up. It was like she'd run up several staircases after eating a hearty dinner. Her magick was rusty and sleepy. Sasha's heart was all that was keeping her alive, so she had to find a magickal creature to feed on and soon. It would be some time before this body could sustain its own power. It would take considerably less power if she'd let this body exist in its natural state, which was dead, or if she let it appear as it originally had. But Nadja wanted to look like herself, not this homely body Sasha had procured for her. She liked looking in the mirror and seeing blond hair and—

Katerina was blond. Why hadn't Sasha just given *her* to Nadja? She had a lovely figure—all but those hideous scars, but Nadja could have taken care of that. Why hadn't—?

Nadja remembered the two brats Katerina had clinging to her skirts. They were inconvenient. She didn't see how it was possible a woman could be tricked into taking care of not one but *two* bits of street trash that hadn't come from her own body. Then again, Nadja hadn't even wanted her biological son. And if Katerina was an odd woman, at least the brats were another ax to hang over her head.

She finally caught her breath. She couldn't have her victim seeing any of her weakness; that might give Katerina the impression she had something to say about her situation, that she had some control. It would take too much work to disabuse her of that notion, so Nadja meant to avoid it.

She knocked on the door. When Katerina opened it, the look on her face was almost worth the years Nadja had spent in the horror of suspended animation.

The blonde's delicate little features sagged like she'd aged twenty years in the second recognition hit. She turned and walked to the kitchen table, sank into a chair. She didn't invite Nadja in, but Nadja wasn't a vampire so she didn't need an invitation. Nadja crossed the threshold and sat in the chair across from Katerina, as if she were there for morning coffee and a raspberry tart. The remains of just such a breakfast were scattered about the table.

"Cozy digs you've got here," Nadja said, taking Katerina's coffee cup. She took a sip and pulled Katerina's plate over to her side of the table. As far as Nadja was concerned, it was all her side.

"What do you want?" the little blonde asked.

"Want? Why do I have to want anything?" Nadja asked, chewing and giving her a cold smile.

"Don't do that, Nadja. We both know you want something," Katerina snapped, defeated.

"Maybe I wanted to visit a friend. We are friends, aren't we?"

"Sure, whatever you say."

Katerina had clearly learned not to contradict her. Good.

"Perhaps I need one little favor. This tart is really tasty. Too bad that brute Petru ate most of them before he left." Katerina's apartment smelled of men and sex; when Nadja focused, it was Petru who came to her mind's eye. She shuddered.

"Yes, too bad," Katerina echoed.

"You need to find me a magickal being. It doesn't really matter what kind. See, since I've come back there's a darkness inside that's burning me with a hunger I've never before known." She grabbed Katerina's hand, which was wrapped around a fork. "But if you're thinking of killing me before I get any stronger, you're too late."

Katerina sighed. "No, Nadja. I've just learned to keep a clean house. The way Ivan taught me." She picked up several other dishes and walked to the sink.

If Nadja didn't know any better, she'd swear that was a jab, an outright rebellion. But she forced herself to ignore it and said, "Good. Because if you fail me, I won't kill you. I won't even kill your children, but you'll wish I had. I'll flay the flesh from their bones and eat it in front of them."

Katerina eased the dishes into the sink, moving very slowly, as if the weight of the world had come to rest on her shoulders. "You are all the bad things that are whispered in the night about the Baba Yaga," she murmured. "Every single one of them."

"Thank you, Katerina," Nadja replied. "You really are very sweet. Perhaps our relationship will be more fun for both of us this time around."

She rose from her chair and made a show of bringing her coffee cup to the sink where she put an arm around Katerina and hugged her. Then she drew back and struck her with the coffee mug, just hard enough to make an impression but not break the cup.

"I want my magickal being tonight, Katerina. If I don't get it, I shall be very upset with you. Even more upset than this."

"I understand." Katerina bit her lip.

"And don't tell anyone else about me. Do you understand?"

Katerina nodded. There wasn't much else she could do.

CHAPTER TWENTY-TWO
Laying the Pipe

J ill sauntered into the dump that Michael called his bar, office, and home. Though it was the middle of the morning, she breezed through the doors as if she owned the place, and as tight as her pants were in the crotch, her balls should have been visible. Or they would have been, had they been more than metaphoric.

Not seeing the bartender, she went around back and poured a shot of vodka. She set it down, then took a swig out of the bottle—she'd never said the shot was for her.

Wiping her mouth on the back of her hand, she decided on having another. After all, it wasn't every day one got to help mastermind a revenge plot against a woman-murdering douche bag. Today was going to be a lovely day, all thanks to Seraphim Stregaria. Jill raised the bottle to her, knowing that somewhere, Seraphim would know. She took another pull and enjoyed the burn that slid all the way down.

"That was quick," Michael said, emerging from his office. "I just shot that guy not five minutes ago. Who hired you?"

She gave him a dazzling smile. "It's a demon thing. I belong to Ethelred. He sent me to help."

Michael squinted, clearly suspicious. "For free? What's the trick?"

He really didn't recognize her. Jill wasn't sure if she should be thankful or insulted. On the one hand, it was convenient as hell. On the other, he'd choked the life from her. One would think that would be memorable.

Or not. He was just another shit bag in a long line of shit bags, and if she hadn't been memorable to any of the others, she didn't know what would make this one remember her. They were users, pure and simple. But that had been a lifetime ago.

"No trick," she announced. "I'll just be watching everything you do. Or is that the trick that you're looking for?" She tried to pour Michael a drink but broke off as she almost slipped in a pool of blood that had gathered behind the bar. Shaking her head she muttered, "Sloppy, honey. Very sloppy, indeed. What would your mother say?"

"What? What did you say?" Michael's full attention was on her now. He suddenly reminded her of a turkey vulture; big, ugly, and always picking at dead things.

"I'm sure your mother didn't raise you to keep a dirty house. Why, what did you think I meant? It's not like I called her a whore." Jill shoved some Russian Tea at him. She'd prepared it just the way he liked.

Michael shrugged. "You can call her a whore if you want, I don't give a shit." He downed the drink and motioned for another. Both of them forgot the body on the floor. "Have you had these before? This is just how I like them."

Jill smiled. Michael returned the expression. They looked like a couple of grinning fools to anyone peering in from the outside, and Jill was even happier on the inside. She couldn't wait to get Michael hot for her. She was going to wreck the man in a way that defied human comprehension.

"I bet I can do it *all* 'just how you like it.'" She made sure her lips caressed those last words, made sure this was an invitation that he couldn't refuse.

"Can you?" Michael moved around the bar and pressed Jill up against the wall, his hand cupping her breast. "You know I like my women to behave like they should."

"Like they should? How is that, *Nana*?" Jill crooned the Russian word for "daddy." Yeah, she'd done her research. That would turn him on. He'd feel the need to see what made her tick. Too bad he hadn't when she was alive. He didn't even remember her. But he'd damn well know her name in a few weeks when the regulars stopped patronizing his clubs. And he'd damn well know it when he was begging her to stop what she planned to do to him. He'd know exactly who she was, and he'd be screaming her name when she was balls deep in his hind end with her prosthetic tools. He'd remember everything about her, but by then it'd be too late. The thought made her smile.

"So you like the Russian, little girl?" he whispered in her ear. "Are we going to be good friends? What's your name, you spicy little demon? Hmm?"

Poor Grace. Why had she ever been with this jackhole? If she didn't liked Grace so much, Jill might have actually thought less of her. How could the quarter-demon granddaughter of the Devil and the Baba Yaga be so naïve?

Jill had never had any illusions. She'd been interested in getting out of the rackets, in being made Michael's woman, and dumping all her other johns. He'd displayed moments of charm and had been halfway decent in bed—at least before the kinky stuff. She'd hoped to save up and start a new life. Not that Michael would have ever known. She'd had a plan to get away, and it had been foolproof. Too bad Michael hadn't let things get that far along.

"Very good friends, Michael," she said, leaning close, taking control of the encounter and pushing him back against the bar. "I'm not like anything you've ever experienced."

She crushed her mouth to his and shoved her hand down his slacks to fondle him as freely as he'd done to her. He made a small startled sound and tried to back away, but he was up against the bar and there was nowhere left for him to go.

"Very nice. I have to go for now," she said as she broke the kiss, and wiped her mouth on the back of her hand like he'd been a good shot of vodka, and licked her lips. "But I'll be seeing you." Then Jill snapped her fingers and pointed them at him like guns and left the bar.

Michael shook his head. What the fuck had just happened to him? He was a little dazed, somewhat confused, and sporting teak hard enough to be used in an industrial nail gun. That hadn't happened to him in a long time, at least not from just one kiss. When he got ahold of that piece again, he was going to pound it until he could see morning through the other side. Saucy little puss, that one. And what really surprised him was that he'd liked her. He didn't usually like surprises. They were bad for business. This demoness was clearly an exception. She reminded him of Grace.

He noticed the table in the corner was empty, as it had been for a few days now. Sasha had wanted leave to play with his new toy, and where Sasha went, Petru followed. But what that meant was absolutely no one was in his bar. No patrons, no workers. The jukebox was dark, the King was quiet. He had scores and scores of people who depended on him for their livelihood, but there was no one around to get rid of a dead body when he needed. It was completely unacceptable.

There was something else, too. For the first time in ages, Michael was completely alone. The silence was like a heavy shroud. He found himself wondering about his mother, wondering where she'd been hidden since her "death," and what it would take to find her. Not for any familial reason, but to drain her power.

He decided to call Grace, to check on her. Her time was almost up and he was surprised that he'd yet to hear from her. That way, if something had indeed happened to her, he could capitalize on his good fortune. If she'd come to her senses, all the better. He'd take advantage of either sequence of events.

He dialed her number and honestly expected her to answer. As if she were still his girl and this whole Nikoli thing had never happened. As if she hadn't been forcibly ejected from his penthouse. As if—

Her voice mail picked up. At the end of her message, he sang softly to her, sang the way she'd liked so much when they first started dating. "Love Me Tender" was always a winner. Then he sighed. "Grace, I don't know what's happened to us, but I love you. Give me another chance. We'll be a family. You, me, and Nikoli."

He hung up. This might work better than all of the strong-arming, which hadn't budged her an inch. He should have kept her in the cocoon of his world, could have been done with all of this by now. Grace could have gone to the headsman with a smile. Now all of that was semen under the bridge.

It was still too damn quiet, so he dialed Sasha's number, which also went straight to voice mail. The man was apparently taking his vacation time very seriously. It was annoying. Michael hated cell phones. They were so intrusive. But he liked being able to reach anyone at any time of the day, night, or in between. Cell phones meant no one was ever unavailable to him. At least, not if they liked their kneecaps. Assuming they didn't turn their phones off. He hadn't thought to tell Sasha to keep his phone on; the guy had never taken personal time. Of course, he'd never asked Michael to buy him a woman before, either.

Michael made a mental note to buy Petru his own phone. It would probably have to be like one of those designed for the elderly, with big numbers and not too many bells and whistles, but the Russian rhino had to be smart enough to answer a phone. Didn't he? For all of his simplicity, Michael liked Petru. The man did his job, kept his head down, and didn't ask questions. His kind was loyal to a fault. That was why it hadn't seemed odd, his absence corresponding with his friend Sasha's. But it was frustrating that he couldn't be reached when he was needed.

Sinking into a booth, Michael surveyed the empty bar and his one-eyed jukebox. Uncharacteristically, he felt a bit out of control. Events in motion now were the culmination of years and years of plotting, conniving, and backbiting, and while this wasn't exactly what he'd intended, he was on the bullet train now. There was no slowing down, no stopping, and certainly no getting off.

CHAPTER TWENTY-THREE

Magickless

"That guy is a total cock. Did he really profane the King on your voice mail? He's desperate, his contract should be up in four days." Caspian snorted and watched Grace move awkwardly around her kitchen. She was shuffling here and there, moving like a six-tailed cat in a room full of haunted rocking chairs. Not really her loveliest moment, and yet, there was still something about her. He wondered if there always would be, or if he was just addled from being locked up with her for three days.

"What's with demonkind and the King?"

Caspian took umbrage. "That guy isn't a demon." No way was that scum stain Grigorovich in the same class as he.

Grace shrugged. "Okay. I still don't get the attraction."

"Talent is universally recognized," Caspian replied.

"No. I didn't say he wasn't talented. I just mean . . . a jukebox that only plays Elvis? I never got why Michael had that installed. What's wrong with a little variety?"

"What's wrong with a little fidelity?" Caspian countered.

She eyed him. "Are you kidding me? One guy's music, forever? That would be boring."

"No, you pick up little nuances that you didn't hear before. It becomes comfortable, and what pleased you about the music the first time should please you always."

"You're serious?" Grace said. "Who listens to just one artist? Especially these days. Variety is the spice of life."

"Next thing you know, Grace, you'll be telling me you love steak but that it would be wrong to eat it at every meal." The thought! Why *not* eat steak at every meal? He'd tried many different things, but steak was the best. Milky Way bars had been a close second but he'd outgrown them. While he remembered the taste fondly, steak was a better pick.

Grace rolled her eyes. "It would be wrong to eat it at every meal. At least, it would be wrong to expect *me* to eat it at every meal."

"You know, Gracie—"

"Don't call me Gracie."

"Your gran did."

"That's Gran."

"Woman, I've seen parts of you that she never has. I think I deserve some special treatment."

"I think I don't like being called Gracie," she retorted.

He sighed. "Fine, whatever. Look, as I was saying—"

"How rude of me. Do go on." Grace bent over to rustle around in the refrigerator, again looking for something edible, or at least nontoxic, for them to throw together and put in their mouths. Something with nutrition.

"You're doing it again." Caspian cocked his head to the side, following the movements of her delectable derriere as she rooted around in the fridge.

"So sorry."

Some boots were made for walkin', but that ass was made for—"Huh?" Caspian had lost his train of thought.

"About the interrupting. You were saying?"

"I forgot."

Grace stood up and moved back to the stove, taking his peep show away—or at least taking it on the move. She was wearing a man's shirt, something he did not like. The bottom of it covered her buttocks, just revealing the sides of her thighs. This he liked very much. He especially liked when she bent over, how he could see tender round flesh. He could stare at that part of a woman for hours.

"Steak?" she prompted.

"Oh, right. As I was saying, that's an analogy that many modern males use to justify cheating on their wives. They don't think it's fair that they should be forced to endure the lifetime supply of the very meat that they picked out and purchased. They should be allowed to get takeout every so often."

"I think monogamy and Elvis are two very different things," Grace said.

"Yes, but you're the one who used the steak analogy."

"I was being snarky!"

"You're always being snarky."

"That's not my fault," Grace grumped as she bent back over into the refrigerator.

"I didn't say it was your fault," Caspian agreed. "I just said that you're always being snarky. It wasn't a complaint, it was just—"

"Wait. What you said about purchased meat." Grace stood up again and turned around. "Was that like 'buying the cow'?"

"No. I never said that." Caspian had a horrible inkling where this was headed.

"I think you did. You just called me a cow. Didn't you?" Her voice was deceptively calm.

"Where did you get that?" he asked.

"Oh, I don't know. You were talking about 'steak at every meal,' and then you were talking about purchasing a lifetime supply of meat in reference to marriage, fidelity, and/or sex. Where does steak come from but cows? So, as you're making a reference to a man/woman relationship, the man is buying the . . . ?"

"Steak."

"Exactly."

"No," he said, realizing her inference.

"No? Then what is he buying?"

Caspian huffed in exasperation. "The *steak*."

"So you called me a cow."

"I did not!"

"Look, is he buying steak or not?"

He was beginning to believe she was looking for things to fight about. "Gracie, what is your problem? That horse is dead. It had a Viking funeral and burned for three days. Shut. Up. About. The. Cow."

"Or what, big, bad demon prince? What are you going to do about it?"

He wanted to show her what he was going to do about it, but he needed to wait until he had his powers back. Caspian didn't fancy getting his tongue stuck anyplace tight again, even if parts of that experience had been most delightful.

Grace hiked her shirt up to show off a bit more leg. Then she bent over and touched the floor, baring her naughty knickered bottom to his admiring view. "Or what, huh? What are you going to do about it? Got no courage without your demonic powers? Afraid you can't hack it without the three-pronged tongue? Afraid you'll seem like a *mortal* lay?"

Not only was she taunting him verbally, every word or two was punctuated by a shake of her ass. It was as if it were the one talking to him, it was the one daring him to come over there and show it a good time. He'd bend her over the couch— Well, maybe not the couch. Their last interaction on that thing hadn't gone so well. But he'd bend her over something, damn it.

She flopped on the couch next to him. "See? You're really not so impressive now."

"Oh, no? I think I hear a challenge," he said. But he didn't move.

"I think you better get your ears checked, because I've been throwing them all day and have gotten no action. But if we're going to just talk . . . are we ever going to talk about what happened on the couch?"

"No. That topic never again need see the light of day."

"I thought you'd leave and never come back."

"Is that what you want?" Caspian asked, keeping his tone light.

She didn't answer but stuck out her tongue, signifying that she wasn't going to answer.

He decided to lighten the mood further. Grabbing her around the waist, he made his hands like tickly little spiders all over her body. She squealed as they tumbled to the floor. She squealed and squirmed and giggled. He liked to hear her laugh. He also liked that little thing she did with her butt when she was trying to get away from him—the way she squirmed and pushed up against him in the most delicious way. So far, she'd done it every time he tickled her, so she could count on constant tickling from here on out.

He finally managed to corral the little harridan exactly where he wanted her, flat on her back underneath him.

"Do you hear that?" she said, finally catching her breath.

"Hear what?" he asked with a frown.

"That thudding sound." Grace looked up at him with wonder, touching her hand to his chest. It stopped where his heart would be.

Where his heart *was*. There was no denying it now.

"It's your heart! It's beating."

"Yeah. It's been beating a couple times every few hours for a while now." Caspian shrugged it off; he didn't want her to know what a big deal it really was. He wasn't quite sure what to make of it.

"It's beating really fast, Caspian."

"Never mind that." He brushed his lips across the fullness of her lower lip. He could feel her resistance but wasn't sure what he'd done. He didn't want to ask, either. They'd been killing their time in quarantine by watching movies, and whenever the film hero stepped in shit, Caspian was expected to just know what the hero had done wrong. Caspian didn't see how he could measure up, but he swore to try and figure it out. Especially since they'd both made fun of the sods who couldn't get their acts together and sweep the heroine off her feet in a reasonable time frame.

"Why did you have to be so hot?" Grace murmured, though she didn't look like she wanted an answer. Then: "What's it like in Hell?"

Okay, he was trying very hard to seduce her, and she wanted to talk about Hell? This wasn't really how he'd planned the night going.

"Not so bad, really," he said. "Once you realize it's all about the PR."

"Are there trees?"

"If you want there to be."

"What about fire?"

"If that's what you think you deserve."

"Huh," Grace said. "What if I don't feel bad for anything I've done?"

"Then you won't be going to Hell."

She took a few moments to ponder that. "What about Michael? He's done some truly horrible things, but they're things he doesn't think are wrong."

"His punishment will come in a more, shall we say, fleshy form?"

Grace laughed. "Yes, but what if I wasn't involved? What if I didn't summon you? Would he still pay?"

"Are you asking me about God?" Caspian said.

"I guess I am. If there's a Hell, then there must be a Heaven."

He didn't want to think about any of this, so he just copped out. "Well, then, you've answered your own question."

"What about Nikoli?" Grace continued. "If he dies, will I ever see him again? Will I go to Hell for being with you? What about for just being what I am? Please, Caspian, tell me what it's like," she pleaded.

"It's . . . it's beautiful."

"Really?"

"Really," he said. "It's much like Oregon. Of course, that's the landscape that appeals to me. It might be different for others. Like I said, Hell is perception. So is Heaven."

"When your powers come back, will you show it to me?" she whispered.

"Yes," he promised. Though he didn't know if his powers would come back. He had a heart now, and it was beating, strong and sure. He might be stuck in this world. To live, to die, to be human. The idea scared him more than being tongue-tied to her crotch again. He'd be human for Grace, but if she didn't want him, he didn't want to stay in the mortal world without her.

"You've already been there," he pointed out.

"When?"

"The dressing room."

"That was Hell?"

Caspian nodded. "What did it look like to you?"

"Well, to me it looked how I always imagined Mount Olympus." She took a deep breath and paused, as if she were considering her next words. After a moment she decided, "I have to ask you something else. I want you to tell me about Nikoli. I want you to tell me the whole truth. Everything you know."

She blinked once and stared into his eyes. To him, she looked like an empty vessel waiting for some great fulfillment, and all he had to give was pain. "You already know, Grace," he said.

"Tell me," she commanded.

"Don't ask me to break you."

"Tell me."

"Where are your pictures of your son, Grace? Why aren't there any around your apartment?" Caspian asked.

"Say it." Her voice had a desperate urgency. "*Say* it, Caspian. I need to hear it."

"I can't. It has to come from your lips, Grace. It won't be real until you say it. Only then will the spell be broken. Only then will you believe the truth."

She opened her mouth to speak. He could see the gears turning in her brain, could practically see infernal smoke shooting out her ears. But it was then that he realized she couldn't do it. Her mouth just wouldn't utter those words. She wouldn't pronounce a sentence like death for the non-corporeal ideal that had become her son.

Caspian didn't want to be the one to do it, either. He didn't want it to be his voice she heard every time she remembered this debacle. It would be as if Caspian had killed the boy, though the boy had never existed in the first place.

It was selfish of him, he realized. This shouldn't matter to him one way or the other. If he admitted that he was having feelings for Grace, if they were true feelings, he should help her as she needed. If he was having no feelings at all, like a good demon, he should be able to just tell her the truth—that her son was a demonically manufactured memory implant—and go about his business. Why was he having such difficulty?

He steeled himself. "Grace, Nikoli isn't real. Never has been."

She buried her face in his chest. Silent sobs shook her body. Caspian wasn't sure what to do. All of the same symptoms he'd seen on an aspirin commercial earlier in the day were manifesting in him. His chest hurt, and his new heart felt as if there was a vise tightening around it. Was it a heart attack? With every moment of Grace's despair, that vise felt worse. It was as if he were being stabbed. All of these human sensations were too much. He didn't know how they stood it, to feel everything so intensely all of the time. It was enough to make any creature insane. Was the joy they seemed to feel worth all of this torment?

Her grip dug into his flesh enough that his fingers started to go numb. She was breaking his arms, she was in so much pain, and yet he couldn't do anything for her. He'd never been so helpless. How did mortals go about their lives knowing that at any time someone could snatch that heart right out of their chest, inflict this sort of intense misery? How did they live knowing such horror?

He thought of his Gracie in such pain and it wasn't something he could accept. Nor could he accept the idea that she was mortal and would one day end, herself. He would rather die than live knowing she wasn't in the world anymore. Which was silly, because all mortal things had a beginning and an end. This was just the way she was made. Unfortunately, he was different. He hoped he was still different.

He traced his fingers up and down the length of her spine, trying to offer what comfort he could, trying desperately to make this pain end, and yet he knew he had to twist the knife further. She had to speak the words or else the spell would remain unbroken; they'd have to go through this all over again.

"You have to say it, Grace."

"Will the pain stop?"

Caspian didn't know. A piece of her soul had been torn away like a strip of dirty sheet, and he didn't know if breaking the spell would mend it. If he'd had his powers, he would have ended Ethelred's sorry existence for even doing this to her, no matter who had given the order, and he'd also find a way for Michael Grigorovich to feel a thousand-fold what he'd inflicted on Grace. Everyone involved would know the depths of his fury.

"I don't know. All I know is that you have to say the words."

"If I don't say them, it's not real. It's *not*. He could be alive. He could . . ." Her grip grew tighter on his arms; it was as if she were trying to draw strength from him. If such a transaction were possible, he'd have indulged her. He'd give anything in the world to ease her pain.

Grace was trembling but took a deep breath. "Nikoli Grigorovich is not . . ." She broke off and drew a few shaking breaths, the tears continuing to roll down her cheeks. "He's not real. My son is not real." Her hands flared with storm clouds black as pitch and roiling for release. It surprised them both, but this was Grace's pain.

Caspian grabbed a quartz crystal from a nearby table. "Release your power into the stone and keep it with you," he commanded. "It will be a powerful weapon."

Grace looked hesitant.

"Otherwise, it will consume you." He closed her hands around the stone and kept them covered with his own until the last of the black energy infused the clear quartz. When next they saw it, the stone was onyx.

"It still hurts," Grace said.

"I know," Caspian replied, pulling her to him.

And the bitch of it was, he did know. His chest still ached—for her and for him both. Grace's power had come back, but he was still this . . . whatever she'd made him.

He felt a sudden certainty that he was human. He would have to deal with it later, though; maybe it was like a cold. He'd caught humanity from Grace and he'd just have to ride it out. Like a fever. He prayed to the Powers That Be that the sickness would go away fast.

She seemed content to sniffle on his chest, so he wasn't inclined to move her. Actually, it was more like she was disinclined to be moved. He tried shifting, but she just shifted with him, her body a boneless mass willing to twist wherever necessary for them to maintain contact.

He hadn't thought that hunger could be a sentient being,

but he reconsidered that position after hearing a sound like Cerberus when two of the beast's heads were fighting over who got the last bone and who was the one that had to lick butt.

Grace sniffled into his shirt. "I didn't know demons got hungry. I mean, not *that* hungry."

"Must have been topside too long."

"I'll make you something," she suggested.

Caspian knew the right thing was to keep holding her close, but he was so hungry and she'd offered. How was it his fault if he accepted?

"You don't have to," he said before he could think better of it.

Look, tongue. For somebody that wants to eat, you're doing a fine job of fouling everything up. Shut it!

She didn't seem to hear him, but rather was lost in her own thoughts. "We've still got a Michael crisis. He's going to kill me if I don't do what he wants, even if he can't really kill my son. You're still going to help me, right?" She blinked as she disentangled herself from him.

"Of course. No problem." *Fucking liar.* What could he possibly do to Michael as a human, shake his finger in a severely disapproving manner?

He could kill him, actually. That's what he could do. He wasn't in service to the Big Boss anymore, so he could do whatever he wanted. It would be a black stain on his soul, but it would keep Grace safe. It was something that he could do to take care of her, something that he would want even if he wasn't under contract. Which, now that he thought of it, if he was really human . . .

Caspian smiled. "Yes, Grace. I'll take care of it."

Michael would never bother her again. She'd be free.

CHAPTER TWENTY-FOUR
Soap in the Mouth, Does It Work?

Grace was amazed at how the pain had gone from excruciating to simply a gnawing ache, all in the few minutes after she drained her fury into that quartz. It felt as if she'd had years to grieve, all played out in just a few moments. The loss of her false child still hurt, but it was bearable now. She couldn't imagine casting a spell on anyone that caused such pain, no matter what they'd done to deserve it. Michael was an even bigger bastard than she'd thought.

She was amazed that Caspian had stayed with her through everything. He was a demon, but for all of his devil-may-care attitude he was also a person. He was a *good* person. He was, in fact, the best man she'd ever been with. Not once through the whole ordeal had he ever tried to hurt her; he'd fulfilled her every fantasy, and it had been he who'd brought up being a one-meal-forever kind of person.

It was after these realizations that she'd realized what she'd stepped in—and how it had dried like Quikrete. There was no chipping her way out; she was completely, irrevocably, damnably in love with Caspian.

She'd never believed in love at first sight, thought it was just a bunch of horse apples that the male of the species invented to speed themselves into a lady's fig leaf. "If you're in love, it's okay." The ultimate excuse. True love came from time, respect, and sacrifice. From trust. None of those things were available upon first sight, no matter how much you wanted to bone someone. You could have lust at first sight, sure, but that was about it.

But now it was past first sight. She trusted Caspian implicitly. He had never lied to her, and when he promised her something, she believed. She felt safe when she was with him, something she hadn't experienced in a long time. Even when she'd tried to banish him and he'd been angry, he hadn't tried to hurt her. When he'd shown her his true form, draped in the glory only known to a Crown Prince of Hell, he'd been careful not to singe her. In fact, he'd been enraged because he thought someone else had been bent on her destruction. He hadn't even abandoned her after getting his tongue stuck inside her, and she had to admit that no one could blame anyone for bailing after that. No, Caspian acted like he was around for a long haul. He seemed to want her for who she was, not just for her body or her magick.

Yup, she'd really stepped in it, especially since Grace knew that there was no chance for them to be together. He was a demon. Even with her dual nature, their having a relationship would still be a big cosmic fuck-you to the Powers That Be. Wouldn't it? She wasn't a virgin, and virgins were the only ones allowed to stay with demons. Ironic, no? But those were the breaks. While Grace had never hesitated to rebel against the natural order of some things, she drew the line at thumbing her nose at the Powers That Be. She supposed she just had to be thankful for the last three days she'd had Caspian all to herself in their self-imposed exile from the rest of the world.

Her epiphany about love came with another realization. She'd been fantastic at potions but sucked when it came to cooking. But they were basically the same thing. For some reason, it had taken years for her mind to make that connection; she'd tried very hard just to make food that was edible. Now the bell had gone off. The elevator finally went all the way to the top.

Spurred by his hunger, tonight she'd made him so much food that she thought he'd be better served by a steam shovel than a fork. He just kept pushing it in. Good thing he was a demon, or his stomach would be rebelling.

She'd made corn dogs she found in the freezer. He'd taken such delight in eating them that she kept making more. He'd eaten the whole package.

He didn't like the macaroni she made, which stung a little. Caspian made a face like a kid confronted with liver and onions, flatly refusing to try the stuff. He said there was something inherently unnatural served by putting cheese sauce on pasta. She'd frowned, just like her grandmother had done to her when she was a child, and with similar results: Caspian had taken a hesitant bite. The face he made was so funny that she forgave him. She supposed demons really did have different taste buds.

He was still hungry, so she'd made French toast. He'd promptly demanded a whole loaf. He kept grabbing her ass while she was trying to cook, though, so she'd had to banish him to his chair upon threat of no more food. The ploy worked. Caspian sat quietly after that, while she cooked and while she delivered the toast, but she'd felt the heat of his gaze on her just the same. Now he was munching on two steaks with a side of her grandmother's pierogies, and her refrigerator was officially a barren wasteland.

He stopped just as he was about to shovel the last bite of pierogi into the bottomless black pit that was his mouth. Dropping his fork, he moaned in abject misery. Apparently, his demonic constitution hadn't been able to process *every* foodstuff her kitchen contained. The poor dear was finally full.

"That'll teach you to eat a whole package of corn dogs," she joked.

His eyes bugged out of his head and he clamped his hand over his mouth. He was shaking his head. "Don't talk about food, Grace. Please."

"See how easy it is to be a glutton?"

He rose and waddled like a pregnant woman to the couch and eased himself down. "I never said it wasn't." Caspian leaned back, and his mouth fell open as he wheezed to get air into his lungs. It wasn't possible because of the great bulk he now carried in front of him. It was cute, really.

Grace sighed. "I lo—" And she crammed a last bit of pierogi in her mouth before her tongue and lips could continue that traitorous train of thought. That little phrase had boarded without a ticket or a passport.

"Huh," Caspian mumbled as a carb-induced coma caused his eyes to flutter closed.

Grace was frozen to the spot. Admitting her feelings to herself was one thing; uttering them where the demon could hear was a hearse of a different color.

Then there was the knowledge that her grandmother was watching. She'd rather Seraphim catch her mid-fellatio than hear her speak such words to a demon. She knew her gran would never approve, so there was only one thing for it. Grace tiptoed to the bathroom and promptly shoved the whole bar of pomegranate-tangerine soap into her mouth. The soap wouldn't change what she was feeling, but it could certainly remind her to keep her fool mouth shut.

It didn't taste anywhere near as good as it smelled.

Her image shimmered in the mirror, and she found a very flustered Baba Yaga staring back at her. The vision of her gran said, "I see you've still got some sense rattling around in that empty melon of yours. What are you thinking?"

Grace shrugged and sighed. Bubbles scattered from the corners of her mouth.

"That is not an answer, young lady!" Seraphim was using her whisper/yell. She was trying to be quiet, but she wanted to make sure that her granddaughter knew she was upset. It was the same voice she'd used when Grace decided she wanted the bottom orange from the display in the market and all of the oranges tumbled down on top of her. Seraphim had just walked away and left her under the pile of oranges. When she'd come back to get her, she'd used this same voice.

"Don't you dare tell him that you love him! Don't you do it, Gracie! You think you like being fucked by him now? Well, he'll keep fucking you, but it'll be in a different way. It won't be in a way that you like. You hear me?"

Grace cringed. Not only because the pomegranate-tangerine soap was burning her taste buds off like warts, but because her grandmother had used the *F* word. It was a first, and not a pleasant first.

"Sera, what are you doing? Come back to bed," a voice echoed through the mirror. It sounded distant. "Are you spying on Grace? Leave that child alone. What's the worst that could happen? Caspian works for me, he won't hurt her. Now, come back and ride—"

Seraphim looked as if she'd been caught naked for her high school valedictory address. She blushed and the mirror blacked out. Grace was thankful. She hadn't wanted to hear Hades finish his suggestion. She could figure out on her own what he wanted her gran to ride, thank you very much, and it was easier to forget if she hadn't actually heard.

She spat soap down into the sink and considered her reflection. What was it with her? First, she'd been drawn to the smokers who hung out in the parking lot before school. Then it had been the guys with the Harleys and tattoos. She'd graduated to a Russian mobster who was trying to kill her, and now a guy who was not just a demon but a Crown Prince of Hell. And who was the best of them? The demon. She had a thing for bad boys, and Grace loved Caspian with her whole being. She'd gone over and over the drawbacks, the reasons why she was certifiably insane, or stupid, depending on whom you asked, but her feelings just weren't going to go away. Still, it wasn't a good idea to tell him. Was it?

The mirror flashed and Grace's grandmother reappeared. "He thinks I'm in the bathroom, and I sort of am—I'm in *your* bathroom. Now, promise me, Grace Eden Stregaria. Right now."

"Promith you whath?" Grace asked innocently, still trying to rub the soap off her tongue with a towel. "I didn't think you were supposed to be able to appear to me unless I summoned you?" She narrowed her eyes. "Or meddle."

"I'm breaking the rules. Deal with it. Now listen to me. You are not getting out of this. I want you to promise that you're not going to—"

"Damn it, woman! What did I say? You are not going to get your way on this, so quit trying." Seraphim cringed as Hades pushed his face into the mirror. So close, he looked like one of those warped puppy pictures with the really big eyes and little head. "Grace, this thing isn't for video calling. Put a black cloth over your mirror. Say what you'd like, do what you'd like. Although, you might want to find that cloth now, your grandmother won't be available for a very long time," he said to Grace. He gave a wink, and Seraphim squealed like Grace had earlier when Caspian tickled her.

Grace shook her head. This was all a little overwhelming. Her grandpa was the Devil and her grandmother was alive, but neither was acting very grandparent-y. Hades was chasing Seraphim like a coed, and Seraphim almost seemed to like it. Grace decided that maybe it would be better if her gran wore the form of the maiden more. Then all of Hades' ardent intentions wouldn't seem so, uh, creepy.

She waved her hand, and all of the mirrors in her house were covered in black gauze. "Sorry, Gran. The Devil made me do it."

CHAPTER TWENTY-FIVE

Billy Goat's Gruff

Katerina didn't feel the least bit bad about inviting the big troll over for dinner, a dinner where he would not dine but be dined upon. Nadja had threatened her and her children, and the threat to Petru was also there. She wasn't stupid—better the nasty troll than herself, though she knew when Nadja had no more use for her, she'd be next. Nadja had emerged from living death with a hunger that could only be sated by consuming magickal beings. Their power fueled the dark magick that enabled her life force.

She didn't know how she was going to get rid of Nadja, but she knew that no matter what the woman said, this would be a never-ending cycle of awfulness, another form of slavery to which Katerina flat-out refused to subject herself and her children. Her kids had known a hard enough life without this evil hag. So as soon as she was convinced Petru wouldn't do anything stupid and overly protective, she was going to ask him how to summon the Baba Yaga. If anyone could take care of the piece of garbage formerly known as Nadja Grigorovich, it would be she.

Of course, Katerina had sworn not to talk about Nadja, so she had to hope that Petru could understand everything she told him and would do what she needed without getting himself killed. She knew many people thought he was slow, but she disagreed. Just because he was a simple man didn't mean he was stupid. He just processed things differently.

She smiled at the giant troll who had stepped through her door. Katerina had never known a troll until this one had become a client. He had a taste for cruelty. After his first visit, Katerina had never wanted to see him again. But then she'd realized other girls weren't as fortunate as she was; she had magick to protect herself. So he kept coming back and she kept seeing him. Magickal clients paid more, too.

"I hadn't expected you to call. Especially not with a freebie," the magickal creature said.

"I hadn't expected to," she admitted. "I was taken by surprise with the intensity of my need."

He growled and charged forward, but he did not catch her. Instead the troll found himself facedown on the living room floor with magickal ribbons binding his hands. While these looked like frills for a girl's hair, they were unbreakable.

"A new game? I don't think I like it."

Katerina shrugged. "I don't think I care." She grabbed her purse and keys and let Nadja in.

She was just about to leave to find Petru, when Nadja blocked her way and put a hand on her arm. "I meant what I said, Katerina."

"I got you a magickal being just as you demanded, Nadja. A powerful one. I didn't have to get you a troll. I have fey, gnomes, brownies, and ghosts on my client list. They come from all over the Midwest to see me. I could have called any of them, but I called this one to show good faith." Katerina jerked free of her grasp. "Hell, Nadja, I could have even poisoned him with the vial of angel's blood I have in the top cabinet. I didn't, though."

The only reason she hadn't was that she wasn't sure such poison would work. If it didn't, she'd be even worse off than before. Rather than killing Nadja, it could give her even more power.

Nadja smiled coldly. "Just see that you keep your teeth bared against those who would stop us from our goal, Katerina. It's too bad I didn't get to know you sooner. We could have wreaked havoc on Ivan, and none of these strong-arm techniques would have been necessary."

Katerina nodded, vowing there would be a Ben & Jerry's in Hell before she ever willingly did anything for Nadja Grigorovich.

She left the apartment to find Petru. Thankfully, he was home.

"Miss Katerina!" the big mobster exclaimed, but he didn't open the door.

"Are you going to let me in?"

"No."

"Why not?"

"It's not clean." Petru looked at his feet.

"It's very important that I talk to you, Petru. Something has happened."

Reluctantly, he opened the door. He hadn't been kidding. His apartment was filthy. There were dishes piled high in the sink, girlie mags spread out across the coffee table, rings from beer bottles on the tables, and the smell . . . it was a mixture of week-old pizza, dirty socks, and beer.

"We'll worry about that later. Where's Sasha?" But as the words escaped her mouth she realized what had happened. Sasha was the reason Nadja was walking free again.

Petru twisted his hands together. "I haven't seen him for days. Not since the night before I came over to ask you to share your meal. I'm worried. He's never been gone this long without letting me know where he is."

"I . . . I think he's dead, Petru," Katerina confessed.

"Don't say that, Katerina," Petru admonished. "You'll make it happen."

"No, honey. I'm sorry, but I just realized the truth myself. I think he's dead. Someone . . . someone he loves is in my apartment."

"The lady he was going to save? She's here? I have to talk to her!"

Katerina put a hand on his chest to stop him, and surprisingly it did. "No, you can't do that. I'm not sure how to say this. I'm not sure what I can say. If I say the wrong thing, it could be very bad for me."

"Did a witch put a spell on you?" Petru asked earnestly.

"Yes, Petru. So I need you to trust me and do as I ask, even if you don't understand why."

This would be a problem for most men, to trust so completely without an explanation. It would be a problem for most women, too. She knew that she was asking a lot.

"I trust you, Miss Katerina," Petru said without hesitation.

"Thank you, Petru." She exhaled deeply, as if she'd just dropped a heavy burden.

"Can you tell me which witch?"

"No."

"It wasn't the Baba Yaga, was it? I thought she'd forgiven me and Sasha both."

Katerina leaped at the opportunity. "No, it wasn't her, but we're going to need to summon her. She's the only one who can take care of this witch."

"Grace Stregaria can't do it? She is very powerful. And she—"

"No," Katerina interrupted. "We need the Baba Yaga."

"Say her name and ask her to protect you."

"Just say her name and ask for protection? That's it? No chalices of lamb's blood, no crying babies, no weird plants gathered in the waning light of an October moon?" Katerina asked.

"Nope. We're all born with one chance to receive her help. All we have to do is ask."

"What about all of those stories that we heard as children?"

"To make you do what you're told, of course. In the heart of all those fairy tales there's both a lesson and a universal fear. The Baba Yaga is traditionally an old woman, and men are frightened of old women because they can no longer be dominated through sex." Petru shrugged.

"Petru." Katerina kissed his cheek. "I think that you're much smarter than anyone gives you credit for."

"You're the only one." He swatted her lightly on the rump.

"So, this isn't going to work like I'd planned. This is both harder and easier at the same time. I need to be in immediate danger before I ask her to protect me. I thought I could just conjure her and she'd take that horrible hag away, that we could then bounce merrily along the happily-ever-after trail. Nothing is ever that easy, is it?"

"No," Petru agreed. "But that doesn't mean we stop hoping."

"No?"

"Nope. And it doesn't mean we stop searching for happiness." Petru picked her up with one hand and threw her over his shoulder like a beloved sack of flour. Hauling her into the bedroom, he said, "We'll start in here."

CHAPTER TWENTY-SIX

Jack and Jill Went Up a Hill, and Michael Came Tumbling Down

It was day three of his seclusion, and not one soul had entered the bar. Not Sasha, not Petru, not Ethelred, and certainly not Grace. She apparently wasn't taking his threat very seriously. But why would she? She was off cavorting with her demon lover.

Speaking of demon lovers, he hadn't seen Jill again, and he wanted to know exactly why not. He'd called for Ethelred, called for him until his voice went hoarse, but still no response. He was running out of options. If he had to, he'd summon the Devil to get this done. Of course, he wasn't sure what he had left to offer as payment. And did it make sense to keep moving up the food chain?

Strangely enough, it hadn't occurred to him to leave. This was where he did business, where he was the most comfortable. He was accustomed to people coming to him. If it had occurred to him to leave, he would have found exit impossible. Jill had used her powers to seal the bar off from the rest of the world. There would be no one in or out until she declared it so. But Michael hadn't spent enough time with himself. Not yet.

It was alone and in a melancholy mood that Michael now sat, jacking off in the middle of his bar, daring Fate to send someone strolling in to catch him with his cock in hand. The direction of his thoughts scared him a bit. He'd always pondered dark things, fantasized about hurting people when he was pleasuring himself, so that didn't bother him. In fact, he'd jacked off on a recent prostitute after he killed her. Nothing as foul as touching the body, no, but her death had excited him so much that he'd wanted to come. But now he was jacking off while imagining that *he* was the strangled whore.

He took a cable and tied it around his neck, tightening it just a little to add to the fantasy. Then he pulled too hard and awoke three hours later with his dick still in hand and hard as a rock. No one had been in or out of the bar. So, he continued his activity but couldn't get off.

Suddenly, the jukebox blazed to life, and Elvis was singing a song he'd never recorded—"I Touch Myself" by the Divinyls. The bar was full; he was surrounded by people. Jill was working the counter and smiling, and there were two "made" guys sitting at Michael's very table. Both paused with their drinks halfway to their lips, staring at him. His cock was out and he was fisting it furiously. There in front of everyone.

"What the fuck are you looking at?" he demanded, and found he could not stop.

"Not sure, Grigorovich. I'm really not." The man nearest put down his drink. "I don't think you know either." A couple of other patrons stopped what they were doing to watch Michael as well.

"I could kill you for your insolence," he growled.

"Yeah, if you could stop beating your dick. Maybe." The guy started to guffaw.

Michael was about to come. For that reason he figured fuck it, he'd already gone this far, he might as well finish the job. But his pistol suddenly wilted like a three-week-old cucumber forgotten in the back of the refrigerator. It made him gasp like a girl being rudely felt up at her first dance.

He kept smacking the shit out of himself, but it wasn't for

pleasure. He was going to will the thing into submission. There was no way he'd ever live it down if he couldn't get it back up, and he intended to make a mess all over the guy smirking in the seat next to him. There didn't seem to be any other way out of this predicament.

Jill slid next to him into the booth. "I think you better go, boys. I'll handle this." The bar was suddenly empty again.

Michael blinked. "What are you doing to me?"

"Nothing," she replied. "I'm just trying to help. Do you want me to stop?" The demonic redhead bit her bottom lip and looked innocently up at him, taking his wilted cucumber in hand.

"No, no," he said. "Keep going."

"You like that, don't you?" she murmured. "I know everything you want."

He moaned, his flesh springing back to life. He was almost ready to come. But Jill pinched the base of his penis to keep him from finding release. "Yeah, I know everything you want, and you're not going to get it. You'll never come again. Not without my say-so. And I'm *never* going to—"

Michael sat up in bed, screaming. He flipped the covers back to check his cock and found it lying sedately against his thigh. He wasn't in his bar, and Jill was nowhere nearby.

A sudden fear found him, so he thought of Grace naked. *Nothing.* His cock didn't even twitch. He thought of strangling Grace. Still nothing. Michael thought of Jill and her knee-high stripper boots, and those tight leather pants hugging her ass, but still the beast would not awaken. It couldn't be stirred.

Just what exactly had he done to deserve this, he wondered. He was a good businessman, he provided incomes for many people who otherwise wouldn't have one, and he was earning a place for himself in the afterlife. Sure he killed a hooker or two, or sometimes his associates, but they were bad people. So, why was he being tormented?

Oh. Maybe things were finally moving into place because Grace had come to her senses. He was being tested by Hell. Michael could deal with that, as it was a temporary situation. It was just a scenario brought up to see what he would do if they cursed him with random impotence. They were seeing if he'd make a good demon, maybe. Ethelred had told him that something like this could happen when he'd cured his demon crabs, after another contract, of course.

He peeked back down at the sleeping snake between his thighs. It was still there, at least. This punishment or testing could have been much worse. Much worse, indeed. He breathed in, breathed out.

Now that he thought about it, the dream had been fairly similar to real life. The bar had indeed been quiet for the past three nights. But it wasn't like Jill was really out to get him, and in the dream she'd been a malicious presence bent on his destruction. She'd seemed pretty hot for him the other night, and he wasn't sure what could change in two days. Then again, women were mercurial creatures.

So, he hadn't seen Ethelred for three days. That had to be a coincidence, right? He'd summon him to see what was up. Maybe they could hang out, take in a boxing match and have some beers, shoot the proverbial shit. The two of them would be peers when everything was said and done, so it made sense that they should hang out and get to know each other better. Right? Right.

Mind made up, Michael settled down into his overstuffed, king-size bed and prepared to go back to sleep. But as he rolled over, something ice cold touched his skin. Ice cold and clammy, like a fish.

He didn't want to look. Michael had that same feeling

he'd had when he looked down and found those demon crabs munching on his nads. But he couldn't just lie there like a prepubescent girl who believed staying very still would keep the monsters from getting her; Michael Grigorovich was one of those monsters, and he knew firsthand that they didn't go away. They just took their time getting ready to pounce.

He opened his eyes slowly and found himself face-to-face with the body of the dead hooker that had made him so hard in his dream. Well, he wasn't hard now, and his mouth was open with no sound coming out.

The corpse was smiling, her red hair plastered to her forehead with what appeared to be sweat. "That was great, lover. Care to go again?" it said. It looked like it was smiling where its lips had rotted away.

Then it was Jill, naked and whole and herself. Though, now she looked more familiar. There was something about her he should recognize, that he should recall, but no matter how he tried, he couldn't put his finger on what it was.

Something was wrong, here. Nothing seemed real. He was lost in a black fugue of pain and confusion. But the worst was the humiliation. His biggest and only fear. It gave him a sick hope.

If this was Hell testing him, he was determined to be worthy of the challenge.

CHAPTER TWENTY-SEVEN
Crime and Punishment

Seraphim found herself on the receiving end of a very sharp slap on the rump, and Hades' fingers felt like they had stingers when he wanted.

"I have to punish you," he said as if he actually regretted it.

"For what?"

"You know exactly for what. For harassing our granddaughter. Leave Grace and her man alone."

"He's not a man, he's a demon. I know the kind of pain she's opening herself up for. It's not worth it." Seraphim wasn't about to bullied on this. Just because she'd fallen back into bed with a demon was no reason for her granddaughter to make the same choice.

"Didn't he get her to realize that Nikoli wasn't real?"

"It broke her heart!" Seraphim said.

Hades stared at her. "Better her heart than her life."

Seraphim shrugged. "I still don't like it. Especially after I specifically told her not to go and consort with him anymore." She felt like sticking her tongue out at him. It worked for Grace.

"It's not your life, Sera. It's hers. Grace has embraced her demon heritage to be with Caspian. And he loves her. He's even grown a heart for her. He's given up his demonhood, his magick, his immortality—"

"What?" Seraphim almost screeched. "How is he going to keep her safe if he's just a man?"

"First you didn't want her to love a demon and now you don't want her to love a man. Which is it, Seraphim? No matter how much you'd like to, you can't relive your own choices through your granddaughter."

"I'm not trying to relive my choices," Seraphim said huffily. "I wouldn't change any of them."

"Even your deal with me?" Hades asked.

"Even that," she admitted. "I wouldn't have had Aurora without you, and I am thankful for every second of her life that I got to share. I guess we did that right."

"We certainly did." Hades sighed. "Look, Sera, I know I don't have the best track record. Persephone dropped me like a bad habit almost right after we were married, but I'd like to think I've changed in a couple of centuries. I really do love you, and I'm asking you to marry me. Again."

"Right now?" Seraphim asked.

"That's not the response I'm looking for, Seraphim Stregaria. I don't want to have to remind you of your promise, but I will if I have to."

"Isn't that what cost you Persephone? Twisting a contract to make her stay against her will?"

"No, it was her unnaturally attached mother, Demeter. She just wouldn't let go. All that six-months-out-of-the-year crap was too much for Persephone to handle. Wanna talk about a meddlesome mother-in-law? She doesn't get her way once and the whole damn world is covered in snow. Talk about a tantrum."

Seraphim eyed him meaningfully. "You know what I mean. Wouldn't it be better if I chose to be with you on my own? If I chose to—"

"Fine," Hades interrupted. "I release you from your vow."

"Thank you." Seraphim picked up a catalog and browsed

the shoes, pretending nonchalance. Secretly she was thrilled. And those pumps were absolutely divine!

"And . . . ?" Hades said, clearly waiting for something.

"And what?"

"I released you. Now you're supposed to capitulate. You're supposed to agree to marry me."

"It doesn't work if you only released me to get something in return," Seraphim said calmly.

"Well, of course I expect something in return. I'm the Devil!"

"A fact that you keep reminding me of. It's bad strategy. Kind of like the customer who gets bad service at a restaurant and keeps saying, 'Don't you know who I am?' After the first time, clearly they know who you are and don't care."

He considered for a moment. "Fine. Now you can say you got the better of me. I don't even care. Just put this on." Hades shoved something at her.

There was no way that she was going to—

It was very lovely, a black diamond in the shape of a heart and set in platinum. The gem changed colors in the light, kind of like an oil slick. There was ornate scrollwork to the side and in the setting, but this was just right for the size of the stone and Seraphim did kind of want to see how it would look on her finger.

Of course, if she tried it on, he'd never let her take it off. That's what a voice was screaming in the back of her head. At the same time, "Maybe I'll just try it on," came out of her mouth.

"That's right you'll try it on," Hades snapped. "And you'll wear it for all eternity. Now, come pay attention to your lord and husband before all Hell breaks loose."

"What?"

"Never mind. We'll deal with Hell later, when and if the

rebellion hits. Right now I want to celebrate my new wife." He swept her off her feet and into his arms.

"Lovely. Now what?" Seraphim said.

"What do you think?" They were already in the bedroom.

Just to be contrary, Seraphim crossed her arms. "What if I don't want to?"

"Yeah and what if . . . ? You know what? You win. You want me to be more understanding and listen to what you say. See? Here is me listening." Hades dropped her unceremoniously on the bed and disappeared.

"Hades!" She got no response. "If you think this is how we're starting eternity, you've got another think coming."

Still no answer. Seraphim seethed on the bed and gritted her teeth. He really wasn't going to play ball.

"Hades!" she commanded. Still nothing.

Okay, he wanted to play hardball? That was fine. She could play *blue* balls. See how he liked that.

Seraphim changed her apparel with a snap of her fingers. She was still trying to learn how to wiggle her nose like the actress in *Bewitched*. It was just for show, of course, but something that she thought was so cute—like dressing as a harem dancer. Seraphim was now covered solely in the gauziest of veils. Each time she moved, her silhouette danced beneath. There were hints of skin, vaguely lush curves and globes.

"Since I'm all alone, I guess I will just have to do my belly dancing workout," Seraphim proclaimed. She began to move her hips, slowly at first, rotating them back, then to the home position, then forward. She moved faster and faster until she was twisting like she'd been raised to dance for kings and gods.

As Seraphim dropped a veil, the temperature in the room went up.

There you are, you sneaky bastard. But she was careful to keep the gloating smile off her face.

She dropped another veil, and still another. When she finally got down to four, the room was sweltering like the inside of a volcano and she turned off the music and slipped into bed. She whispered, "Yes, it's too bad I'm alone. I might have taken the rest of my veils off for my new husband."

"Damn it, Seraphim!"

"Do I win?" she asked, turning to Hades.

"Yes."

"Good." She turned out the light.

"Sex isn't always going to get you your way, you know. I'm the Devil. I'm slick. I got game."

Seraphim smirked. "Of course, you do, sweetheart. You just come over here and show me. That's right." She patted his hand and spoke as if to a child.

"You should know better than to challenge me," Hades warned.

Seraphim rolled over halfway and gave him a saucy grin over her shoulder. "Should I?" she asked with a giggle. "Maybe you better explain why again. Or better yet, *show* me."

He did exactly that.

CHAPTER TWENTY-EIGHT
A Tighter Knot

Grace was still watching Caspian sleep. It was just as unacceptable as ever, even though she didn't have to worry about asking him to save her son's life. That was both a blessing and a curse.

Thinking of Nikoli caused a tightness in her chest that she imagined would always be there. She knew it wasn't rational to still feel pain for someone who'd never existed, but he'd been real enough to her. She supposed that was the point of the spell.

She rested her hand on Caspian's chest where his heart beat in a strong, regular rhythm. She liked the feel of it under her hand, liked the way it sounded. She'd noticed lately that her own heart hadn't sounded so strong, but she didn't worry because she didn't feel any different. It still beat, if slowly, quietly, as if she were sleeping and dreaming of soft things.

But change was coming. She could feel the rush whenever Caspian was inside her, and she knew the time for a choice was approaching. She was losing some of her humanity, and she might yet choose to be a demon.

Grace rested her head where her hand had been, so she could listen to the sure, confident thud of his heart. She wasn't sure what it meant, this pounding in Caspian's chest, but she was glad that he was experiencing it. For some reason it made her feel closer to him.

She kissed the edge of his jaw, rubbing their cheeks together. He tasted different now—no less tantalizing, but different. The salt of his skin, even the scent of him had taken on different aspects. She moved to kiss him on the mouth and was surprised to find he tasted like steak—steak in a can that had been left out in one-hundred-degree heat for a week. Yuck.

He made a sound of pleasure and tightened his arms around her. Securing her ass against his thighs, he locked her into a kiss even as she turned her head and struggled to break free.

"You're a naughty little witch to wake me up like that, grinding against me like you're begging for some action, and then denying me. It's just cruel."

"Caspian, I don't know how to tell you this, so I'm just going to say it. You need to brush your teeth. For the first time ever, your breath is . . . well, it's not what I would call minty fresh."

He looked scandalized, as if he'd never before had teeth wearing a cashmere sweater and a tongue with a matching muff. Maybe he hadn't. She wondered why he did now.

Shrugging, she laughed. "It happens to the best of us. Just brush your teeth. I have an extra toothbrush in the bathroom."

"A brush for teeth? Okay." He didn't sound as if he thought she was sane, but he went into the bathroom anyway.

When he'd been gone for longer than a man with a hard-on should be, Grace found him in the bathroom, holding up an object quizzically.

"Grace, I just don't think it's going to work." He turned it over and over in his hands, holding it up to the light, this way and that.

She stifled a giggle. "Caspian, that brush is for the toilet."

He dropped the thing as if bitten and glanced from it to Grace and then back. "Why would you even *have* something like that?"

"To clean with."

"The water cleans the toilet when it flushes, doesn't it?" he asked. He was beginning to look mortified. And maybe a bit angry.

"You didn't put it in your mouth, did you?"

"No! I was thinking about it, though. You said to brush my teeth!"

"With a *tooth*brush, Caspian."

"I've never actually seen a toothbrush. Well, I've seen them on TV, but you know things never look the same in person. This is the only brush it could be. I see your hairbrush, your comb, your curling brush, a brush for your eyebrows, a brush for your eyelashes, but I see nothing for teeth!"

Grace opened the vanity and pulled out a new toothbrush. She kept some just in case. Not that she'd planned on having a demon sleeping over last time she was at the drugstore. For that reason, they were all pink with little hearts.

She opened the package and handed over the toothbrush. "I suppose you want me to show you how to use it, too?" She fought a giggle.

"No. I will read the instructions, thank you. Watching you put something into your mouth will not be productive. Not in the way you want, anyway."

"Why not—? Oh." Grace blushed. "Okay, well, if you need any more help, just yell." She went back out.

In the living room she waited, but the sounds he made almost forced her to go back in and check on him. When he came out, he smiled. "Grace, I like this toothbrushing. It feels very nice."

She laughed and moved into his arms. "Now you can kiss me."

"I might need to brush my teeth again," he was saying. "I could do that all day."

"I've created a monster!" she said. "Too bad. He'll have to champ at the bit, because I've got other plans for that mouth."

Grace tilted her chin up to meet his lips and squealed a little as his hands found the waist of her jeans. Usually Caspian just magicked her naked, but she'd always wanted him to strip her with his hands. She was getting her wish.

The heat of his fingers through the fabric was delicious, especially moving ever closer to her flesh. It was such a tease! The palm of one hand slid over the ball of her shoulder and pushed the strap of her tank down. Every contact sent a new shiver down her spine, and when his fingers grazed the edge of her breast, her nipples tightened in response.

Caspian hooked his thumbs through the belt loops of her jeans and tugged them down. His fingers trailing lightly over her mound, he knelt in front of her and hooked her leg over his shoulder. She was kind of impressed that he would risk putting his face back down there, what with everything that had happened. Not that she was complaining. Far from it. The sensation was rapturous.

Grace couldn't stand up any longer. She wanted to lie down, but she also wanted to bring him the same pleasure he brought her. He always made sure that she came first, and she wanted them to come together, so she unhooked her leg from around his shoulder and pushed him onto his back. It was a good thing she had long legs, because straddling his wide chest was quite the feat. Like she had during their first encounter, Grace rocked forward on her knees and worked herself back against him so he could continue his work while she did, too. That time she'd managed to crack him first.

She rested her weight atop him and used one hand to

guide his cock into her mouth. She traced her tongue around the base of the shaft and up to the head. Then she took it as deep as she was able into her throat, suckling the head, laving the entire surface with her tongue, and paying special attention to each ridge and valley.

The speed and intensity of his mouth matched hers. He seemed to be following her lead, so if she wanted him to flick his tongue across her clit faster, she did just the same to the head of his cock. And whenever she took down the full length of him, he did the same with her clit.

Grace loved the silky feel of him against her lips, loved watching his sac tighten as he fought not to come. Inside her mouth his engorged cock became even more swollen, and his fingers dug into her hips. But he was working her, too, and she was just about to burst. She rocked into his movements, grinding herself against his mouth as he pulled her closer. Continually, she worked his cock, but the need to come was testing her resolve.

She was about to come, but with each stroke, she was sure the next one would send him over the edge. Caspian bucked against her. His balls were so tight, his cock so hard in her mouth, Grace thought she might win. She had a chance. He was resilient, though, fighting her talented mouth and hands with his own. At last she decided to let him win.

She felt a familiar starburst inside her. Caspian kept licking, kept pushing deeper, even though her womanhood was shuddering against his mouth. She didn't stop sucking, guessing she could still attain her goal; she wanted him to come in her mouth while she was orgasming, and it looked like it was possible. Grace stroked faster with her hand and kept moving him in and out of her mouth.

He spilled for her just as she was riding the final waves of ecstasy—but Caspian wasn't done. His hips bucked a final time; then he guided her movements, turning and positioning her for a kiss. He tangled her hair in his hand and drew her in. And just as she could taste her honey all over his lips, he could surely taste himself. They were sharing each other, and she found the idea more intoxicating than anything else.

Somehow his cock was hard again. He tried to move her atop him, and she'd come so hard she was fine with whatever he wanted. Demons! Grace didn't know how he did it, but the heat was building again, though he'd just put out the first fire.

"Now that it's work, you want me to do it, is that it?" he teased as she sat motionless astride him. When she just nodded, he obliged by lifting her legs up over his shoulders. But this time, instead of tasting her, he entered her. The angle was impossibly steep, and every thrust hit her core.

Grace thought she was going to die. She arched up to meet his body, and dark blasts exploded behind her closed eyelids every time he moved. She wanted to open her eyes and look at him, but she couldn't—couldn't think, couldn't breathe—all she could do was feel. It was as if the alpha and omega of the Universe was in her quim; every sensation started there and ricocheted through her before ending again where it was born.

She'd been holding on to his forearms and then his shoulders as he drilled her, but she released him as a last pleasure stole away her strength and voice. Her mouth was open in a silent scream, and a galaxy was born and died in those precious moments. Time stopped, and sensation was all that mattered. They lay spent in each other's arms, limbs tangled, in the middle of her living room floor.

After a short but quiet period of luxuriating, Grace roused herself enough to ask, "When this thing with Michael is over, how long will you stay?" It was both her biggest hope and biggest fear.

"I don't think I'll have any choice about that."

She fought annoyance. This was what she'd expected from Caspian at the beginning. Lately, she'd had more hope. "Why are you always so freaking cryptic? Can't you just answer the question?"

"I'm trying to!" he said. "I can't go back to Hell because I'm not a demon anymore."

The statement took her by surprise. *"What?"*

"I don't have any demonic powers anymore. I'm human."

"How did that happen?"

"I don't know."

Grace was quiet for a long moment that seemed to stretch into eternity. Hope flared in her breast. An impossible hope. "Oh. Well, you could stay with me. If you wanted."

Caspian's silence stretched into eternity.

"You don't have to answer now. I can't even believe I said that. Stupid idea, just forget it." All her words were bursting free in a rush.

"Grace, why don't we talk after I take care of Michael?"

"Oh, you can't have anything to do with Michael. Not now." Grace didn't want him anywhere near that bastard Grigorovich.

"Why not?"

"You just said that you're human!"

Caspian shrugged. "I'm not going to magick him anymore, Grace. I'm going to kill him."

"But you're human," Grace repeated.

"You keep saying that as if it makes a difference."

"It does make a difference! Caspian, he could kill you."

"What sort of man would I be if I couldn't protect my woman just because I don't have demon magick? I wouldn't deserve you. I'll be worthy, Grace. I promise you."

CHAPTER TWENTY-NINE
A Troll a Day

Nadja Grigorovich had just put her schedule on fast-forward. The troll she'd gorged on earlier had filled her to the brim with magick, sating the dark beast that dwelled where her soul had been and that was now always looking for something to gnaw on. Sated it for the nonce. She just might have to eat a troll every day, because she felt so lovely. They would always be on the menu when she became the Baba Yaga—an event that had been moved forward to tonight.

At her son's bar, Nadja sensed demon magick all around. The doors opened after she blasted them with a shot of her own power. The mighty hammer of her will was unstoppable.

She did not like what she'd found inside. Not one bit. She'd raised her son better. The bar was empty other than Michael; his head was in his hands and he had two empty bottles of vodka on the table before him. His hair was wild and greasy, and he looked like he hadn't slept for days. His eyes were bloodshot and ringed with dark circles, and he was sloppy drunk.

One of the bottles went sailing past her head, and exploded into a thousand shards on the wall behind her.

"Get out. You're not real."

She ignored this. "Where is Grace?"

"How the fuck should I know?" he said, taking a drink from a third bottle that sat on the booth bench next to him.

"It's your job to know, at least if you still want to be a demon."

"*Mamulya?*" Michael asked. He was really fucked up. He hadn't called her anything but Nadja since he was six. "I missed you, *Mamulya*. My heart is full to see you."

Nadja raised a brow and wondered if she slapped the spit out of his mouth whether anything he'd learned would come back to him. Maybe he'd remember where he'd hidden his balls. She was tempted to call and ask Grace to get them out of her purse. Whatever had happened to the delightfully menacing bastard she'd left behind, and who was this needy little bitch who had taken his place?

She sighed, deciding to try a different tack. A little subtlety might just be what was needed. Something catastrophic had happened to her little monster, and she needed to find out what it was.

"*Mamulya* is here, Mikal," she said, speaking to him as if he were five years old all over again. "Come tell me all about it."

She slipped into the booth beside her son and gently pried the bottle out of his hands. As she set it on the table, she thought she saw a redhead behind the bar, but the woman was gone in a flash, if she'd ever been there.

"Grace is fucking a demon," Michael complained.

"That's a problem?"

"Hell, yes. He gave me demonic crabs, the fiery shits, and screwed Grace in my very own hot tub. Ethelred told me she screamed his name and that he's better than me."

Nadja felt a faint stirring of an emotion close to maternal solicitude, at least as close as she ever got. No one was better than her son at anything.

Michael continued. "Sasha disappeared with a girl I bought for him, Petru followed them, and I shot my bartender only to have him replaced by a demon whore who's tormenting me for some imagined wrong I did her. I'm in hock up to my ears with Ethelred and there's no end in sight. Grace cast a Karma spell on me, so that when I tried to tag the back door of the new girl, *I* felt it. How fair is that? It's not!"

He drunkenly flopped his head back on the table. "I've tried to do everything you asked, *Mamulya*. I've lied, cheated, stolen, killed, and punished as you said. I'm no closer to demonhood."

Nadja petted her son's head and rubbed small circles on his back like she had when he was a child with a cold. Ivan hit her every time Michael coughed, so it had behooved her to take care of him. Just like it did now.

"No, it's not fair, Michael," she said. "I will raise her for you after I am Baba Yaga. I promise, my son. If you want Grace, you shall have her. For eternity."

Her boy's eyes were haunted. "Will you also make the whore stop tormenting me?"

"Which one, Michael?"

"That one," he said, motioning to the bar. "That red-headed bitch I killed and put in a Dumpster. She haunts me. She gives me dreams, visions, chokes me while she touches me. And worse . . ."

"How did she die, my son? Did you strangle her?"

Michael nodded miserably. Then he glanced over toward the bar. "I told you I would tell my mother, you bitch. Ha," he cackled. His head lolled back drunkenly.

"Answer the question or I can't hurt her." She tugged on his hair to make Michael pay attention.

"Yes, I strangled her and dumped her with the rest of the trash. Or my men did."

"She's angry then. But how did this dead hooker get magick?" Nadja kept petting her son's head, hoping to soothe him.

"I don't know, but she has it. She's a demon now. She says she's going to stay with me until I kill myself." He nodded to a gold-plated nine-millimeter that was on the table, and he looked like he'd been pretty close to using it.

"No, son of my flesh! You mustn't ever kill yourself. Not when you can kill others," Nadia advised. *"Come here, little whore."*

The words were a magickal command. To her surprise, Jill found herself corporeal and bound, her personal power quiescent, unreachable. She was trapped. Trapped in this bar, trapped in a private hell. It was worse than the real one.

"Why are you tormenting my son?" Nadja compelled her to answer.

"He killed me. He strangled me because the demon crabs made him angry. Or maybe just because he's an evil bastard."

Nadja grimaced. "That was your lot in life, girl. You must accept it. He is stronger than you."

"Not anymore," Jill crowed.

"No, not anymore, demon. But I—*I* am stronger than you. You will serve. I bind you to him for all eternity."

And with that simple sentence, a silver chain sprang from Michael to the inside of Jill's stomach, attaching them. She belonged to him forever. Only the Devil could break this chain.

"Wait for his leisure!" Nadja screeched in closure. The bar's heavy atmosphere instantly lightened, and Jill was sentenced to some shadowy place where she'd never again see the light of day. Not unless Michael asked for her or the Devil recalled her to Hell.

"Is that better, my son?"

"Yes." Michael took a deep breath, his head fell forward, and he began to snore lightly on the table.

That whore had kept him up and tormented him for days. Nadja decided to let him sleep for a few hours. She couldn't believe that the prostitute had managed to push her strong son almost to the point of breaking. If Nadja hadn't shown up when she did, his brains would be splattered all over the wall behind them.

Well, she didn't need him for this part of her plan anyway. Nadja concentrated very hard and changed form into that of an old woman with a basket of apples. Ingenious, if she did say so herself. Very old-world magick—something that Grace wouldn't see coming until after it choked her to death.

She threw some more magick around the bar, making sure her son was protected at least until she got back, then headed out the door. Slowly, she made her way across town, enjoying the freedom of this cronelike form. Nobody paid her much mind at all. She liked the attention she got wearing the shape of the body Sasha had bought for her—men all liked to stare at her ass—but it was nice to be inconspicuous, too.

Not that anyone respected the elderly in this country. Most were treated like children who couldn't do for themselves, not as the great sages they were in her culture. In her village, everyone gave grandmothers respect. They had seen so much, had so much knowledge to share. . . .

Also, you never knew who or what was wearing that skin. It was well-known in magickal circles that many creatures preferred the form of an old woman. In her village, an old woman knocking on your door at night was something to be feared. Here it was just a hassle. No one believed anymore.

That was something that she was going to change when she was Baba Yaga. People would remember to fear the night and its creatures. That old saying about how there was nothing in the dark that wasn't there in the light? It was bullshit. There were all sorts of horrors that crawled in the shadows, just waiting to be acknowledged, waiting to spill out into the world in an ink-dark stain of evil. They would all answer to her, Nadja Grigorovich, descendant of Rasputin, and ruling Baba Yaga.

But for now, gaining the trust of a younger person was best accomplished in an old and withered form. She would see if Grace Stregaria had taken lessons from her grandmother's knee, or if she was like every other modern youngster who would open the door to an old woman and her basket of apples.

She scattered a few pieces of fruit in the hallway, easing her old frame to the ground as if she'd fallen. When she gave a giggle, the sound emerged as a deranged cackle, but this suited her just fine. She pounded hopefully on Grace's door.

The door didn't open, which surprised Nadja. Perhaps Grace had taken to her lessons, after all. The possibility hadn't really seemed likely; she had to stop assuming people were as stupid as they seemed.

She pounded again, hoping no one else stumbled on her. Nadja didn't think she could play nice twice; it had just about killed her earlier with Michael. Scratching a final time in desperation, she gave a sigh of relief when the door finally opened.

It was no wonder that Grace was screwing this demon instead of her son. Not that Michael wasn't handsome; he was. She was proud of his features. But this demon was . . . something else. Maybe he'd be free for a hookup after she'd taken her rightful place as the world's preeminent witch.

He took one look and shut the door in her face.

"Help, I've fallen!" Nadja thought about adding, "And I can't get up," but she was sure that would be pushing it. Plus, she'd giggle. She flopped down all the way to the ground and let out a small mewling sound.

"Old woman, sell your sob story elsewhere. As if I'd let you anywhere near either of us with an apple."

"He's so mean," she howled, hoping she might attract the neighbors and force his hand. "I've fallen and he won't help me."

"Yes, I am mean. I'm the scourge of old ladies everywhere. Beat it, or I'm going to shove those apples somewhere no one has explored since the Dark Ages. Beat feet, hag!" Caspian called through the door. "I know better than to trust your kind."

It had probably been too much to hope that this was going to work on Caspian, seeing as he was a demon. But Nadja wasn't giving up. She howled again in a voice so high pitched and irritating that she annoyed herself. The door opened again, and she peered up into Caspian's smiling face.

She didn't know what the hell he had to be so happy about—until he dumped a pitcher of rose water on her. To add insult to injury, he tossed salt on afterward. And not just a pinch of the stuff. He got some in her mouth. Her magickal disguise began to shimmer, and she knew the jig was up. For now, anyway.

"I'll get you," she said as she disappeared.

So, now what? If it had been Grace alone, the girl would have been too weak to deny her pleading entreaties. But with the demon there, apparently protecting her . . . ? She had to find a way around him.

Inspiration struck like a blinding light. She'd turn into Sasha and use Petru! Except, she was sure Katerina would have warned the big lug somehow; she wouldn't leave him to muddle along uninformed. The woman hadn't been in love with Sasha, and she would have warned *him*. Now Katerina had *love-struck* stamped all over her forehead, so it seemed like a foregone conclusion. She likely did it without breaking her vow of silence, too.

So, no. That plan wouldn't work, but something similar might. She needed someone or something big that could just burst in and take Grace out of Caspian's hands. Something that could get past the hex bags she'd smelled. Or . . . she could just say fuck it and burn the place down. That sounded like the most expedient of plans. Why bother being tricksy? Seraphim's magick was strong, but not even hex bags could survive a healthy dose of arson.

Nadja hobbled down the stairs, not daring to change forms. Someone might see her, and that wouldn't do. She meant to keep her powers a secret. As she exited the stairs, she blew a kiss in the general direction of the building, and magickal flames sprang up wherever she looked. They crawled high up the walls, spreading in an elegant ballet of death that would consume all it touched.

She would have made an excellent getaway if she hadn't tripped over a homeless man who'd been watching the whole thing.

"I didn't see shit," he said as she stood up.

"I know," she whispered, and then added a few words of magick. His eyes glazed over with a white film. "And you never will again."

The delay was fortuitous. She turned just in time to see a very interesting development—Grace jumping off the roof and gliding down into the nearby alley sporting lavender wings. But that wasn't what impressed her most. What fascinated her was that Grace's demonic sex god was holding on to her for dear life. He had no wings.

No wings. Had Caspian gone native for Grace? It was an interesting and intriguing question, one to which she needed to find the answer. So thrilled with the day's events was she, Nadja almost clapped like a giddy schoolgirl. Granted, she'd made an ass of herself in the hallway, but everything else seemed to be coming along nicely.

She watched the demon and Grace make their way to the hotel across the street, made sure that Caspian did nothing magickal or demonic. He didn't. At last, Nadja was satisfied. Smiling to herself, she headed back to her son's bar. It was time for Michael to go get his girl. He'd have no trouble taking her now.

CHAPTER THIRTY

Every Time a Witch Cries, a Demon Gets His Wings

After the fire took her apartment, Grace was about to crack like a rotten nut. She'd had *enough*. She'd had load after load of the most heinous crap that could befall any one person, and it had been raining down on her for the past four years.

Okay, so, she knew she was not a normal person. She knew she had extremely powerful relatives, and that this increased the likelihood of having bizarre shit cropping up, but this was getting ridiculous. She just wanted a tiny bit of relief. She'd be happy if she could just manage one day where absolutely nothing out of the ordinary happened to her, good or bad. She wanted just one mundane, banal day. A day to herself. No grandmothers (Love you, Gran!), no Devil (Love you, too, Gramps!), no demons (Fuck it, love you three, Caspian!), and certainly no fires, carriages, hex bags, wings, sex toys, or sex.

Well, maybe not no sex. Sex might be okay. But normal-ish sex. Nothing that fucked with the basic foundations of how she saw the world. Was that just too much to ask?

Apparently it was, because just as the thought entered her head, a bullet entered Caspian's. It burst right through the door, burrowed through his head, and embedded itself into the wall of the hotel where they'd taken refuge.

The door splintered. Michael stepped through the debris with a smile on his face. "Took care of your demon problem, Grace. And you've got one day left."

She screamed as Caspian fell, a startled look on his face and his blood spraying across her hands and shirt. She called on her power, but Michael was atop her in an instant. He held her down and pinched her nose closed, forcing her to open her mouth to breathe.

She remembered that she didn't have to breathe much as a quasi-demon, tried to call the Powers That Be and trade her soul for the rest of her demonhood—or even her life for Caspian's—but nothing happened. And when her mouth fell open to suck in a big ol' breath, Michael shoved a peanut-butter ball inside. As Grace tried to spit it out, the power that had been gathering at her fingertips sputtered and died like she had a faulty battery.

All she could think about was Caspian. She begged the Universe to let him live, swore that she'd do anything for him. He couldn't be dead; not now that she'd discovered she loved him. He was a demon, so he couldn't die.

No, he was human. He'd regained his humanity by being with her. Which meant it was her fault that he was dead.

"I told you to get rid of him, Grace," Michael was saying. "Didn't I tell you? Now, will you just come home and do what's right for our son?"

Grace began fighting. She kneed her onetime lover in the balls, but that didn't faze him. It didn't even piss him off, which surprised her. Nonetheless, she vowed she was going to kill him. If she never did anything else with her life, Michael Ivan Grigorovich would die by her hand.

When she didn't respond to his comment about Nikoli, Michael shook his head. "I see you've broken my spell. Good, I'm glad. Then your magick is all the more powerful." He hit her with the back of his hand, hard. "But see what you made me do, Grace? I wouldn't have wanted this for you, but you disobeyed me. Not only that, you were unfaithful with your demon."

Grace had to live, even if it was just long enough to kill this bastard. She stared at the floor, not wanting to provoke him into doing something precipitous. Though she imagined his plan for her was dire in the long run as well.

"Can you see that, demon? She knows her place. Your body isn't even cold and soon she'll be screaming beneath me! From pleasure or pain, I have not decided, but she is mine."

Grace couldn't look at Caspian's body. It was terribly wrong that he'd lived so many centuries as a demon, then been human for only a few days before dying. He hadn't been given a chance to experience what the best parts were like. He hadn't felt what it was to be well loved. She hadn't even told him that she loved him!

Suddenly, all of her reasons for not telling him were insignificant. It didn't matter if he felt the same. Love wasn't something you confessed to while hoping for something in return, not even hoping to hear it back. It was a gift to be given freely, unconditionally, and with no expectation. And if anyone had ever earned it, Caspian had. She'd never thought her infatuation with Michael had been love; she'd known better. But Caspian, no matter what he was . . . he was the one. He was it. He was her *forever*.

"Help him, Lucy. Please," she begged, hoping against hope that her grandfather could hear, that he would answer her summons. She wouldn't say that she loved Caspian now, not aloud; that was too much like admitting she'd never have another chance and that Caspian was really dead. She wouldn't let him die; she would do whatever she must to get him back. Bullet or no bullet, he was going to be fine. He had to be.

"Who is Lucy? Who else is here?" Michael demanded, shaking her roughly.

Wouldn't you just like to know, you bastard, she thought. *Wouldn't you just.*

"Eh, no matter. My mother is waiting." Michael secured magickal chains around her wrists and ankles. She looked like an inmate from a women's prison, and it seemed like that was the angle he was trying to play up to take her out of the downtown hotel.

Dragging her by the hair, he led her out the door and down the stairs. "Don't fight me, Grace," he warned. "It will just go harder on you."

Go harder? How could it go harder?

As Grace watched Michael continue talking, she couldn't hear any of the sounds that were coming out of his mouth. It didn't matter, though, because the words didn't matter. She had one objective and one objective alone: killing Michael Grigorovich. He was going to pay for all of the pain he'd caused, the damage he'd done to numerous families. She'd seen the face of evil and this was it.

It was a good thing she believed true evil never went unpunished.

CHAPTER THIRTY-ONE

Caspian's Deal

Time was meaningless to Caspian. He lay in the dark nothingness between life and death. He wasn't alive and wasn't dead. He wasn't a demon, but nor was he human. Not really.

The heart he'd grown had stopped beating. It still felt full of love for Grace, though. He remembered the look on her face as he'd fallen, and he knew regret for the first time in a long time. He knew loss and he knew despair. He knew these things, and he knew them because of her. He knew them *for* her.

There was a bright light getting ever brighter in his field of vision, but he felt none of the peace he'd heard humans experience when they die.

"Don't go gettin' all excited just yet, Caspian, me lad." He saw the face of Hades peering down at him. "Eesh, with those glassy eyes . . . you look for all the world like you're dead. I know it's a bright light. Isn't that a kicker? It's for sinners, making them think they've hit the jackpot and got one over on the Bigger Boss. I *am* the Morning Star, after all. Why does no one remember that but me? Everyone remembers the Lord of the Flies thing from the horror flicks, but never that I'm supposed to be hot—in an official capacity, even! Hmm. I'm starting to feel very put off."

Hades glanced around before speaking again, as if he

were about to reveal top-secret information. "I think you're in love with my granddaughter."

Caspian couldn't speak, he couldn't move, couldn't do anything to acknowledge his old boss. He wanted to. He could feel his last tenuous hold on this life, this plane, slipping away with the silence of the heart that had grown to beat so strongly in his chest. He wanted another chance, if only to tell Grace what he'd been afraid to admit: He loved her.

"You're dying for her, eh? Very romantic, but unnecessary. So, you'd die for her. Would you live for her? Would you sell this humanity you've earned for another chance to be with her?

"I see that you would." Hades made a show of straightening his collar before he continued, humming a chipper little tune. "I've got a deal for you, and you even get to keep your soul. What do you think about that? There is a catch, of course, but isn't there always?"

Caspian didn't speak. Instead, his body erupted into flames.

CHAPTER THIRTY-TWO

Weekend at Nadja's

"Grace, I really didn't want it to be this way. I've come to realize since we've been apart that I do care for you. I wish you didn't have to die. Nadja says she'll bring you back for me when she's the Baba Yaga, though."

"My grandmother will smite her, Michael. Be prepared for that."

Her ex-boyfriend snorted, easing Grace down the stairs into the cellar of his bar. "She's come back from living death. She's stronger than your hag of a grandmother."

"We shall see." It was hard for Grace not to say something slick about the Devil coming to kick his ass, but she didn't want to give away any advantage she might have. If they knew Hades was coming, they might have time to prepare. Of course, none of this mattered if Hades hadn't helped Caspian.

"Where's your demon now, Grace?" Michael crowed. He dropped her on a frigid marble slab. "Your Crown Prince of Hell? You made him soft, you let me kill him."

His words were like a thousand daggers, but only because they felt true. If Caspian hadn't been with her, this wouldn't have happened. "I know that, Michael," she admitted.

"Was that your plan from the start—you just wanted to make me jealous so I'd take you back? Well, it worked." He looked both pleased and annoyed. After a moment, he said,

"But there will have to be a punishment for that stunt you pulled in the hot tub."

"Why? You like to be jealous," Grace said, trying to play along. "You like knowing that you've had what everyone else wants. That you could have it again."

"I can at that." He secured her wrists one at a time to manacles that were hanging from a marble altar like macabre bracelets. Michael sank to his haunches to pull her hair out from beneath her head, and when he did, he caressed its silky texture. "Your dying will not be easy. In fact, you will wish that you were dead many times over before it ends."

Grace didn't say anything.

"The book says that there are one thousand cuts to be made to your flesh before you are a worthy sacrifice to the Dark."

"Are you trying to scare me, Michael?" she said.

"Oh, yes."

His previous words hadn't struck dread in her heart, but that simple answer did. He stood, and she could see that he had an erection.

Grace wanted to vomit. He was disgusting. He always had been. How had she ever been so blind?

"Yes. Now you've seen what I like, the biggest secret I was keeping from you. This is all for you, and when you get back from your little trip, you and I are going to have such a good time." He laughed. "You won't even be able to die to escape me. I'll do as I like with you until the stars blink into nothingness and the world burns."

She'd seen what he was, and she defied it. "Such a pretty tongue. Too bad all you can do with it is talk."

"Trying to make me angry so I will kill you before the ceremony? It won't work." Michael smiled and shoved a ball gag into her mouth. "See, it just won't work."

Grace knew that if she started to cry, she'd choke, but the

wild sobs filling her chest were about to erupt. She was terrified. She didn't want to die, she didn't want Caspian to be
dead, and she didn't want any of this. She wondered if Jill
had felt anything similar as the life seeped out of her. Where
was Jill? If only they could have taken their well-earned revenge.

She slowly breathed in and out. It seemed as if sense and
logic traveled on that precious air, because the deeper her
breaths, the calmer she felt. She breathed until peace settled
through all her limbs and her mind shook off the foggy
helplessness fear had instilled. She breathed until she no
longer felt her body. She breathed until she remembered
evil never won.

A light went on in her head as bright as a Las Vegas landing strip. If she could just invoke her grandmother, Gran
would come and handle everything. She was glad now that
she hadn't known Seraphim was alive; otherwise, she would
be unable to call on her. She would surely have used her
one Baba Yaga call for something stupid. But now all she
had to do was work the ball gag out of her mouth.

She fiddled with that hated silicone ball for what must
have been hours. Her limbs went numb and so did her lips.
She saw a movement in the corner, and her eyes scanned
the darkness for a form in the shadows. It seemed to be a
woman. Could it be Jill?

As the figure stepped into the light, all of the happy hope
that had been buzzing like little bees in her chest crashed
into her stomach with a sickening plop. It wasn't Jill. It was
Nadja.

"Do go on, little Grace. Don't let me stop you. Work that
gag out of your mouth, girl, and let's see what you've got."

Grace stared at her with defiant eyes.

"You certainly have a lot of your grandmother in you.
You look just like she did when she was pregnant with Aurora. Too bad there was never anything in that dried-up old

womb of yours. You and Michael would have had very powerful children." The evil woman laughed. "Wait, you almost did. If only you'd died for Nikoli, you could have made him real. Your last breath would have been his first. The magick that made you believe was the same magick that would have given him life. They didn't tell you that, though, did they?" She searched Grace's face for a response. "No, the do-gooders never do."

Grace knew in her heart that Nadja was just being vindictive, that she was looking for any and everything sharp and homing in on her soft places, that Nadja just wanted to make her hurt. The unfortunate thing was the hag was succeeding.

Nadja neared the altar and continued to inspect her, from the texture of her skin, to her hands and fingernails, to her hair. Nadja's fingers were cold, colder than the marble Grace was lying on. Her touch was like frostbite.

"Would you like some help with that, Grace?" the witch asked, watching her struggle with the ball gag. Her icy fingers pulled the device free and dropped it to the floor. Her first finger traced across Grace's lips. "There you go. Is that better?"

She waited for a response but, not receiving any, continued. "From what Michael said about you, I really thought you'd bite. Don't you want to bite?" Nadja pushed her finger inside Grace's mouth and made a point to touch all of her teeth, almost like she was checking the breeding of a horse. "What a good girl you are! I don't know why Michael had so much trouble with you. You're not giving me any at all." She smiled, baring her teeth like a dog. "I want to see your wings again. If I ask nicely, will you show them?"

Grace was thankful now that Michael had fed her the peanut-butter ball, because she knew when Nadja saw her wings, she would covet them. They were unlike anything else, or so Caspian had told her, and the peanut butter took away her control. But, how had Nadia known she had wings? Who could have told her?

Unless . . . she'd seen them after the fire. That was how Michael had been confident a bullet would kill Caspian. That was how he'd known her demon had chosen humanity.

"I can't," she said simply.

Nadja slapped her hard across the cheek. A small trickle of blood seeped from her nose. "Why not?" she asked.

"Michael force-fed me peanut butter."

Nadja sighed, shaking her head. "That means I can't eat you. Too bad, I would have liked to have had those wings. They really were lovely. I've never seen another creature with wings like that." She paused. "I wonder if he did that just to block me."

"He did it so I wouldn't fry his ass. He killed the man I loved."

"I suppose that makes sense," Nadja agreed. "But you can never tell with Michael. Are you sure you can't try? If I eat you, it will be over very quickly. Michael's little sacrifice party is going to take a really long time."

"You could wait the three days until the peanut butter wears off and try again," Grace said.

Nadja laughed. "Helpful, aren't you? But, no. See, if we keep you hanging around, there's bound to be someone drinking a hot cup of hero who will think he can save you. Then, if he actually did . . . well, I'd be out of luck on the wings and my son's contract would be up with nothing to pay off the balance. So that gamble won't work for me."

"I see," Grace replied. She was scared enough to pee her pants.

"Good. Glad you understand. Well . . . get on with it." Nadja stared at her expectantly.

"Get on with what?"

"The summoning of your grandmother. I don't have all day."

Grace knew better than to ask, she really did, but the words just came out. "I thought you didn't want anyone drinking a cup of hero."

"You're under the misguided impression that she'll win."

Nadja rubbed a spot on her chest and the neckline of her dress plunged just enough to give Grace a glimpse of a brightly burning jewel. There was no way she was going to summon Seraphim. Nadja seemed way too confident about her magick, and Grace had seen gems like those in books. Someone had died for that stone, and she was pretty sure someone else would die because of it.

She wondered if Sasha had been the one to be sacrificed. Had he been taken unawares, or had he sacrificed himself for love? Her previous comments came back to haunt her. She'd said that he and Petru deserved whatever they got because of the lives they'd chosen to lead, but now that judgment left a cold awareness inside her. Even if they did deserve it, it wasn't her place to say so. Didn't everyone deserve a chance at redemption?

Grace had to wonder why the Universe was bothering suggesting life lessons when her life was about to come to a screeching, glaring halt. For some reason, it gave her another beehive of hope, irrational though that sounded. But she still wasn't summoning Seraphim.

"Digging in your heels, hmm? I can tell by the set of your chin. I guess we'll have to find out what exactly it will take. By the end, you *will* call for your grandmother, though. Let's start with your childhood." She dipped her fingers into Grace as if Grace was a well and the dark horrors that haunted her were sweet, cool waters that she brought to her lips and drank. Nadja looked deep into her eyes, and Grace started screaming. But she didn't scream for Seraphim.

CHAPTER THIRTY-THREE

Breaking Point

"I'd be very impressed with how tough she is if it weren't thwarting me." Nadja sighed. "The horrors I've put her through would make you cry like a bitch, Michael. Maybe your demon will have better luck."

"I'm not letting that thing out of its cage."

"Oh, yes, you are," Nadja said. "Your contract is due tonight, and you're not going to pay with Grace until she calls for Seraphim Stregaria. *You make this happen.*" She stamped her foot.

Michael eyed his mother with disdain, then grabbed her by the hair. "You have disrespected me one too many times, Nadja." He shoved her down into a chair and got an inch from her face. "If you do it again, I'll pluck that magick stone from your breast and swallow it whole. Now, I'll get you Seraphim, but *after* I have achieved my demonhood. I'll not roast in the fires of Hell for your revenge plot. Do you understand me?"

Nadja was so startled and proud that she had tears in her eyes. Her boy was strong! "Yes, Michael. You're such a good boy." He tugged her hair hard enough to pull some strands out before letting go.

Going into the back room, Michael came back with a leather-bound package containing tools and special instructions for his sacrifice. But as he was about to head down the stairs to the cellar, Ethelred appeared. The demon stood in his way.

"You shouldn't kill her. Not now."

"I've only got three hours. To do the carving right, I'll need all of them. And, why shouldn't I do it now?" Michael was frustrated, but he would also hear out what the demon had to say. He'd been smart enough in writing his contract to demand Ethelred warn him when he was about to put his foot in it.

"Your sacrifice is meaningless without Seraphim. The Baba Yaga must bear witness. So, Nadja, you will get your wish."

Ethelred sat down at one of the bar tables, giving a slight nod toward the resurrected witch. He looked around the bar and turned up his nose, then waved his hands and performed some magick. A tablecloth stitched by Carmelite nuns appeared on the table, along with his trusty china and a piping hot pot full of Irish Breakfast tea. "I believe you should be expecting company. Would you care for some, Nadja? No? Suit yourself."

"Are you going to make her call on her granny, or am I?" Nadja asked her son.

"*I'll* do it!" Katerina said as she came through the door.

"Company. What did I say?" Ethelred shrugged.

Nadja was speechless, and Michael just gaped.

"Lay a hand on me, Michael, and leprosy will rot your dick off. Got it?" Katerina warned.

He was still too startled to answer, because this was the second time this week someone had threatened to do unspeakable things to his cock.

"Where is she?" Katerina asked.

"The cellar."

"Tea?" Ethelred turned to offer her some.

"No—but thank you. Maybe Petru would like some. He'll be here shortly."

"You're a good woman, Miss Katerina." Ethelred winked.

"She's a whore. Don't you call her Miss-anything," Nadja commanded.

"Nadja, you always were big for your britches. Miss Katerina may sell her body, but she's a lady through and through. You'll not be treating her badly any longer."

"Is it an epidemic? First that idiot demon of Grace's grows a heart and now you, *you're* telling me that I need to be kind?" she sneered. "You're from Hell."

"That doesn't mean I have to be rude or unkind." Ethelred took another sip of his tea.

"Yeah, I think it does. Otherwise, you're missing the whole bloody point."

"Or you are," he returned.

That was when Ethelred noticed something peculiar. His hands had changed. His fingers were longer, more elegant. Not that he'd been bad looking before, though most men with sausage fingers were unattractive. As a demon, he was marked by his hands. They were nature's way of showing the world just how poisonous he was.

But, this could only mean that Caspian was dead. Even if the other demon had chosen a human existence, his crown wouldn't pass until his mortal life ended. Ethelred felt a heaviness in his chest where a heart might have been. He'd wished Caspian nothing but the best with Grace, and he'd also harbored a secret hope that someday they all would find a certain companionship.

A heart? He supposed maybe you could be a demon and have one; it just wasn't widely publicized. It made their jobs easier if no one knew that they had feelings. Also, after living so long, one could go numb, feel like one's heart was gone entirely—but that didn't mean it was.

CHAPTER THIRTY-FOUR
Betrayal

Katerina didn't even wait to hit the last stair before she called Seraphim. "Baba Yaga, protect us!" Even though she wasn't in any direct danger, Nadja's presence was enough to warrant Seraphim's attention.

"No!" Grace screamed. She'd fought so hard to prevent this, and all for naught.

There was no fanfare accompanying her grandmother's arrival, none of the earthshaking showmanship that had marked her appearance in Grace's apartment; the materialization was a quiet affair. Seraphim appeared—and as soon as she did, Nadja was on her like a nuclear-mutated leech.

Before Grace's grandmother could react, Nadja bit into her flesh. Her magick was ready, ramped up, and waiting, and within moments she was consuming the power and life force of the world's last Baba Yaga. Katerina shrieked as she saw what she'd done, saw all hope draining away into the evil that was Nadja.

Seraphim cried out and clawed her attacker, tried to use her magick, but she'd already lost too much strength. The beast that inhabited and empowered Nadja fed ravenously, and when Katerina tried to pull the Baba Yaga free, Nadja was as strong as three men. She tossed the blonde away like a rag doll, watched her collapse against the hard stone floor.

Seraphim Stregaria fell next, the last of her blood oozing

out in a dark pool. The power that had sustained her was gone.

Her strength doubled, Nadja took in all the magick of the Baba Yaga. It changed her in a way that it hadn't Seraphim. It made her stronger, yes. It made her bigger, too, and less feminine. Her eyebrows thickened, meeting in the middle and growing slightly down the bridge of her nose. Her forehead creased and crinkled, and her arms elongated, her knuckles dragging on the floor. Her beautiful hair fell out in clumps, and sores erupted on her creamy skin. A great wart stood out from her cheek, and her spine bent and curved, forcing her to lean forward. Now all of Nadja's ugliness was on the outside, but she had what she wanted. She was the world's preeminent witch.

"*This* is the horror described to me as a child," Katerina whispered.

But, there was hope. The gem still flashed with color in Nadja's chest and surged with power. Katerina said a small prayer before closing her eyes and lurching upright, staggering forward and digging her fingers into the soft, rotten flesh of her enemy's chest. She tore the jewel free.

Nadja should have fallen over dead, but it was too late; the powers of the Baba Yaga kept her alive. She staggered, but remained upright. Katerina ran to Grace, trying to untie her before the creature reached them. It was difficult, because her hands kept shaking, but at last she succeeded.

Grace was staring at her grandmother. The old woman's crumpled form was motionless, and it seemed clear she was dead. The pain of that loss reminded her of another, and of the quartz she had in her pocket. All of that pain, all of that despair . . . It gave her the idea of shoving it into the hole where Nadja's other heart-stone had been. Wouldn't that wreak all Grace's pain and suffering down on Nadja? She would rot in misery—and no one deserved it more.

Grace had the stone in hand; she even held it up with every intention of slamming it into Nadja's body for everything she'd done. Her hand fairly shook with the need to make the witch pay, but before she could act she remembered what she'd learned lying on that slab. Who was she to pass judgment on another? Who was she to condemn, especially when she didn't know what had made this evil woman what she was?

It wasn't what she wanted to do. If she'd thought about it beforehand, this would never have been her plan, and she would never have thought herself able to follow through. But what she did was hug the monstrous woman. She turned and threw her arms around Nadja Grigorovich, threw her arms around her and hugged her. The Universe had been clear in its lesson.

Visions lurched through her brain. She saw Michael's father doing terrible things to Nadja. She saw Michael doing terrible things, including making the pact that cast the memory spell regarding Nikoli. She saw Nadja doing terrible things. This family was evil. Theirs was a cycle of violence, a cycle of horrors that seemed to have no end. But who was Grace to do anything but pity these people, to offer them sympathy and love and hope? Wasn't love what had given her a shot at happiness with Caspian, even if events had turned out so horribly? Wasn't love what allowed her to get past the evil spell making her believe she and Michael had a child? It was a horrible risk—and yet her only hope. It was humanity's only hope.

The quartz of suffering shattered in her hand, and the pieces scattered from her palm like so much dust. There was a flash of light and her grandmother's body vanished. So did Nadja Grigorovich.

Grace shook her head. She didn't know what had happened but decided not to hang around and ponder her good fortune. Instead, she should get out of Dodge, do not pass Go, do not collect two hundred dollars. Whatever had happened, it was all fine with her.

She didn't know the blond woman who'd come to help her, but she grabbed her hand and pulled her toward the stairs. Only to crash into Michael.

"Where are you going, Grace? We have a date."

The blond woman stepped between them. "Remember what I said about the leprosy and your dick falling off? Did you think that was a joke? Just let us go. Make it easier on yourself."

Michael smiled savagely and ripped a charm from her neck. Crunching it beneath his boot like a dead leaf, he waited a second and then grabbed the blonde by the wrist. Forcing her hand against his cock he said, "It's still there, bitch. And maybe I'll be taking it for a test drive on you later. Cutting this one up will be hot work, and it's been a while since we were together, Katerina."

The blonde's earlier bravado was gone. She screamed as Michael twisted her wrist.

Grace slumped in defeat. Had all those beautiful words about love been a joke? Was evil to win after all? "Stop, Michael. Just stop. I won't fight you anymore. Don't hurt anyone else. Let her go, please."

"Turn around. We have a sacrifice to begin."

Grace thought that was an apt description. This was indeed a sacrifice. She wished it would bring back the people she loved, but she knew that was impossible. But maybe it could help this other woman. Maybe. Grace felt a kinship with Katerina, and she prayed that her acquiescence would do the blond woman some good. And while she'd never thought she'd walk willingly to her own death, not for anyone but perhaps her fictitious child, there had been so much suffering. And Caspian was gone, gone, gone. What was left? What was left but to do some good with the life she had left?

"Michael, promise me that you'll let her go."

"Why should I?"

"Because I'm making a deal. My cooperation . . . my soul for her life. It's a good deal, Michael."

He stared at her for a moment. "In blood," he said, drawing a knife from a leather pouch.

"In blood," she agreed.

He drew a first dark sigil on the inside of her wrist, deep enough to draw blood but too shallow to nick a vein. By the time he was done, her entire body would be covered in such markings and she would be praying for it to be over. She already was.

A bright white light burned her eyes, gathering to illuminate the shadows.

Michael saw it, too. He said, "Morning Star comes to make me a demon."

The light grew brighter and brighter until Grace had to close her eyes; it was like looking into the sun. Michael stopped in his cutting, used his arm to shield his eyes. There came a great shaking, an earthquake ten times more intense than the show Seraphim once put on for her benefit.

Pieces of the building began to fall down all around them, and the ceiling splintered. Whole parts of the bar just vanished as if they had never been. A warm yellow light balanced out the agony of white. Out of nowhere there came a thousand voices singing Mozart in her ear.

"Enough! I have had enough!"

A tall figure with golden skin and white hair flowing down his back stepped out of the light. Grace could only see the waves of his hair and she wondered if he was a demon, too. But then he turned and she saw his eyes. It wasn't hellfire that glittered there, but moonbeams and

clouds. He had a sharp nose and high cheekbones. His eyelashes looked like snowflakes. He was almost as beautiful as
Caspian.

"You have learned all the lessons we could possibly ask,
Grace Eden. You've found the courage to sacrifice yourself
for others, to love even when all you love has been taken
away and there is no expectation of recompense. You have
earned all that I am about to give you."

Michael looked both surprised and horrified. He tried to
stab the figure with his ceremonial knife, but the weapon
bounced off the newcomer's skin like it was a toy and the
luminous being shackled Michael with a collar that erupted
in spiny bone spikes out of his throat—as if it were part of
his flesh.

"I am Raphael," the figure said, his attention back on
Grace. Wings spread behind him like a banner. "A Crown
Prince of Heaven."

Through the tears slipping down her face, she saw his
wings weren't the same color as the great white sea behind
him. They were downy, but they radiated a lavender aura.
Just like her own.

Caspian suddenly materialized. The first thing he said
was, "Hell."

"Caspian? How?" Grace looked at Raphael, who nodded
his assent before she ran to him.

"Adversary," the Crown Prince of Heaven acknowledged.

Caspian returned the pleasantry. "Your Highness."

"What? Why did he call you that?" Grace collapsed against
her beloved, smearing her blood on him from where
Michael had mutilated her but not caring in the least. She
doubted he cared, either. She felt suddenly whole. Her life
had been renewed.

"Sorry I was late," Caspian said. "I had a serious case of

dead." He supported her weight easily as he swept her into his arms.

"Take care of my daughter," Raphael said, and then he was gone. So was Michael.

"Always," Caspian said, as if the vanished prince could still hear. He glanced back down at Grace. "Looks like you're both demon and angel, my love."

She smiled up at him. "Just like every other woman that's ever walked the earth."

Caspian laughed. "All of this and still a saucy reply. What would I do without you?"

"Be miserable and bored until the end of your days."

"There is that. Definitely."

She sighed in that moonstruck heiferlike way she'd been trying to avoid, but what did she care anymore? "I love you, Caspian." Why hadn't she told him before? Why hadn't she told him a thousand times?

"I went through Hell for you, so you'd better."

He held her tighter and just breathed in her scent, which was a lot like peanut butter at the moment. He was clearly waiting for her to be upset that he didn't say it back, but she was just content to be in his arms.

"You know that I love you, Grace. Don't you?"

"That doesn't mean that I don't want to hear it," Grace said. "Will you say it again?"

"Yeah," he replied. "I'll tell you as often as you'd like. *I love you.*"

She looked up, drinking him in. She'd thought she'd never see his face again. Never see his smile, or feel his lips . . . Brushing a curl from his forehead, she held thankful joy in her heart.

That was when she saw the burning crown that hovered over his head.

"What's this?"

Caspian didn't answer. He said, "I came here fully prepared to bring Armageddon to this little part of the world, but Raphael beat me to it. He was a lot calmer about the whole thing. Should we send him a thank-you note, do you think?"

"Bring Armageddon? Hades . . . ?" Grace asked.

"He has retired to a ranch in Texas—with Seraphim," he added, seeing the sadness in her heart.

"How?"

"Always asking how. Hades was right, though. It's cute. And I think all of the answers will come in time. Your father's gifts are going to make a big difference in your life."

"My father. I'd like to get to know him," Grace mused.

Caspian shook his head. "Look here, girly. I need you to not be thinking about him for a while." He grinned at her. "I've been dead for some time, but now I'm back as the Prince of Darkness. It's time to raise a little hell." He gave a sly wink and glanced down at her breasts, then at his crotch. Grace could just imagine what was going on beneath his jeans. In fact, she spent a little time doing just that.

She tilted her face up to his, and when their lips met, that was when she knew that Happily Ever After was like love. It wasn't a destination, but a journey. And the whole thing was heaven.

Where Are They Now?

There's popcorn on the floor. The tissue in one hand is wet from the scene where a frothy beverage spewed out your nose, and the tissue in the other is moist from wiping away your tears when Caspian died and you got really mad at the author. We all got sniffly there, and maybe a bit mad, suffered a raging case of "Hey, writer lady, you'd better fix this or I'm going to light your book on fire and send you hate mail." Trust me: Even the muse got an earful. But as the credits are rolling, there's great music playing and hijinks did most certainly ensue.

"But what happened?" you cry. We want to know exactly how Seraphim isn't dead and how Aurora and Raphael got together and so much more. And while Michael's fate would be better suited to the horror genre—this *is* a romance novel, after all—one little peek wouldn't hurt, would it?

Hades did indeed retire to Texas. He'd wanted a ranch outside Dallas with some cattle. He didn't seem to mind that the animals didn't care much for his presence and Seraphim wasn't very big on all the moo poop. She still had a job to do, and she needed to look and smell her very best. She was sure he just liked being around other things with horns. He wore a false pair around the house, always saying, "Guess who's horny today?" All Seraphim could do was shake her head and smile.

Seraphim? She's still the Baba Yaga. The Powers That Be couldn't let her go out like that. So, the Universe shook with their purpose and goodness reigned. The Powers don't do that too often, but sometimes it's necessary. Grace was so good and sweet and, hey, they just didn't like an unhappy ending. No one else would have either, except for Nadja, but her vote didn't count. Hades wanted his woman to retire and stay home with him, but Seraphim had a feeling this retirement stuff was just a phase—more like a vacation. He'd find some way to get back in the game, both feet first, and Seraphim wasn't about to let him do it alone.

Michael's mother was strapped to the Wheel for another few thousand turns, and this made her pretty dizzy. She got a mulligan, a do-over. Some thought she didn't deserve it, but there was a price yet to be paid. Her next incarnation would find her in the previous century as a young girl with visions—a dangerous occupation for a woman in the Burning Times.

Jill was indeed bound to Michael for all eternity, but Nadja's magick spell died with her. She was gifted with Michael's soul in return. When he forfeited on his contract—he couldn't exactly fulfill it while throat-chained by Raphael—Ethelred was kind enough to hand it over. The two now live together in a lovely house in Detroit. Jill is the Web mistress for a forced-sissy site, and Michael is her star performer three times a day. Her screen name is DoubleD_Dominatrix666.

Katerina taught Petru how to cook, and they started a soup kitchen that doubles as a shelter for prostitutes wanting to get out of the life. The pimps don't argue after a serious conversation with Petru. They got married, and Petru adopted her sons as his own. Katerina and Grace have since become very close. Petru misses Sasha daily, and they have a small shrine in their home where a candle is kept burning for Sasha's soul. But he doesn't need it. Sasha will have another turn on the Wheel, too, and he'll find Nadja again and again until they earn their redemption.

Ethelred is happy with his new Crown Prince status, but he's kind of lonely, though Grace and Caspian have him over for dinner parties. They all play Taboo, and he's really good at it. He's also taken to growing his own tea. He wanted to say something slick about blowing the angel Gabriel's horn, but I think we'll give that a miss—for the time being.

Grace and Caspian spend most of their time in a castle in the Netherworld, or in Hell as it's better known. It really is a lovely place, as Caspian suggested. He can rule from there, taking care of this and that. He handled the brewing insurrection that Hades had been sweating, parceling several companies and selling them off, absorbing others and giving great severance packages. All in all, he turned out not to be all that bad a guy to work for, even if he spends a lot of time at home in the bedroom with Grace.

Heaven and Hell being a state of mind, in a surprise development Raphael and Aurora moved in across the street and Grace has gotten to know them. While she loves both parents intensely, she still shoots fireballs when they pester her for grand-imps or cherubim. She's not quite ready to start her new family, as she's just been reunited with the loved ones she'd lost. But she figures it's coming soon.

All in all, everyone got their Happily Ever After. At least, everyone who deserved one.

And don't miss HOW TO MARRY A WARLOCK IN 10 DAYS, coming October 2012!

GOT WARLOCK?

Middy Cherrywood does. She's got more warlock than she can hex with Dred Shadowins. He isn't just a billionaire playboy and *Weekly Warlock* centerfold. He's a spy for the High Chancellor, and he convinces Middy to pose as his fiancée for his latest mission. Too bad no one told his mother before she slipped Middy a potion that will make their sham engagement all too real in just ten days.

Dred Shadowins already has his hands full with cursed objects, possessed nuns, and dreams where Merlin makes him pay for taking his name in vain by relating his sexcapades with Nimue. But by the end of the mission, he's convinced his most difficult challenge is the hero's cape Middy's draped over his shoulders. Because he wants nothing more than to give her the one thing he may not be capable of providing: Happily Ever After.